CLASSIC CYBORG

LIQUID COOL: THE CYBERPUNK
DETECTIVE SERIES

From the Crazy Maniac Files
BOOK ONE

AUSTIN DRAGON

Published by Well-Tailored Books, California

Classic Cyborg
Liquid Cool: The Cyberpunk Detective Series
From the Crazy Maniac Files (Book One)

978-1-946590-63-3 (paperback)
978-1-946590-61-9 (ebook)

http://www.austindragon.com

Book cover design by Leslie K.

Printed in the United States of America

CONTENTS

I'M CRUZ, METROPOLIS P.I., AND LIQUID COOL IS MY DETECTIVE AGENCY

Metropolis.

I was born in this supercity, raised here, and I would die here—hopefully, many decades in the future. As a late thirty-something private detective working these "mean streets," I wouldn't work anywhere else on the planet. Not even those booshy Up-Top colonies in space, the moon or Mars could ever coax me away. I complained like every other bona fide resident, but I loved the place.

As the largest municipality on planet Earth, Metropolis was an unwieldy monolith of a supercity, but it was overflowing with life in constant motion. People were stacked on top of one another in flashing superskyscrapers that reached into the dark rainy skies, some as tall as three hundred stories.

From the ground, the dark, urban landscape was offset by flashing neon and video signs. In the "good" districts, street lampposts hung over nearly every city corner, and lights liberally adorned the surfaces of buildings, usually in some kind of geometric design. If that wasn't enough visual madness, there was the glowing eye-wear of the people themselves. Bright lights scared away the gloom and doom of the dark and cloudy skies—nine out of ten city psychologists said so. Fifty-million people populated this "neon jungle"—living, breathing, and dying beneath its ever-present rain. Above it all, was the hovercar sky traffic—twenty to fifty feet up.

This was our modern paradise—Metropolis, the largest and most powerful supercity on Earth, designed to be the city of the future for today. It was also the headquarters and home of Liquid Cool. My "fame" came at me like a mugger in the night. One day I was a hovercar restorer, the next I was dodging bullets and laser fire with bad guys while solving cases.

I'm Cruz. The president, CEO, COO, and detective-on-the-go of the Liquid Cool Detective Agency. Besides my own one-man detective firm, I have a wife, a kid, a classic hovervehicle, and a cool hat. I've had some big, high-profile cases in my relatively short three-year career as a Metropolis private detective. But for the real detective working the "mean streets," it's never about the big cases. Those cases got the attention and the special names, like "Blade Gunner," "NeuroDancer," "The Electric Sheep Massacre," "I, Alien Hunter," or even my first major case, the "Police Watch Conspiracy," which was really two cases that turned out to be one. Those cases were big events that came along every so often, but in between were the smaller ones, and they were every bit as dangerous. I'd met many...I'd call crazy maniacs—criminals and clients alike—from all walks of life, all kinds of neighborhoods. Slimy, low-life gangster-wannabes; shifty working-class Average Joes and Janes; and off-world, filthy rich tycoons from Lunar Colony or Mars. Most were forgettable. I solved the case and moved on, storing the file away in the archives of my mobile computer, and the mental file in the trash bin of my memory. Sometimes, however, one of those "smaller" cases stuck in my mind and wouldn't be forgotten.

Storms were rare in Metropolis—after all, it rained all the time. The weather was far too tired from working every day without a break to give us any of those "Storms of the Centuries" like Earth used to have. But it was during the calm before the storm when a particular "small" case strutted into my Liquid Cool office one day.

His street name was Classic Cyborg.

It was late morning, and I was in the field doing what any good detective would be doing—working. Since I was "famous," I didn't have to beg or hunt for cases much anymore; plenty came my way. However, I remained picky. I wanted to remain a generalist detective. I worked the Average Joe cases of all kinds; megacorporation cases, mostly corporate espionage; and government cases, mostly skiptracing for the municipal courts. I hated cheating spouse surveillance cases, but they were so plentiful that I had to accept the fact they'd always be at least a quarter of my monthly caseload. They also always paid promptly. One type of case I refused to take: bodyguard jobs. Far too dangerous for me. I got shot at enough without volunteering to be a human shield for anyone. But life was always filled with exceptions.

I was on bodyguard duty at a birthday party for an eight-year-old in a community park located on the roof of a hundred-story mega-tower penthouse residence. In other words, I was babysitting a bunch of annoying kids. The couple was rich and referred by a friend of a friend, so I took the case. Apparently, one of the kids had a stalker, and the parents wanted me to be near their daughter at all times, including at her birthday party with all her friends and not-friends. Almost a hundred screaming kids were on the roof playground. They were all from the local private school, and there were a half dozen teachers on chaperone duty too.

My work "uniform" was my trademark tan fedora and tan slicker. My clothes underneath changed, often a vest over a dress shirt; casual, fitted, stretch pants; and non-slip gripping shoes. However, people only remembered my tan fedora and slicker. In Metropolis, most people didn't wear hats—hoodies were the preferred choice, and people stuck with dark-colored slickers. The masses never wanted to stand out in the crowd, but I was a contrarian, despite never wanting to stand out. Yes, I was a paradox.

"How many guns do you carry?" the little red-nosed kid asked me.

I had stationed myself at the outer perimeter of the park as the kids, ages three to eight, played on a giant inflatable castle with secret passageways, slides, swings, and trampolines. All the kids were happy to exhaust themselves on their high-end castle balloon toy, except for one. He locked eyes on me the moment I arrived. I didn't like it then, and I didn't like it now. He walked over to me and stared at me with his arms folded. I wanted him to go away. He either had a cold, was recovering from one, or was getting one. Whichever it was, I didn't want his nasty germs near me.

"Go play with your friends," I said to him.

"You didn't answer me."

"I don't want to."

"How many people have you shot?"

"You know I can see your diapers. Pull up your pants properly."

"Diapers?" A shocked expression flashed on the kid's face as he looked down at his pants. They were on properly, and he wasn't wearing a diaper. He was seven, after all, but the look on his face was beyond priceless. "I don't wear diapers." He looked up at me with a mean expression. "I don't wear diapers."

"Go play with your friends."

"I don't have friends."

"I can see why. Go play. You're interfering with my work."

"Are you going to shoot people?"

"I'm going to shoot you."

"My father is a lawyer, and he knows people's rights. He sues people like you for a living."

"People like me? What does that mean? Don't answer. I'm here to protect people, including you, you brat. If you don't go play, I'm going to spread rumors at your school that you still wear diapers and sleep in a crib, sucking a pacifier."

Now the kid was listening to me. He glared at me and started to walk away. I kept my eyes on him until he got to the inflatable castle, but he wasn't playing. He sat down on the faux-grass of the roof and watched me.

At least he wasn't my client's kid, or I would have promptly left so the stalker could get him. My attention returned to work. Kids were everywhere in and around the inflatable castle, but some were running around in the park a bit further away. There were also plenty of adults on hand, parents mostly, but this was the tower's public park. Residents of the building were here too—sitting on benches reading, playing chess or socializing at the outdoor tables, doing their daily walks or jogs. There were a lot of people around, and I kept my real focus on my client's daughter, who was quite the social butterfly with a dozen girls around her, following wherever she went. It seemed very unlikely that anyone would try something here in such a public place.

One of the birthday kids ran to me. "Mister," she said.

"Yes."

"There's a suspicious perpetrator over there." She pointed to the far end of the roof.

"Is that so? Are you playing a joke on me?"

"I'm not lying."

"'Suspicious perpetrator' are big words for a kid."

"They're not big. I can spell both of them. S-U-S-P-I-C-I-O-U-S, P-E-R-P-E-T-R-A-T-O-R."

"What does it mean?"

"Suspicious. Someone or something attracting attention because of unusual appearance or action. Perpetrator. Someone doing bad. Over there." She pointed again.

"What's the something bad he's doing?" I stood where I was and simply took my binoculars from my jacket. I had a clear view, but heard her giggling.

"Go play!" I shouted at her, putting my binoculars away. She ran away, still giggling.

What did I expect? If I was a kid at a birthday party, high on tons of birthday cake and candy, and the adults told me there was a private detective here, I'd want to mess with him too.

The boy pest had gotten up from his spot and marched over to me again. "I demand to know how many guns you have!"

When I pulled my omega-gun from my jacket, his face went white and he ran away faster than a cyborg with supersonic bionic legs. The weapon was literally not of this Earth, illegally acquired on the Up-Top black market from an associate named Phishy, but the silver weapon could be modified to shoot any kind of solid or laser round. I had seen him. I fired clear across to the other side of the roof as I ran. One of the joggers in a blacker slicker was hit in the back. When I finally reached the person, I turned him on his back so I could clearly see his face.

"You shot me!" he yelled at me, shaking from the pain. "Why did you shoot me? Is that legal?"

I was surrounded by residents, parents, and kids as I knelt down near him and dug into his pockets.

"Oh, look at this," I said and handed a picture of my client's daughter to her father. Both parents were standing behind me. "Here's more." I pulled out more pictures. "Are you a fan of this girl?"

"It's not against the law to carry pictures of children."

I stood up from the ground. "I spotted you outside the building when I arrived. I'm sorry, did you think you were invited to the birthday party? Well, you weren't, and you're not a resident of this building. I bet trespassing isn't your only crime. I bet you have a police record a mile long. Stalking is a crime and stalking a child is a bigger crime."

"I'm not stalking anyone." He sat up, slowly.

"Keep your hands where I can see them," I said.

From the corner of my eye, I saw the client's daughter come out of the crowd with a gun in her hand. "You're dead, you old, dirty bastard!"

I snatched it from her. "Give me that! And watch the language."

She kicked me in the leg. "Ouch!" I cried out. "Behave yourself!" I yelled at her.

I happened to glance back and saw the father aiming another gun at the stalker! I snatched it. "Stop it! What's wrong with all of you? There are cameras on this roof. We've made a legal citizen's arrest, but if you shot him, he can call the police on you."

My eye immediately switched to the mother. If father and daughter were crazy maniacs, then she was probably one too. Her hands were empty, but she watched me with a smirk. Her eyes and mouth widened. "Gun!" she yelled.

I jerked my body to the side as I fired into the stalker's chest. I jumped up and quickly looked at the object in his hand. It was only a pair of dark shades. I turned to look behind me. The mother was smiling. The father was smiling, and the daughter was smiling. In fact, everyone on the roof was smiling—except me.

"I'm living in a world of crazy maniacs. Call the police, ambulance, whatever. I'm outta here." I pointed at the parents. "Don't think that setting aside half that yummy chocolate birthday cake for me and my family is a bonus. I want the real bonus you promised, meaning cash."

Police hated police shows and police "reality" shows even more for good reason. They gave the general public lots of ideas, but usually all the wrong ones. Yelling out "gun" was a public favorite to get the police to shoot someone for you. I was a licensed private detective, with a carry and conceal permit for any legal weapon on Earth, and I was always armed. That made me a pseudo-cop, and everyone knew it. I didn't like being manipulated by anyone, even if I was well paid for it.

The stalker wasn't dead, but he wouldn't be leaving his future hospital room any time soon. Police found his hovercar, and there were a lot more than just pictures inside—lots of illegal weapons, which he didn't have permits for. So, his future hospital recovery room was going to be Metro Prison.

The life of a street detective in Metropolis was one of keeping one eye on the bad guy, another on the victim, and another on the client. You never knew which one of them would do something stupid, including trying to shoot you. I didn't like getting shot.

PUNCH JUDY, MY CYBORG SECRETARY

My "Birthday Stalker" case was closed. I got my bonus, and a box of chocolate cake to be devoured by my wife and son. Maybe I'd sneak a slice or two. I looked at the digital display of my slicker's pocket watch. (I was all into the retro-fashion and saw no reason to change. It was part of my trademark style now.) I'd wrapped up the case in less than two hours but got paid my day rate with a bonus. Not a bad way to start the workday, and it wasn't even lunchtime yet.

The best thing was that I didn't have to wait around for the police. The parents were eager to pay me the bonus and see me out. I didn't care what lies they'd weave for the arriving officers as to who shot who and why. The parents' lawyers were also at the party, and I saw the anxiousness in their faces to get everyone's stories coordinated and legally acceptable. They wanted the stalker off the street, and he was.

It had been my idea to post a big, fat neon sign in front of the building publicizing the birthday party. Stalkers were always on surveillance. With my trap set, all I had to do was take the time before the start of the party to circle the building in my vehicle as many times as necessary, make a record of everyone hanging around, cross-check their photos with the police for criminals and those with criminal complaints, see which one showed up at the roof birthday party, shoot them with a non-lethal round, call the police, and collect my money. Simple.

"It's going to be bad!" PJ yelled from her desk.

The Storm of the Century was on its way, and we were busy (not really) at work in my Liquid Cool office in Buzz Town. As far as districts went in Metropolis, it wasn't the best of areas, but it wasn't the worst either. I liked to think that my presence as a new detective classed up the neighborhood a bit.

I started the Liquid Cool Detective Agency not even three years ago, leaving my previous line as a classic hovervehicle restorer and sometime illegal hovercar racer behind. All I had done was a simple favor for a friend, but it led to me being a full-fledged licensed private detective in the largest supercity on the planet. Already I had solved some of the biggest and most dangerous cases that not even the big, fancy detective firms with a thousand agents could boast. Besides myself, PJ was my only full-time employee.

My office was on the hundredth floor of one of many office mega-towers on Circuit Circle. From my private office, I sat at my desk staring out at the window with a cup of silk coffee in hand. PJ was right. A storm was coming, and it was going to be bad. I had a rare, clear view of the line of monolith office towers through the tinted windows. No rain yet, but the cloud cover above was so dark and dank that it seemed all the water on the planet was building up to crash down upon Metropolis any minute.

I swiveled around in my chair to see PJ appear at my open doorway. She was hired as a secretary, though I had no idea what she had promoted herself to these days. We started out as frenemies, but now she was my second in command. She had short, crimson hair, a simulated mole—a dot above her lips, today, matching her crimson lipstick-covered lips. Hip, female business suits were what she wore nowadays—sleeveless, knee-high skirts. The only reminder of her previous life were her heeled leather boots. That previous life she was a soldier in the punk-posh gang *Les Enfantes Terribles* in Neo-Paris, France. She loved her sleeveless tops to show off her buff, bionic arms. PJ's street name was Punch Judy, because she liked to punch people and could, in fact, punch a three-hundred-pound cyborg through a steel and concrete wall.

But PJ wasn't just about the violence. Like me, that was only when needed. She had become the master...mistress...of customer service and "client acquisition." She had turned the main office area into a shrine to all my high-profile cases. There were framed pictures covering practically every inch of the reception area. Pictures of me at press conferences, at police scenes, with megacorporation senior executives, with the Council of Corporation president, me shaking hands with the Mayor...but my favorites were those with just the Average Joes and Janes of the supercity, including the client from my very first major case, Carol Num, after I successfully rescued her kidnapped daughter. These were the cases that made it all worthwhile, despite all the crazy maniacs I had to deal with and getting shot. I didn't like getting shot.

"Don't I have a client?" I asked.

"He's late, but look at the weather. We're lucky anyone is leaving their home."

"But nothing's happened and it's barely raining."

"But it's going to be bad. I bet there's more water hovering in the sky up there than in the ocean."

"PJ, rain doesn't hover. It only comes down and wets you and causes accidents."

She pointed at the window to the sky. "That's hovering. Look at that."

"Where are my clients? We can't make money with an empty office. I should be out there getting clients or solving cases."

"No, no. You don't need to get clients anymore. You're famous. The clients come to you."

"Clients? You mean a lot of crazy maniacs, sometimes crazier than the criminals."

"That's one time—NeuroDancer."

"Blade Gunner case?"

"She saved you."

"Her brother?"

"He tried to, but he didn't know it was you. Besides, you became buddies."

"Electric Sheep Massacre?"

"Okay, he was crazy, but you've had hundreds of clients. Those are only a few." We heard the front door buzzer. "I'm not going to allow you to infect me with your negativity. It's not even lunchtime, and that may be your client." She pointed at me. "No negativity with the clients."

"Yeah, yeah. Until we get paid. I know that. But if it isn't the client, I'm outta here to find some non-crazy maniac clients."

"Let me see if a *Monsieur Mania Fou* is out there."

"No French allowed so early in the morning," I said, as she disappeared from my private office.

While I waited I reviewed messages from the previous day. I usually did so as soon as I got into the office in the morning, but today I was clearly under the influence of procrastination. It happened, and it was normal. I wanted to be out on the streets working a case, but my last seven or so I had basically solved from my desk or mobile computer. Hopefully, PJ was talking to a real client, someone who wasn't too criminal or too crazy, and more importantly, could pay my fees.

"Boss." PJ was at my open doorway again. "Your next appointment is here." I looked up. "Mr. Classic."

A CLASSIC CLIENT

In my classic hovervehicle restoring and hovercar racing days, back when I was building my reputation and client base, I'd met many colorful characters. I had seen Mr. Classic's type many times before; he was like an O.G., "original gangster," though in the classic hovervehicle collector and aficionado world, most had never been real gangsters. It was their attitude—all bravado, machismo, that air of indestructibility. Ladies loved them, and men wanted to be them.

Mr. Classic Cyborg strolled into my office, lighter than air and a smirk on his face, as he took off his psychedelic, retro shades. He wore an expensive smoke gray suit, but no shirt or top underneath. PJ liked to show off her bionic arms with her sleeveless attire. He had to show off his metallic, ripped chest—a design I had never seen in any cyborg before. His eyes had a reflective quality like a night owl, so they were probably bionic too. But I doubted he was shirtless to show off his bionic torso; it was to show off all the neon tattoos. He was a walking billboard of street art. Most of it actually looked quite good—much better than what qualified for high art in any booshy Metropolis art gallery. He had a naturally bald head and graying stubble, as if he just shaved off a beard and mustache. I'd guess he was in his 50s, based on his style, but with cyborgs like him, and in his state of fitness, he could easily be much older.

Liquid Cool was a fortress of an office, especially since I was a "famous" detective and had already put down quite a few bad guys. We had all kinds of security cameras, sensors, and measures, including lasers and pulse shot-guns. If the man was sitting in my office, it meant that PJ had already scanned him thoroughly to determine the kind of cyborg he was. The amount of illegal street modifications available to the criminal cyborg class was endless, but if PJ allowed him in, it meant he had none of those.

However, I was apprehensive at this part. "Mr. Cruz," he said as he extended his arm. Even a "normal" cyborg could do tremendous bodily harm to a normal like me.

I shook his bionic hand. "Mr. Classic." I gestured for him to take a seat in one of the two plush chairs in front of my desk.

"Thank you." Though he walked around with no shirt under his jacket, he moved with class. He unfastened the button of his suit jacket as he sat. I noticed his neon tattoos had disappeared. So, he could turn them off too.

"I notice an accent," I remarked.

"Yes, Polish," he answered. "My old country. Yours is Puerto Rico I understand."

"Yes, but no cool accent. Only boring Metropolis-ese, if I can make up a word."

"My father was very strict. He wanted all his children to speak the mother tongue and as many others as we could learn. Why learn to speak one language when you can learn ten, he'd tell us."

"I'm surrounded by family and friends who can all speak more than my one."

Classic smiled. "You do speak more than one language, Mr. Cruz. The most important one of them all. You speak the language of the streets. That's why you're the boss and not them."

"I've done okay."

"You're too modest, Mr. Cruz. People like us don't need to be modest. We can let others do that for us. We both started from humble beginnings, some would say we started out at a great disadvantage from everyone else in our class, but here we sit—at the top."

"Am I at the top?"

"Yes. 'The top' doesn't mean money or power, necessarily. If you wanted that, you'd have that too. 'The top' means the best at whatever you set your mind to."

"What are you at the top of, Mr. Classic?"

"My former life or the current one? I also had a former life, like you. My previous life was more along the lines of the previous one of your French operations manager out there."

"Operations manager?" I laughed. "Thanks for letting me know. I hired her for one job, but she's been unilaterally promoting herself ever since."

He smiled. "She's like us—creating her way. Not allowing it to be created for her. I was a criminal, Mr. Cruz. I started out as muscle-for-hire, contracted by all the major crime gangs a long time ago. Classic Cyborg became my street name. I was a very scary person back then, but I soon grew tired of taking orders. The people I worked for—no one was scared of them. Everyone was scared of me, so why shouldn't I be running the big show. I formed my own gang, involved in all the criminal vice that there was, but did it better than anyone else. When I started, there were over two dozen cyborg gangs working our territories. When I was done instilling a new order to our corner of the mean streets, there was only one—mine."

"Police never got you?"

"When you're the boss of a successful criminal gang, you better get used to being in court, in jail, or on the way in or out of both. I was no different, but nothing that I'd call serious. In or out of jail, I ran my empire."

"What happened to make you leave that life behind?"

Classic reached into his jacket and produced a digital plastic photo. "She happened." I looked at the picture of a young woman in his twenties. "All she had to do was be born. Classic Cyborg the Sadist became Daddy Classic the Softy."

"How can I help you, Mr. Classic?"

He returned the photo to his jacket's inner pocket.

"Yes, how can you? I want to hire you, Mr. Cruz. I didn't finish my story."

"I knew you'd tell the other half—or I'd find out after PJ finished the background check on you."

He smiled again. "If you didn't do a background check on every client who walked in here, I wouldn't be here. My case involves my new life. My enemies of the past are after me today by attempting to destroy my present life—my family, daughter, livelihood, all of it. I don't care about me, I deserve it in a way. But not my daughter. That's a cosmic line you never cross."

"Did you ever cross it in your previous life?" I asked.

We stared at each other for what seemed to be forever, before he answered. "No. I threatened people that I would, but I never crossed it. That's what everyone else did back in those days. I brought in a new order. Animals need not behave like animals all the time."

I opened the top drawer of my desk and took out my notepad. "I'll jot down any notes, if I have to. Give me all the particulars. What is your livelihood?"

"Cyber-psychosis. Have you heard of it?"

"I've known people who've suffered from it," I replied.

"People think that everyone is a cyborg on Earth these days, but outside the criminal class, we're still rare. People have a bionic part here and there, but that's not the same thing. For the real cyborg, a significant percentage suffer from mental issues: depression is the most common, but there's the more serious, like a specific kind of REM behavior disorder where the cyborg tries to claw or rip off their cybernetic part or parts.

"That's my business. I help cyborgs. I'm a seventy-percenter myself, so I have credibility within the community. I started with retired criminals like myself, then expanded to the general cyborg community."

"How do you help them?" I asked.

"I'm a cyborg counselor. I help those with mental problems associated with being a cyborg live normal lives. It could be anything from a simple talk to full psychotherapy sessions. It could even be helping change their bionic part to make them less cyborg-looking. I'm very good at my new vocation. I was a high school dropout and a felon, but I now have multiple PhDs and am a certified counselor for the city of Metropolis—only in this country could such a ridiculous thing occur."

"You're Dr. Classic, then."

"Doctor. Yes, I suppose."

"What happened to make you come here today?"

I could tell that Classic was a smoker. He did that thing with his index finger and thumb, rubbing them together, then including the middle finger. I could see because of the look of his faux-manicured nails.

"It's a non-smoking office," I said before he could even ask.

He laughed. "But you wear that old-style gangster hat. You should smoke too. It adds character to a person."

"Some other time."

He sighed. "Mr. Cruz, someone's trying to kill me." He saw me waiting to hear the details. "I'm Classic Cyborg, Mr. Cruz. I've been out of the game for a long time, but my rep remains on the streets to this day, no matter how reformed I am in my new life. There are a lot of punks on those streets who could instantly make a name for themselves if they could kill a legend. That's how street punks do things today. They don't work to gain a rep with real deeds. They're always looking for ways to cheat their way to the top."

"Mr. Classic, what you've described sounds like a police matter."

"Mr. Cruz, the police aren't private investigators for the public, and they're not about to do anything for me. I want to hire you to find out who it is, so I can protect my family on my own."

"Protect?"

"No, Mr. Cruz. No vigilantism. I'm out of the game for good. If I have to, I'll move out of Metropolis, but I need to know who, for sure."

"Have there been any attempts on your life already?"

"Two. My clientele are all cyborgs. They planted a fake client on a house visit. He tried to gun me down. I barely escaped. If I have to fear my own clients, then my livelihood is effectively over. The second was a drive-by shooting at another visit. I was too busy diving for cover to get the license ID of the hovercar."

"Did you report the drive by?"

"I didn't have to. Other people were there and they called the police."

"Is there more? Is there an actual contract out on the street to kill you?"

"A message. A note was left on my hovercar a couple of weeks back. 'I'm going to be the one who kills Classic Cyborg,' it said. Not very original, but that's how street punks talk these days. In my day, we had much more class."

"But far more violence too."

"True, but we did it with class."

"Do you already have an idea who? Who do you suspect?"

"I have my suspicions. I was a legend. Who on the streets would benefit from killing an old legend? It wouldn't take long to come up with such a list."

"How many people on this list? I know you already have it."

"Three names."

I sat there, watching him closely. He probably sensed my distrust and reached into his jacket again. Out came a slim, faux-steel credit card.

"Do I pay you or her outside?"

I paused for a moment. "Her, outside."

DETECTIVE TRENDY, METRO PD CYBORG GANG UNIT

As I flew out of the parking bay in my bright red, classic Ford Pony, the sky made it seem like we were all on another planet. Above the sky traffic was a dark, almost black cloud cover, and below it was clear. The rain was sporadic, no more than a mist. It surely did look like something bad was coming.

My vehicle was a sleek, bright red muscle coupe with a high-performance, super-charged, advanced nitro-acceleration hydrogen engine. I had found the shell in a junkyard when I was a kid in middle school, rebuilt and restored it by high school, and had been upgrading it ever since. My Pony had been featured (without my permission) in so many hovercar magazines that I lost count. It was also my mobile office when needed.

Mr. Classic paid his retainer to PJ, which made me officially on the case. However, I took it as a given that the client rarely told me the whole truth. If I wanted to work for only truth-tellers in Metropolis, I'd be forever unemployed, and non-criminal clients were often the worst when it came to honesty. We had done the standard background check on all potential clients, but I needed to dig deeper. He did tell me he was a "legend."

I made a few calls to acquaintances in the hovercar scene, who I guessed might have heard of him, and they had. One went so far as to say that I should return his retainer and stay away. Others told me that if his old life was creeping back into his new life, then I better make sure to do a lot more than a standard background check. That meant a trip to Metro Police Central.

Even with the heavy traffic, it didn't take me all that long to get to Downtown Metro. Also known as Police One, Metropolis Police Central stood at the opposite end of the avenue from City Hall and looked like a cubical fortress. It was home to the supercity's 500,000 plus police force—the largest not just in the nation, but on the planet.

Due to all my work with and on behalf of Metro PD, I finally had a status beyond that of the common licensed private investigator. I was popular with the rank-and-file police who worked a beat, but not so much with the police brass, who despised me. It meant I had to always keep a low-key presence inside police headquarters. I didn't have to wait in the general lobby area inside, which was more like a zoo with the constant march of police and a steady stream of captured criminals in and out. The security was solid—armed police guards, security cameras, armed sentries at the end of the hallways near the elevators and scanning archways. However, I was buzzed in and allowed to pass into the inner waiting room behind the main counter and wall. Beyond it was a bull pen of dual cubicles where the street police sat and worked. Further away were elevated single cubicles where the detectives sat, and beyond that were the offices for the higher-ups.

Today was not my lucky day, because all the police officers I normally talked to were out in the field, which is exactly where they should be. I waited until a senior officer was available from the Gang Unit.

"Mr. Cruz." A Caucasian officer with dreadlocks appeared in civilian clothes and, like most in the squad, looked like a real gang member himself, with tattoos and piercings everywhere. "I'm Detective Trendy."

"Thanks, detective, for taking the time."

"Follow me back."

Usually, detectives were not so friendly with me or willing to help. Trendy looked amiable enough when not in "undercover mode," but I doubted that my good standing with the street police or my personal charm were the reason behind this VIP treatment. He led me from the waiting area to the empty rooms used for meetings, interviews, and questioning.

"Coffee?" he asked.

"I'm good."

"What's it about, Cruz?"

"Classic Cyborg."

Trendy had sat down and leaned back to put his feet up on the table. He was wearing those boots that looked like clawed feet. "That's ancient news, Cruz. But when he was news, he was one of the most vicious gangsters around. Started out as a bodyguard, promoted himself to crime boss, and took over a territory that had been run by dozens of different gangs. When he was done, there was only one—his."

"When did he go straight? Or did he?"

"He better have gone straight. He's on the city payroll as a licensed counselor and even gives anti-gang talks in middle and high schools." Trendy could see me almost laughing. "I'm serious. The kids love a real ex-gangster standing in their class giving speeches and answering their questions. He's very popular. He's been out of the crime business for twenty-five years. There hasn't been so much as a whisper of him even being next to anyone doing something remotely illegal in that time."

"Twenty-five years ago, but you remember all his history."

"Of course I do. I work with him every week. He's a worker, always out there. Also, I'm in the Gang Unit. We know the history of hundreds of ex-gangsters, alive and dead, all cyborgs. He's one of them because of what he was."

"Cyborg Gang Unit."

"Yeah."

"You're definitely the right detective to talk to. His new reformed life is real then?"

"It's real. You can't fake something for so long. He gave up his old life when his daughter was born."

"What happened to the mother?"

"She died while giving birth. A rare condition, so rare the medical staff didn't even know it existed anymore."

"Was the mother in the crime biz too?"

"Not really. More of a gangster groupie than anything."

"You say Classic was vicious. How vicious?"

"Never convicted, but he allegedly killed a lot of people on his way to the top. Crushing people's skulls with his bare bionic hands, disemboweling them with a bionic kick...vicious. Cyborg thugs back then were all into their illegal modifications of samurai swords, buzz saws, and hatchets that popped out of an arm or chest. He didn't do any of that. That's why he was so scary. No modifications, nothing fancy, no weird tech. He'd just ripped your buzz saw modification out of your chest, then kill you and your entire crew with it."

"Then we're not talking allegedly."

"Never convicted."

"How did he get licensed with the city and accepted on the kiddie speaking tour? Wasn't there any police or prosecutor uproar?"

"There was, huge. It was a scandal. Lots of people refused to work with him, but again, he's good. He's helped a lot of people. He's never complained. But more importantly, he's never even got a speeding ticket ever again. Then the direct investigators and prosecutors involved in trying to get him for all those years started to retire. Cruz, people have very short attention spans, even the police. You stay under the radar and do only the right thing, let the years go by, everyone forgets. Also, in his case, he was never accused of killing a cop."

"Only other criminals."

"We still have cops, myself included, who don't necessarily view that as a bad thing."

"Twenty-five years clean."

"Yeah. Why are you here asking about him?"

"He hired me."

"Hired you? For what?"

"Someone put out a contract on him."

"Contract? What does he want you to do?"

"Find out who it is."

"Then what?"

"He said he'd decide when he knows, even if it means leaving Metropolis with his family."

"You believe that?"

"You're the one who said he's been an angel for twenty-five years."

"Yeah, I did."

"From what you know of the gang world, especially those who love being cyborg criminal maniacs, who would be at the top of the list—"

"In wanting to off an old cyborg gangster out of the biz for twenty-five years?"

"That's what he believes. Kill the legend of the man by killing the man."

"He was smart to hire you then. Let me look at the reports. I'll be back in a few." Trendy pulled his feet off the table and walked out of the room, leaving the door open.

Trendy didn't take as long as I had expected. In fifteen minutes he returned with a folding tablet in hand. I had spent the time reviewing messages on my mobile phone, so at least some of my daily work got done.

"Cruz, I got good news and bad news." He sat back down at the table.

I had always hated that phrase because it invariably meant that even the good news wasn't really that good or was irrelevant. "Doesn't sound good."

"It is. I have three names for you, and I'd wager it's one or a combination of the three behind any contract on him."

"Why are you so positive?"

"They're fans of his."

"Fans? Fans who'd want to kill him?"

"It's the crime world, Cruz. It doesn't have to make sense to us because it makes sense to them."

"Who are they?"

"That's the bad news. Cruz, these individuals are not normal criminals. They're classified as 'C&D'—cyborg and dangerous, extremely dangerous. You don't want to tangle with any of them. They're unpredictable and linked with more homicides than I think even you would be comfortable with."

"I've dealt with crazy maniacs before, and cyborg ones too."

"I can't tell you what to do, but I'm not sure that even Classic Cyborg from twenty-five years ago would have an easy time with any one of these."

"Who are they—least dangerous of the three first?"

"The bottom of the three would either be Harder Steel or Pink Machete."

"I love the street names these punks come up with."

"They'd be tied. At the top of the list is Franken-borg. Cruz, I think you need to take a pass on this case. Seriously, they're too dangerous."

"One of them?"

"I would wager on it."

"Why now?"

"This is the twenty-fifth year anniversary of his retirement. You wouldn't know that, or the average person on the street, but in the crime world, such things are remembered, and celebrated."

"Celebrated by killing. Do you think Classic would know these three names?"

"I don't know. He might, or might not know everything about them."

"If these three cyborgs are on the Metro PD watch list, why aren't they in the system?"

"On what? Classic is a felon, but not one of those convictions was for murder. We know these three psychos have killed people, but there isn't a molecule of evidence that we could present in a court of law."

"Maybe that needs to change."

"Cruz, don't make the mistake of thinking you can beat any of these guys in a shoot-out."

"Can you give me their bionic specs?"

"Cruz, I can't give you access to a private citizen's health records."

"Can't you?"

"No, I can't. However, I'm going to leave this tablet on the table here while I go out and get something to drink. It contains confidential health records of private citizens, so guard it for me until I get back."

"Will do, detective."

DOCTOR SILVER-ROSE, METRO CITY PSYCH

The Metropolis Gang Unit was a huge division, and its Cyborg Gang Unit was its largest sub-division. The police who worked in the unit not only knew everything about every cyborg gangster and wannabe there was, but specialized in taking them down—meaning shooting to kill. They were so good at their job that even the scariest cyborg criminal was scared of them. I took Trendy's warning seriously when he said, "cyborg and dangerous"—C and D. If he was afraid of them, I better be too, so I was never going to forget the designation.

All cyborgs in Metropolis, Earth, and even Up-Top had to have permits for all the bionics they had in their bodies. But illegal modifications weren't just something criminals did; most people did it. Mandatory cyborg permit registration was the only way to prosecute someone for those illegal modifications. On paper, Franken-borg, Harder Steel, and Pink Machete were "normal" cyborgs, but the Metro Cyborg Gang Unit had compiled a lengthy list of what the street said these "fine, upstanding citizen" cyborgs could do to a person. It was all very nasty, and meant that before I went anywhere near them, I'd have to do my own modifications to my weaponry.

For the moment, my next stop was to City One. I left the Pony where it was parked and took the public shuttle—normally I walked, but even I was starting to believe the general consensus that when the storm hit, it had the potential of washing every average pedestrian away, straight to the Great Oceans.

The person who had educated me on all things that had to do with mental health and cyborgs was PJ. Before she was gainfully employed by me, she had struggled in her post-gangster life. I wasn't responsible for the terrible accident that led to her becoming a cyborg, but I was directly responsible for her becoming a cyborg, as I was the one who cut off her arms with a laser-saw to free her from the burning wreck of a crash that was her hovercar. Understandably, after such a traumatic event I would have struggled too. Our friendship was far different then than it was today; we were at best "frenemies" then. "Oh, my boss saved my life, but he cut off my arms to do it." All that was behind us, though—no one could think of PJ any other way but with her buff bionic arms that she liked to show off.

My inspirational business "Bible," *How to be a Great Detective with 100 Rules,* written by my posthumous mentor, Mr. Wilford G., a ninety-two-year-old private eye who had worked the streets of Metropolis for seventy years, had a very simple axiom: "Verify everything, especially your clients." That's what I was doing. Everyone said how good Classic was as a counselor. I wanted to hear it for myself from Metro Psych

Services. I was amused by the fact that he also spoke to school children. The kids wanted to meet a real-life gangster. I doubted they could even tell you what he said in his talk five minutes after he left. All they cared about was that they had met a real gangster.

It was universally known as Metro Psych, but the real name of the department was Metropolis Mental Health Services Division, with Psych Services being one department and Cyborg Psych being a sub-department. Like all health offices for the city, there was lots of white and nothing else—white walls, white floors, even people wearing white.

"I'm here to see Dr. Silver-Rose," I said to one of the receptionists at the main counter when I entered.

They had me wait in the lobby, which had only two other people besides myself. One was a well-dressed woman who wore dark glasses, kept her gaze on her tablet, and never moved. The other was a clean-shaven man in a business suit who had his eyes glued on me from the time I sat down. As long as she wasn't drooling and he wasn't talking to an imaginary friend, I was fine.

"Mr. Cruz," one of the receptionists called. When I stood, she gestured to a door and buzzed me in.

Dr. Silver-Rose was Japanese and German. Tall, slender, dark hair and eyes. She led me through the hallway of Cyborg-Psych to her office/consulting room. She only spoke after she gestured to the chair in front of her desk and we both sat. The room didn't have that sterile feel of the exterior of the office; rather, it was filled with colors and curios all around. As I glanced around at the different objects on the desk, shelves, wall, and hanging from the ceiling, I felt that she was observing my subtle reactions.

"What information do you need from me, Mr. Cruz?"

"About Mr. Classic."

"Yes."

"Can you give me some background on him?"

"For what purpose?"

"He's a client, and I need to know all about him to help him. You're his boss."

"I am the head of the department, not his boss. He is an independent contractor with the city. Technically, the City Council is his boss."

"No one oversees him."

"We all oversee each other."

"What does that mean?"

"Exactly what I said. We observe the work of each other in the field, findings are shared as a group, and reports are compiled as a group."

I laughed. "Everyone is employee and boss at the same time. Shrinks."

"No, Mr. Cruz. We are scientists and psychiatrists."

"Dr., can you give me any non-group opinions on Mr. Classic?"

"Mr. Cruz, it would be helpful if you simply asked a direct question."

I felt like I was talking to a five-year old. She knew full well what I wanted without me having to spell it out.

"Many people have told me that Mr. Classic is very good at what he does. Can you elaborate, please?"

"Mr. Classic is a natural at connecting with his patients on an emotional and practical level. He's very adaptable and doesn't conform to a specific program or routine. He creates a different program to suit the patient for as short or long of a time as needed, always modifying along the way. He has positively channeled his own ego to be a very effective spokesperson on cyborg mental health issues. He's respected by the cyborg community and by the cyborg mental health provider community. What else do you wish to know, Mr. Cruz?"

"Of all the people who do what he does for Cyborg Psych, how would he rank?"

"Cyborg Psych?"

"That's what us Average Joes and Janes call you."

"Interesting. I would rank Mr. Classic in the top one percent."

"Better than you?"

"Of course. I'm not a cyborg."

"You have to be a cyborg for the job?"

"No, but he can provide empathic services to those who prefer a fellow cyborg."

"Do you like him?"

"What's the relevance of the question, Mr. Cruz?"

"It's a normal question, Dr."

"I don't think so, but I'll answer it. No, I don't like him, but I don't like most people."

"If that's the case, then you're right: my question wasn't relevant."

"Mr. Cruz, Mr. Classic is a valuable member of my team. If there were any concerns about his own mental state, he wouldn't be working here."

"Do you believe someone could be evil and simply turn it off and become good?"

"Another odd question to ask, since you said he's your client."

"You don't like most people. I don't trust most people."

"Fair enough. We may have colonized other planets, but we still can't read a person's mind. We can only observe and draw conclusions from present observations and prior behavior. What are you suggesting? Mr. Classic has been faking his transformation for a quarter century?"

"Dr., I'm about to embark on an extremely dangerous case on his behalf and I want to make sure that things are as presented, and that I'm not surprised in the end. I've had clients try to shoot me, shoot at me, try to involve me in illegal activities, try to get me to do illegal activities for them. I just want to make sure I have the full picture."

"Then Mr. Cruz, I'm sorry I can't help you. Human beings, cyborg or not, are the most complex of organisms. In the journals, I once read of a man sentenced to life in a maximum security facility. He was involved in a severe brawl and was put in a coma. The prison medical staff were positive he was faking. He lay in his room for fifteen years, until the last of the original medical staff retired. The new team came in and moved him to a low-security wing. The man escaped the prison, killing two guards inside and three on the outside before being killed by police.

"Another journal report I read in school, had a man sentenced to life for rape and mass murder over twenty years, starting at the age of ten. He became a chaplain in prison. There was a prison riot and the inmates took over. That man single-handedly led another group of prisoners to rescue the prison guards, subdue the inmates who had taken over, and turn the control of the prison back over to authorities. He was offered a pardon, but refused, saying, 'None of my victims get to go home. Why should I?' He died in prison.

"The problem, as you already know, Mr. Cruz, is which is which."

"Then Dr., let's build that mind-reading machine. We can split the profits fifty-fifty."

At least I got her to smile, which on second thought, might have been some kind of shrink trick to observe my behavior.

THE ELECTRIC LADY, GANGSTER GROUPIE

Classic was charming and charismatic. With his fancy suits and flashy smile, it would've been easy to get some city bureaucrat to overlook his past. They focused on current criminality, not events from long ago. But there was one more person I wanted to visit before I really got started on his case. I had to be convinced that Classic wasn't using me, like other clients had tried in the past. Even without reviewing Trendy's files, I knew I was about to go face-to-face with some very, very bad guys. It'd be nice to know that my client was on the level while I was doing so.

I was landing the Pony in Metal-Ville when my vehicle ID scanner beeped. It was what all Metro PD hovercruisers were equipped with to scan every hovercar and hovervehicle in range to identify outstanding tickets, stolen vehicles, or vehicles wanted by authorities. It was my latest modification to the Pony (meaning illegal), but it sure came in handy. My dashboard display screen said that the large silver hovercar that was leaving the parking curb belonged to Harder Steel—one of the crazy maniacs that might be after Classic. *How interesting.*

I made a mental note. In the detective business, you spent a lot of time in bars, restaurants, and clubs. Classic Cyborg reformed to become a city shrink. I had expected his daughter to go into a line of business that was more typical to an ex-hood's child, but her company was unexpected. I had never been to a glass factory before.

Inside the building, I found myself in a massive open area with so much noise, so many robotic arms working an assembly belt, and so many hoverbots buzzing about that I actually felt in danger. A worker in a yellow jumpsuit appeared and put a red hard hat on my head—yes, he put it on top of and crushed my tan fedora—then pointed me to what I assumed was the main office.

When I arrived, I was in a bad mood. I hated hard hats. I hated that my real hat was crushed. And I hated all the noise. I entered the office and closed the door. A heavyset woman stood behind the counter in a yellow jumpsuit and red hard hat, like every other human I had seen.

"Who are you?" she asked.

"Your man crushed my hat."

"Is that all?"

"Yeah."

"Give me the number for your mommy, and I'll call her down for you and your hurt feelings."

Another male worker appeared from an open door. "Maybe we should have left you out there. Ever suffered from a real head trauma? It's not like in the movies. No doctor's going to be able to fix your brain. It gets damaged, it stays damaged. Go on back out there and have one of the hoverbots crash into your head and see how it feels."

"Don't modern robots have sensors to prevent that from happening?"

"Listen to him," the woman said. "So you're a bum inspector."

"I'm not an inspector."

"You liar," she shouted at me. "We've been inspected already last week. Get out of here, you bum inspector!"

I was about to let loose on her but stopped myself. I closed my eyes and gave a loud sigh. I opened my eyes. "I'm sorry," I said without the attitude. "This is all my fault. I ignored the signs. Came into the area unprotected and then got mad. I'm sorry. I'm not an inspector. I'm a private detective and I'm here to see the owner." I placed my license and ID on the counter.

The woman looked at them, and the man from the office came closer and inspected them too.

"Private detective?"

"Her father hired me."

"Classic?" the man asked.

"Yes."

My change of attitude made them calm down too. She scooped up my license and ID and gave them back to me. "Wait here."

They both walked away from the counter and into the rear office. I took a seat on a waiting room bench—it was made out of neon orange glass. It felt like plastic to the touch but it was as solid as metal.

The main office door opened and there she was—The Electric Lady. That's what everyone called her. Her first name was Justyna. She was in standard yellow jumpsuit and red hard hat attire, but she had some fashionable heels and orange-tinted shades on.

"You," she said.

I stood to shake her hand, but she folded her arms.

"My father hired you?"

"Yes."

"You go tell my father that I'm a grown woman, and I can see whoever I want."

"Oh, the boyfriend," I said.

"He told you."

"No. I saw him leave in the silver hovercar."

"Yes, the boyfriend. You tell him to stay out of my life."

"Do you always date criminal cyborg maniacs?"

That was a mistake. She snatched me and literally threw me through the front doorway. The only lucky part for me was that the door didn't break as I flew out and landed hard on the ground outside. I was immediately overcome by the noise and the sight of flying hoverbots everywhere. *Yep, Electric Lady was a cyborg too*, I said to myself.

I decided the best approach was to stay on the ground. She stood over me as I lay there as if I were relaxing.

"Comfortable?"

"I am, actually."

"Get up off my ground and get out of my factory now. I won't throw you the next time. I'll kick you and shatter your ribcage."

I reached over and tapped each leg under her jumpsuit—the sound of metal.

"I promise to leave, after I talk to you for five minutes. Your father hired me, but he didn't hire me about your boyfriend."

"Why then?"

"Because someone is trying to kill him, and—please don't kick me—your boyfriend is on the suspect list."

She reached down and picked me up like a rag doll.

"What are you talking about? That's a lie. My father is spreading lies."

"Miss, I don't want to get in the middle of a family dispute. Can we talk for ten minutes?"

"You said five minutes."

"I lied."

"Follow me," she commanded and marched off.

I had to return my crushed fedora-hard hat combo to my head as I followed her along the outer perimeter of the factory wall to another set of doors. As I walked, I looked at the activity of the robots—large and small robot arms everywhere.

"I've never been to a glass factory. What type of glass?" I asked. I had to do something to keep her from even thinking of throwing or kicking me.

"Piorun Glass is a leader in the industry. Optical glass for Up-Top spaceships and satellites, fiberglass for Metropolis and around the world, glass steel for law enforcement and the military, structural glass for construction, and much more. Here."

She had led me down a hall to another office, but this time it was high-class all the way, one fit for a megacorp president. Every piece of furniture was made of some kind of colored glass. Her office colors were blues and whites.

"Tell me about these lies from my father," she snapped as soon as she sat down.

I sat in the single chair in front of her desk. "Your father feels his life is in danger."

"From my boyfriend? A lie!"

"Not from your boyfriend. From a small list of people that includes your boyfriend."

"He wouldn't dare."

"Your boyfriend? Why?"

"I'd kill him."

"Would you? Kill your boyfriend, go to prison for a few decades, and lose all this? That's tough talk from someone not involved in the crime world. Prison actually isn't fun, in case that's what you heard. How long have you been seeing your boyfriend?"

"None of your business."

"You want me to rule out your boyfriend as a suspect? Then answer me."

"A year."

"Has he ever talked about your father, ever?"

"I pursued him. He didn't even know who my father was."

"And why would you do that?"

"Do what?"

"Pursue him."

"Because—"

"Because of what? Because he's a gangster? It's kids like you who give kids like you a bad name. That's just plain stupid. There are other ways to annoy your father besides dating a gangster killer, or didn't they teach you that in private school."

"What's your name?"

"Cruz."

"Mr. Cruz, I have a growing impulse to knock your head off."

"Who's Pink Machete?"

"What?"

"Who's Pink Machete?"

"What is that?"

"Who's Franken-borg?"

This time she said nothing.

"Oh, so you know that one. You're a gangster groupie, is that it? Like your mother."

She jumped up from her chair. "Your ten minutes are up. Tell my father to stay out of my life."

"Miss. If your father wants to poke into your life, I don't think there is anything you, with your fancy bionics, or me, with my fancy guns, is going to do to stop him."

I stood from my chair, but stopped at the door.

"Miss, you need to dump the boyfriend and stay away from all of them. I look around and see a twenty-five-year old running her own successful company. You'd risk all that and your life just to spite your father. That's not just stupid, that's psychotic. You better seek counseling. These people will get you killed, and daddy won't be there to save you."

PINK MACHETE, CRAZY MANIAC #1

I t was something I liked to do: confront bad guys. I don't know why, and many told me that one day I'd confront the wrong one because they'd throw me out a two hundred-story window. I did it anyway. I had a knack for upsetting them. And upset criminals always made mistakes, which is how you caught them and foiled their criminal plans. However, in this case, I rationalized that I wasn't confronting the bad guy; rather, I was simply sizing up criminal psycho gangsters who might be trying to kill my client. All I was going to do was talk, create my own profile on them, and leave it to the police. But how wise was it to talk to a cyborg with the street name of Pink Machete?

It always amazed me that I had lived in Metropolis all my life and there were still districts I didn't even know existed, like Thunder Town. It was larger than most—a working-class neighborhood of old East Europeans—and it was where Classic was born, grew up, and still lived—in the north of the district. In the south, was where Pink Machete's gang sometimes hung out when they weren't committing crimes.

The storm still hung above the city like an alien force ready to pounce, a black barrier, and the rain remained a light drizzle. As I flew the Pony into the south of the district, I rehearsed in my mind how I was going to play it. I should have had an army of bodyguards with me, but that would have only made things worse before they had even begun. I had to be calm and casual.

There was one establishment they all liked to hang out in, or more precisely, liked to hang out in front of, laughing, drinking, and smoking as loudly and wildly as possible without having someone call the police on them. The whole street was a loud mess of all ages, and the real gangsters weren't even the rowdiest. The fact that there were secure parking lots with armed guards put the town on my "good" list. My Pony would be safe as I went to work.

"How long?" a huge security guard asked when I passed by the guard post at the elevators.

"Not sure."

"No overnight parking. Parking is allowed for twelve hours only. After, the twelve hours, the vehicle belongs to us, until you pay the fee."

I had dealt with guys like this before. You did not want to get on the wrong side of guys who were protecting your vehicle.

"I'll be out of here before then, sir."

There was a very simple rule that applied to most of Metropolis. Establishments with bright, neon signage with their name were legit; those without a name were shady or criminal. The club that the street gang was loitering in front of had no name. The gangsters were all dressed differently, but they all wore black and had on pink neon shades. Some were bald; some had wild hair, tattoos, piercings, or nothing at all. Some of them had hulking frames. Others were as skinny as a twig. As I approached, I wondered how they could be this frightening gang that I had heard of. Then I remembered. It wasn't them, it was their boss everyone was afraid of.

"Hey," I said as I reached them, my hands in my pockets.

At first, they ignored me. A few of them glanced my way but didn't say anything back. They were all talking in at least one other language, so I wouldn't be able to learn anything from them that way. I simply stood there.

"What do you want?" one of them finally asked.

"I'd like to talk with Mr. Pink Machete."

They were all paying attention to me now and started laughing hard.

"*Mr.* Pink Machete? What do you want from Mr. Pink Machete? Do you owe him money?"

"Nothing like that. I wanted to clear his name."

"What are you talking about?"

"Someone thinks Mr. Pink Machete is trying to kill him. I don't believe that, but my client is convinced and is very angry about it. I'm trying to keep him calm."

"You a detective?" another thug asked.

"I am."

"Who's your client?"

"Classic Cyborg."

It was like I had dropped a neutron bomb on them. The laughter and attitude was gone. They tried to hide it, but they were scared to the bone.

"You better tell the boss directly." The thug pushed a button on the back of his hand and it started blinking.

I kept my eyes on the gang. They nervously kept smoking, but no one talked.

"Who might you be?" a voice said behind me.

I turned to see Pink Machete. He was over six feet tall, clad in a pink slicker, dark shades, and bleached blond hair. If I had seen him on the street, I would have laughed, but Detective Trendy wouldn't be so concerned by some clown. I was seeing the "pink," but not the "machete."

"Cruz," I answered calmly.

"What is a Cruz?"

"A detective hired by Classic Cyborg. He thinks you're trying to kill him."

"Does he?" Unlike his men, Pink Machete was anything but afraid. His smile got wider, as if he was admitting that he had a contract out on my client.

"He does."

"Why are you here then? Here to plead for his life?"

"Hardly. I'm here to talk. Maybe talk some sense. Classic's been out of the racket since before you were born."

"Classic Cyborg is a legend."

"Yeah, maybe, but let's think this through. You leave him alone, and he continues playing shrink to a bunch of cyborgs with mental issues. Twenty-five years becomes thirty, then forty, then fifty. No one will ever remember him. You, on the other hand, will make an even bigger name for yourself. But if you don't leave him alone, then you're asking for him to get back in the game, or at the very least to retaliate. Why?"

"Why what?"

"Why would you make that play? Start a war with someone who's not even in business anymore. Make yourself vulnerable to your rivals. Put your name at the top of the police's Person of Interest list. Why? It makes no sense."

"It makes a lot of sense. Whoever did it would be the Man Who Killed Classic Cyborg."

"You'd kill someone to be known as the person who killed him? Lose your gang, your turf, and probably your life for a title?"

"You don't know much, do you, Cruz? Look at all the mass murders in history. No one ever knows the name of even one victim, but everyone remembers the mass murderer. Titles mean everything."

"You're right. I don't know much. I apologize for bothering you. I had hoped I'd be able to keep my client calm, but it seems this case won't be as easy as I hoped."

I didn't bother saying anything more. I turned and walked back the way I had come.

"You'll be back shortly," he said.

I glanced back, but didn't say anything.

The walk back to the parking garage took me the same ten minutes. I was concerned about being ambushed, but there were plenty of people around. I even saw a police cruiser coast nearby. When I got to the elevators, there were no guards. The two men I saw earlier were nowhere to be seen. Looking through the window of their guard post, everything was on, and a cup of coffee was on the counter.

I exited the elevators and couldn't walk fast enough, but then I stopped. I saw my Pony, but there was something on the roof and something on the hood. I ran to it. Before I got a clear view, I had already realized what the masses were. It was the guards, cut in half, their upper torsos thrown on my vehicle.

The rage that pulsed through my veins was barely controllable. There was nothing I could do for the poor men. They were dead. Now I knew what Pink Machete meant when he said I'd be back. I wanted to run back there and blow him away with every fiber of my being, which is exactly why I couldn't.

I took out my mobile and called the police.

HARDER STEEL, CRAZY MANIAC #2

Not only did the entire parking garage become a massive crime scene, but my Pony was now the center of a double homicide investigation with Evidence Collection crawling all over it. I might not see my vehicle for weeks or more. However, that wasn't what I was concerned about as I quietly sat on the pavement with two officers standing nearby waiting for the detectives to arrive.

The investigating officer turned out to be Trendy. I saw him as soon as he exited a landing police cruiser. Another man in civilian clothes got out, looking every bit like a gang member too, so I assumed he was his partner—a tall, muscled, Samoan-looking bald guy.

"I hope he's paying you enough," Trendy said when he and his partner reached me.

"This entire building and parking lot had surveillance. Tell me that it caught who did this on disk," I said.

"Nothing," Trendy said. "All the cameras went dead before the attack."

"It doesn't matter. I know who did it."

"Who's that, Cruz?"

"Pink Machete! He did it himself. I'm positive of that."

"He always does, Cruz."

"What are you going to do?" I snapped at him.

"Unless you recorded the whole murder on your mobile, nothing. But you know that."

"Then can I go home?"

"Cruz, you know better than that. You'll be interviewed for your statement, then you can call a hovercab or someone to collect you at Police Central."

"I get my vehicle taken, lose hours of my day, and the crazy maniac who did this gets to laugh away out there in a pink outfit."

"Yeah, Cruz. That's how it works. Welcome to the real world. Let's get out of here before you do something unwise and illegal and get yourself arrested."

I'd been "chauffeured" to Metro PD many times before, but this was different. Both men who had been killed had families and that made me angrier. Trendy was right, the best place for me was to be in some kind of police custody. I was too dangerous to be wandering the streets in my frame of mind.

It seemed I was right back in the exact same interview room that Trendy and I had spoken in earlier. His partner sat in the chair next to him as he continued.

"Why do you all do this? I gave my statement already—five different times."

"Cruz, you know why, so I'm going to ignore you. I have a few more questions for you. You believe Pink Machete killed the two guards before he showed up at the club."

"Detective, you don't need to be a detective to figure that one out."

"Then that would mean he was at the parking lot as soon as you arrived and killed them right after you left. Right?"

I was already ahead of him and had come to the same conclusion.

"I take your silence as agreement. How did he know you were coming to see him? Did you tell anyone?"

"No."

"Then how?"

"I have my own theories."

"Care to share?"

"No."

"Cruz."

"Detective, criminals can figure out things too. You told me there were three gangsters. I stumbled on the girlfriend of one, who told the boyfriend, and the other must have found out from there."

"Girlfriend? Electric Lady is dating one of these psychos. Harder Steel?"

"Yes."

"Pink Machete admitted to plotting to kill Classic."

"Yes, he did. He wants to be the Man Who Killed Classic Cyborg."

"What about the others?"

"One down, two more to talk to."

"Cruz, I'm going to tell you again. You need to walk from this one. The body count is two, but if you don't stop—"

"Detective, the body count isn't because of me. We have to keep the body count from rising, but that isn't going to happen if we walk away and pretend that some kind of gang war isn't coming."

"You said Classic would move out of Metropolis."

"I said that. I didn't say I believed it."

"You don't believe it."

"Of course, not. Would you leave your home and your daughter behind to run away from these punks?"

"What are you going to do now?"

"Why? Are you going to give me a police security detail?"

"That would be a 'no.' You're going to see Harder Steel?"

"That would be a better move than visiting the one that I don't want to be in the same district as."

"Cruz, Cruz. Do not, do not, shake his hand."

"What?"

"Do not let Harder Steel shake your hand."

"That would be bad, huh?"

"It would be very bad."

"Detective, at least with him, I won't be alone. I'll have the girlfriend there."

"You don't know much about Electric Lady, do you?"

"She's a megacorp CEO. She'll behave, and he'll behave because she's there."

"She hates her father, and you were hired by her father. I think you're completely underestimating the danger you'll be in."

"Trendy, after this, I won't be underestimating anything ever again when it comes to this case."

Without my Pony for at least a month, I was relegated to permanent hovertaxi use. The only consolation was that Trendy told me that they'd collect the evidence and wouldn't pull my Pony apart to see all my nice (and illegal) vehicle modifications. For transportation, I could have used a Let It Ride taxi for free, but I wasn't about to bring my best friend's company into this case. I felt like I was playing a game where all the participants knew all the rules and tricks except for me, but I was a quick learner.

I found out why Classic's daughter was called the Electric Lady. The driver dropped me at another no-name club, but this one couldn't be called seedy (even though it was) because it had more flashing neon and lights than I had ever seen. There was the Electric Lady, without the red hard hat and orange jumpsuit. She strolled to the main entrance in a half black slicker and underneath—a shimmering, extra-tight, thigh-high dress and glowing heels. Her arms, legs, neck, chin, and points on her temple all flickered blue. She was a walking light show.

I'd almost forgotten my mission. She was arm-in-arm with her boyfriend, Harder Steel. He wasn't as tall as Pink Machete, but he was much bigger in width. He was bald and wore dark glasses, a silver slicker opened to show his bare-chest underneath, silver pants, and black platform shoes. She was an elegant cyborg; he was a blocky, Neanderthal of a cyborg.

I was not about to talk to either of them once they went inside, which is why I waited for them at the main entrance. She noticed me right away, and I could see her look of disgust. He noticed her expression then took off his shades to glare at me with his two eye-socket-enclosed bionic eyes.

"I told my boyfriend what my father said," she said.

"Thanks. That'll save time."

The gangster let go of her hand and stepped over to me. "A detective, huh? What if I do have a contract out on him? What would that old man Classic do about it?"

I looked at her. "Are you okay with what he's saying? He's saying it's okay to want to kill your father."

"Don't talk to her. Talk to me." His bionic arm grasped my shoulder. It was heavy but it stopped short of squeezing.

"Mr. Steel, I don't want any trouble. I'm talking."

"If you didn't want any trouble, you wouldn't have come down here when my girlfriend and I are enjoying ourselves at our club. If you didn't want any trouble, you wouldn't have gone to my girlfriend's company and disrespected her."

"Your girlfriend threw me through a door, so I'd say we're even."

"But I didn't get to throw you around yet."

"I actually came down to give your girlfriend a photo."

"Photo?" Steel asked.

"Yes." I already had it in my hand and gave it to her. "The photo is of two men that an acquaintance of your boyfriend, named Pink Machete, killed earlier today. Both men had families, never bothered anyone, never hurt anyone. Now they're dead for no reason. Actually, they're dead because of you. You called your boyfriend about our conversation, then your boyfriend let Pink Machete know, and then Pink Machete killed them to send a message to your father. Pink Machete killed the men, but you two caused their death. I'll leave you both to enjoy yourselves. You can keep the photo."

Electric Lady was partly human. I could see her eyes tearing up. Harder Steel said nothing, but he was turning red.

Maybe a guilt trip would work on them, maybe not. What was clear to me was that Classic was absolutely right: two of his "suspects" were out to kill him. Worse, his daughter knew about it and didn't seem to care. It was possible she was even involved in the plot herself.

In nightlife districts like this one, hovertaxis were everywhere. I signaled one and it descended in no time. I opened the passenger door and was about to hop in when the driver rocketed upwards. My hand instinctively held onto the door handle and I was hoisted up into the air just as a hovercar crashed down where I had been a moment before. Then my hand involuntarily let go and I dropped ten feet to the ground, falling back and landing on my butt.

"I'm going to kill you for upsetting my girlfriend!"

I didn't need to look. I knew who it was. I jumped to my feet, turned, and started firing from my omega-gun, already in hand. Both rounds hit him in the chest, but he laughed.

"You have to do better than that, detective. Here, my turn."

I watched the cyborg jump into the air, realizing that his platform shoes were not a fashion accessory at all, so he could be taller than the girl, but were hovershoes. He grabbed a hovercar that was landing and with sheer might threw it in my direction. The driver must have mistakenly hit the accelerator rather than the air brakes, because the hovercar came at me so fast I barely jumped out of the way. The car hit the pavement, flipped twice, and crashed through the bay window of a diner. I lost count of how many pedestrians were hit by the hovercar projectile, and how many were now injured in the diner. All I heard were screams.

I aimed my omega-gun in the direction of Harder Steel—this time on a setting that would send him straight to hell. But he was nowhere to be seen.

FRANKEN-BORG, CRAZY MANIAC #3

In my very first case as a detective, the "Case of the Guy Who Scratched My Vehicle" (I'm much better at naming my cases nowadays), I witnessed something like this, but there wasn't anything funny this time. Police arrived to secure the scene—fifteen wounded and three dead.

I saved myself the grief and left the scene before the police arrived. If I had stayed, even though I had nothing to do with the homicides, all that would have mattered to the police was that I was involved. I would have been at Police Central for the rest of the night and probably wouldn't get out of interrogation—no more friendly interviews—until noon the next day.

I had met one cyborg who could cut people in half and another who could jump into the air, grab flying hovercars, and throw them at you. These gangsters weren't afraid of the police, which most criminals were; they were afraid of the police catching them and stripping their bodies of all their illegal bionics. That's why Harder Steel did his vanishing routine, and

I'm sure the Electric Lady would be all but impossible to locate too.

I had PJ call Classic, and when he called back, find out where I could meet him. So, where was Mr. Classic Cyborg? He was leading a Tai chi exercise class at the Metro Senior Living Center. Right up until my hovertaxi landed and I walked in, I couldn't believe it. However, I couldn't deny what was right in front of my eyes. An auditorium filled with exercising cyborgs of all types—none under the age of sixty—in row after row, standing on purple mats that covered the entire floor.

Classic was at the front in a white martial arts robe, showing off that bionic chest of his. Tai chi was very popular—the slow movement exercises and controlled breathing; it wasn't viewed as martial arts anymore, but pure meditation and life stress reduction.

I stood at the back watching them. To see them all move in unison was actually quite compelling. Everyone in their colored martial arts uniforms of whites, yellows, blues, purples, silvers, and pinks made you want to join in. I could've watched them exercise all day, so I sat cross-legged on the floor to do so.

Mr. Classic finished the Chinese exercise class, did a Japanese bow, and the class returned the gesture, then the chatter erupted. The only group chattier than little kids were the other end of the spectrum—senior citizens. Classic saw me, but he had to do his thing—shaking hands, patting shoulders and backs of his students.

"Mr. Cruz," he said as he shook my hand too. "You're here to give me an update."

"Yes."

"There's an office we can use."

I followed him to an empty office on the floor. It was a reading room with bean bag chairs in the center. Along the walls were traditional long tables with stools. Of course, we sat in the bean bag chairs.

"Tai chi too," I said. I loved how bean bag chairs swallowed you up. "When you transformed yourself, you really did transform yourself."

"I needed something to replace all that anger at my core. Always thought of martial arts as a way to kill a man. Never knew it could be used for anything else, but that's what I've done all these years. Replaced the anger with the serenity of purpose."

"You've done that without a doubt."

"But?"

"Are we in the process of being pulled back in?"

"You seem to be angry with me, Mr. Cruz."

"I'm here to tell you that I've closed your case. Yes, they're trying to kill you."

He laughed as he went into a shoulder rolling exercise, forward then backward. "That kind of sloppiness is not your reputation, Mr. Cruz. I was told you are very precise in these things. Just because they want to kill me, or want you or others to believe it, is not the same as identifying the real identity behind the two attempts and current contract on my life. I need to know who."

"When were you going to tell me your own daughter is dating one of them?"

"Why? You're a detective. You found that out without me having to say anything. I'm sure you've added her name to the suspect list."

"Five people are dead, Mr. Classic."

"Did you kill them?"

I wasn't really liking my client at the moment.

"Mr. Cruz, you're a professional. People get killed all the time. Innocent people get killed all the time too. Who have you met with so far—of the suspects?"

"Your daughter, her boyfriend Harder Steel, and Pink."

He smiled. "Yes, I can see why you say that. You haven't seen his machete yet."

"But the two parking lot guards that he sliced in half did."

"You are angry with me. Mr. Cruz, it's not your fault or mine. Me hiring you. You taking the case. You working the case. We didn't kill these people. They did. And if it wasn't these people, it would have been others, whether I hired you or not, whether you took the case or not. You need to continue."

"Why?"

"Mr. Cruz, they know you're working for me now. You can't stop until you're done. We must see it to the end. Seems like you have one more person left to question."

"I don't find that funny."

"It wasn't meant to be."

"There is no way that I'm going anywhere near a gangster named Franken-borg, especially after my encounters with the other two. Stupid isn't brave where I come from."

"I hear you're very thorough, so I know you will. I'm counting on you, Mr. Cruz, for a good result. Franken-borg isn't all that scary. I heard you've dealt with scarier cyborgs that him, or me, Up-Top."

"Those cyborgs I didn't deal with. We kept them from setting foot on the space station. If they had, I probably wouldn't be sitting here. My body would be orbiting Pluto, along with the army of police and corporate samurai soldiers who were with me."

"The point is, Mr. Cruz, that you found a way among the options available to you that the others didn't. You'll do it again. You should call your office manager."

"Why?"

"Call her."

Classic hopped to his feet. I looked at them and they looked like metal skeleton toes and feet. He was doing more exercises, standing up on his tiptoes. He stopped, turned, and left me in the room.

I dialed the office on my mobile. PJ's face appeared on the tiny display.

"PJ."

"What's up, boss?"

"Mr. Classic told me to call you. Why? What happened?"

"Nothing happened. He added a bonus, a big bonus."

"*Muy grande.*"

"Very good, Cruz. I'll tell your mother you're finally learning another language. Yes, *muy grande, très grand*."

Once the French started, it meant I had to end the call.

Ironically, the scariest cyborg of the three had the thinnest file. I was thankful that Detective Trendy had allowed me to see the files, but there wasn't much in them that I could use. They were filled with a lot of rumors, but very little confirmed fact. Franken-borg's file didn't even have an actual photo, which made me even more apprehensive about walking around. Pink Machete had been tracking me, Harder Steel would have his gang looking for me, so I had to assume that somewhere out there was the third. That's what worried me.

I sat in my loaner hovercar across the street from the entrance to the parking bay of my Liquid Cool office tower. If you were being hunted, then look for your hunter where they're likely to be waiting for you. That's what I was doing; I was on stakeout. As I sat there and watched, I wished that it had been raining. It was overcast, the storm clouds of the century hanging above the supercity, but now there wasn't a single droplet falling. I didn't like it. I glanced at the clock on the dashboard. I had been waiting for almost three hours but figured it wouldn't be long before something happened.

"Hello, my name's Cruz," I said, "and I'm a private detective hired by Classic Cyborg. He's hired me because he's heard from credible sources that you're planning on making an attempt on his life, but he feels it's all a big misunderstanding. On behalf of my client, I'd like to talk to you and clear this whole thing up. I'll be at my office all day, so give me a call at your earliest convenience. We need to keep the police out of this."

It was the message I prerecorded and sent to Franken-borg's audio-only number that my own credible sources said was this maniac's "business" line. I had PJ send it two hours ago after I was comfortably settled in at my current stakeout post.

My eyes were constantly scanning the area—the ground for pedestrians and the sky for hovertraffic. Suddenly, a hoverlimo slowly and illegally coasted two feet above my windshield. I watched it continue away and disappear. It was actually a hearse, not a limo. My heart was already lying at the bottom of my stomach when the hoverhearse flew by—these maniacs liked drive-by shootings. I decided to go with my instincts and abandon my hovercar.

I had just stepped out of my hovercar when another—or the same—hoverhearse appeared. All I heard was a click. My body hit the asphalt fast as my loaner hovercar was sprayed with bullets and lasers.

My omega-gun was called the gun to end all private guns, or that's what it said in its manual. What made my Up-Top weapon so special was its accessories, and the ability to switch its settings with a flick of a thumb. I fired my omega-gun once and heard a grunt. I heard yelling inside the vehicle, but I had already switched to automatic-mode and fired my own laser volley into the open windows. The hoverhearse lurched forward, but I kept firing, blowing out the back windows. Then the vehicle caught fire. Pedestrians were running away screaming as I watched the fire engulf it as it flew away.

From my slicker, I pulled out my special glasses and put them on. Those were the men, but where was the boss? *I saw him.* Across the street from me in the shadows was a massive figure of a man—more than seven feet tall with a barreling chest. As he stepped out from where he was waiting, I could see that his bionic arms made him look like he had the body of an ape—his arms actually touched the ground.

There were no pictures of Franken-borg. He was considered the most frightening cyborg criminal in Metropolis. Here I stood watching him as I'm sure so many others had done before, but they were all dead. I'm sure many of them had formidable weapons too, probably quite a few were powerful cyborgs, but Franken-borg had killed all of them. My glasses allowed me to zoom in on his face and see into the shadows where he stood. He was grinning—so he had night-sight too.

He expected me to run like a rabbit. Instead, I started marching toward him. His smile disappeared, and both eyebrows rose. Then I started running at him as fast as I could. His face went wild, and he raised both arms. I threw the items at him and dove.

Franken-borg's arms fired some kind of circular pulse laser weapon that I had never seen before. My first grenade was obliterated instantly. The second one was hit by his beam and it exploded as it ricocheted back. The third he concentrated all his firepower on and shot it apart.

"Do you think you're the first person to try that?" he bellowed. He was about to laugh when I jumped up and hit him in the face with an orange.

"No, but I'm sure that was," I yelled. The guidance systems in his bionic eye or eyes defended against and homed in on metal and alloys, not a piece of fruit.

There was no running from this cyborg. I was sure it was a fatal mistake that many others had made. I hit the button on my jetpack and flew into the sky, but I never once took my eye off Franken-borg. I had to wear a jetpack, but his was probably welded to his body. He followed after me, yelling a string of obscenities as to what he was going to do to me the second he caught me.

I hopped onto the roof of the mega-tower, two hundred stories up. At that very moment, it started. Franken-borg landed on the roof just as the sky erupted in the loudest thunderclap I had ever heard in my life. Hovercar alarms began going off everywhere as the torrential rain poured down.

Franken-borg was distracted. It was as if he had never seen lightning before. He looked back down as he wiped the blood off his neck. I had been firing at him the second his gaze looked up. He laughed as he raised his ape arms again, but dropped them.

"What did you do to me?" he yelled. He started to shake his head violently, his eyes closed, his teeth clenched.

"You shouldn't have tried to kill Classic."

"I didn't try to kill Classic," he answered. His eyes closed and his head shaking became more violent. "If I had tried to kill him, he'd be dead. But I was about to make my move soon."

"Then you shouldn't have tried to kill me."

"I'm *going* to kill you." He stopped shaking his head and half-opened his eyes in the rain.

"Not in this life, because I already killed you."

"What did you do to me?" he yelled again. His arms rose and he screamed. The circular pulse blasts would have cut me in half had I not dropped to the ground.

Lightning flashed. He stopped to look at it again. Another thunderclap pounded. My omega-gun in its normal configuration didn't have enough kick, but my collapsible laser shotgun did. I extended it and fired one blast after another at him. First in the head, then I concentrated everything else into his chest. He couldn't see, but he kept firing at me. I blasted him off the roof and saw his body fall, but I knew I wouldn't be that lucky.

"What did you do to me?" I heard him yell as he went over.

He flew up in the air but his eyes were swollen shut. His mouth and nostrils were foaming. I had one more for him and threw it. The grenade exploded and down he went. I ran to the edge of the roof to watch the cyborg crash to the ground. Time itself slowed, and it felt as if I watched his falling body become a tiny dot for a long time. Having heard it before, he made the sound that a full hovercar would have made if it too "returned to the surface." I waited a bit, but there was no movement. Franken-borg was dead.

DEAD POOL DAX

I sat in my private office with the door closed watching the news on my desk computer. If I had known what was being reported, I don't think I would've been able to dispatch Franken-borg to the morgue where he belonged. I would've been too scared. The circular blasts from his arm guns were deadlier than I could have imagined. I had dodged them, but the pulse waves bombarded past to the buildings across the street. I watched as media cameras showed the entire impact area dissolving to dust. The police had to condemn not one, but two mega-towers. I felt sick at the prospect that I could have been dissolved. I had done worse to someone in my last major case, but that was a Martian weapon against a bad guy.

"Mr. Cruz, the police are here to see you," PJ's voice came over my desk intercom in her "professional voice." But before I could respond, the door opened.

Detective Trendy waltzed in with his Samoan-looking partner. I was expecting to see a whole army of police officers behind them in their silver-and-gray armored uniforms. However, it was only the two of them. Trendy sat in the chair in front of my desk. His partner walked to the lounge area of my office and threw himself onto the couch.

I turned off the news on my computer. "Is your partner about to take a nap?" I asked.

"He's getting comfortable," Trendy answered. "Watching the news?"

"Yes, I have to stay informed. Violent crime is all around us."

"Yeah, and right down the street from you too."

"It used to be right at my front door, so I'm making progress."

Trendy watched me, smiling. "Where were you today?"

"I was right here in my office all day. Came in at eight a.m. and have been here ever since. I haven't even gone to lunch yet."

"Yes, officer. That is true." PJ was standing at the open doorway.

Trendy glanced at her with his smile and looked back at me. "Already got your stories straight."

"Detective, what do you mean?"

"Save it, Cruz. I'm not even going to waste my time. You know that other cyborg, Harder Steel. It seems he tried to kill someone with a hovercar, but missed and ended up killing a few innocent civilians near a club. People are telling us that you were that person he was trying to kill."

"It wasn't me. I know nothing about it."

"Then we come here and someone has killed the 'unkillable' Franken-borg. I didn't tell you this, but even Classic was scared of him. There isn't a crime boss or gang that wasn't scared of him. Now he's dead."

"Dead? How did it happen?"

"Cruz, you're not that good of an actor. We're checking to see if your face was picked up on any camera anywhere, but I'm sure Franken-borg already took care of that for you. He thought he was going to kill you, and look what you did to him."

"It wasn't me," I insisted.

"There isn't much left of him, but the medics did find traces of Devil Spit, that's the street name, on the body. A person's throat and nostrils swell shut, and the person either suffocates or drowns on their own saliva. It's classified as a bio-toxin and is a banned substance on Earth and Up-Top. So if the two hundred-story fall didn't kill him, he was dead anyway. Cruz, I have to hand it to you, I would never have thought of that one myself. And they say you're a germophobe. But my partner and I didn't come here for any of that."

"It wasn't me, detective."

"Save it, Cruz. Everyone knows."

"Everyone knows what?"

"Everyone knows you killed him. The unkillable Franken-borg, the cyborg monster himself, was killed by the famous Cruz, the detective. Everyone knows. It's already all over streets."

I was starting to feel sick.

"But it gets better." Trendy was smiling again. "Franken-borg has a brother. Guess what his street name is? Robo-Stein. Thought I should warn you as we sweep up his brother from the pavement down the street."

They heard me swallow hard. Trendy hopped up from the chair. "Cruz, you're the Man Who Killed Franken-borg. Now you're *really* famous, just not in the way you'd like."

I heard the partner pick himself up off my couch. He was smiling too. They walked out.

"When do I get my vehicle back from forensics?" I yelled.

PJ looked back at me with her mouth hanging open. "You killed Franken-borg?"

PJ was like a hyped-up kid after too much candy. She was on the phone to friends of friends of friends. I did what I could to find out about Robo-Stein by first calling Metro PD. When I got the public file over the Net, there was less information on him than Franken-borg. I had to rely on PJ's connections to get me some kind of information.

She appeared in my office with her electric steno-pad. "I got it," she declared. "Robo-Stein ran their gang with his brother, Franken-borg. How did you kill him? Everybody's talking about you."

"Criminals you mean."

"Of course."

"I don't care about the criminals."

"Thirty percent of our clients are criminals."

"Don't remind me. What about Robo-Stein? What's his cyborg specialty?"

"He's bionic from the neck up. They say his brain is bionic and he's super smart."

"Remember Red Rabbit? He supposedly had a bionic brain too, but where is he? A living vegetable in a prison clinic."

"No one's scared of Robo-Stein, even though he's supposed to be genius smart. They were scared of his brother, and you killed him. How? How did you do it?"

"I'm smarter than Robo-Stein."

"People are scared of you now."

"Why can't I find any pictures of these guys? Police only had a sketch of Franken-borg—"

"They got good pictures of him now, as human mush on the pavement."

"There's not even a description of what Robo-Stein looks like. How can we watch out for him?"

"You can't."

"Why?"

"He changes his head."

I looked up at her. "What?"

"He wears a different head depending on his mood. His outer head is removable and changeable. That's why there's no description."

"PJ, are you serious?"

"The man has no head. A bad accident as a kid. Same accident that made his brother a cyborg too."

"We're looking for a cyborg crime boss who changes his heads. Great! PJ?"

"Yes."

"I hate the future."

She laughed.

I had my door closed again, but this time I was doing research on the computer. If I stood close to the glass, I could see the red and blue light show at the corner of Circuit Circle. Two entire buildings were being red-tagged as city hovervehicles arrived on the scene to begin repairs. I had bested a cyborg who literally could take down an entire mega-tower.

I sat in my chair and sighed. My posthumous mentor, Wilford G., warned in his book, *How to be a Great Detective with 100 Rules,* "Sometimes you get a case you just don't want to do anymore, and want to run from as quickly as possible, or pretend it doesn't exist or pray the client fires you." His advice: "Double-down, work the case hard and fast, and close it."

"PJ!" The door opened and PJ stuck her head in. "Get Mr. Classic in here."

"Closing this case?"

"Case is closed, but now I have the pleasure of having three crazy cyborg maniacs after me."

"Tell the cops."

"What are they going to do? The street police may like me, but they're not my bodyguards. We're on our own here."

"What are you going to do?"

"I need to make these cyborgs the police's problem, not mine."

"How? These are very bad people."

"Exactly, so I'm going to be doing my civic duty for the police. Find someone they robbed, assaulted, or did some kind of crime to. I need these three off the streets as quick as possible."

"I'll see what I can find out."

"You're not a criminal anymore PJ, and when you were, it was in France. No, you wouldn't know any of the people we need to find, and neither would any of your friends. This is the real mean streets. Neither one of us knows that world. We can't pretend, and rumors on the street about what's going on there don't count. We need experts. I want these guys in jail or dead, period. And their gangs too."

"You're killing invincible cyborgs and going after their gangs."

"They cut two men in half and threw their upper torsos on the Pony. They pulled a hovercar from the air and made it crash into a restaurant, killing more people. I don't forget that."

"It wasn't your fault."

"No, but I feel responsible. I want these three."

"What about the daughter?"

"I'm not sure how she fits in yet, so Mr. Classic's going to handle that one on his own. Whether he wants to or not."

"I guess I'll keep my shotgun handy at my desk from now on."

"I'll be doing the same."

"Hunting aliens last time, now bad cyborgs. You're Cyborg Hunter."

"Three leaders and their gangs."

"I think Mr. Classic is the genius," PJ said and I already realized what she profoundly was referring to but asked anyway.

"Why do you say that?"

"He was concerned that three criminal cyborgs were trying to kill him. He hires you, and so begins the end of those three criminal cyborgs and their gangs. Lucky for him, or very clever of him."

I nodded. "Yes, very."

With the madness on Circuit Circle, the safest place for me was to stay in my office. PJ had gotten us lunch, and I even had her reschedule my clients for the rest of the day.

"Boss." I heard PJ call from the main office, but she wasn't at the doorway. I had heard one or more people enter—walk-ins were common in this business, but I was taking no chances. I came out with my omega-gun pointing.

Standing near the main door was a man in a cheap striped suit with his slicker draped over one arm. He had a thug-in-a suit with him holding a black briefcase. "Oh, please, please," he said. "Mr. Cruz, this is a friendly visit."

"Everyone knows my name. Who are you?"

"My name's Dead Pool Dax."

"All these colorful street names."

"In my racket, I wouldn't get far by just going by Dax."

"Tell me what you want and leave. I'm very nervous these days, and that makes my trigger finger even more nervous."

"I'm sure. Actually, that's why I'm here. Have you ever heard of the Dead Pool?"

"Hence, your name Dead Pool Dax. No, what is it?"

"You're a legit operator, so that's not surprising. There's the legal gambling world, then the illegal one. In the illegal gambling world, bettors can bet on anything at all. There's even the Dead

Pool where bettors can bet on who will be killed first and so on in the many street battles that plague our great supercity."

"My trigger finger is getting tired."

"Bear with me, Mr. Cruz. The punch line will be well worth your time. This Dead Pool pits the old crime legend Classic Cyborg against three who wish to take his life and his name: Pink Machete, Harder Steel, and Franken-borg. Lots of money has already gone into the pot to predict who'll die first and who'll be the last man standing. This week another player was added to the pool as a side bet. Yes, Mr. Cruz—*you*. I never knew a legit operator like you had killed so many bad guys out there. Very impressive, Mr. Cruz, but nothing compared to today. All the big money was not just on Franken-borg killing you, but everyone else in the pool. All the serious money said Franken-borg would be last man standing. But the serious money was wrong. You're still standing, Mr. Cruz, while Franken-borg lies in pieces at the City Morgue."

"Why are you here?" I asked.

"Your winnings, Mr. Cruz."

"What?"

"I brought your winnings."

The thug lifted his arm with the briefcase and opened it. PJ and I both gasped at the amount of money in the case.

"Yours, Mr. Cruz."

"Why would I get money from this Dead Pool? I didn't bet."

"You're legit so you don't understand the rules. You don't have to join in the bet to get winnings. If your name is added to the Dead Pool, meaning you can be killed, then you automatically become a participant. People bet money that Franken-borg would kill you, you killed him, they lost, so a percentage of the money in the pot is yours."

The thug closed the briefcase, and PJ took it from him.

"But it doesn't make sense," PJ said.

"If people are going to make money from the deaths of those in the pool, the least we can do is allow the survivors of the pool to get in on the action."

I was at a complete loss of words.

"Yes, it's exciting isn't it?" Dead Pool Dax smiled.

"When did this Dead Pool begin."

"The first of the year."

"January 1st?"

"Yes."

"That's nine months ago."

"It's not unusual for someone to set up a Dead Pool before it goes live. They have to put up the initial cash, get things set up, prepare. We've also had Dead Pools set up and wrapped up in ten minutes."

"When did it go live?"

"A month ago."

"Is this year significant in some way?"

"Mr. Cruz, it's Classic Cyborg's twenty-fifth year anniversary of his retirement. The perfect time to kill him and take his name."

"You say that as if it's done all the time."

"Because it is, Mr. Cruz."

"What happens now?"

"Money will continue to be paid out as people die."

"Who opened, if that's the term, this Dead Pool?"

"You're a quick study, Mr. Cruz, but unfortunately that's the one question I can't answer."

"The identity is a secret."

"It is."

"You know who it is, don't you?"

"I do. I'm Dead Pool Dax, but I never tell or there would be no Dead Pool."

"This is a lot of fun for you, isn't it?"

"Yes, it is." Dax was laughing under his breath.

"Who do the odds favor to win now?"

"Mr. Cruz, you have turned the whole pool upside down now that you killed Franken-borg. His brother, Robo-Stein, was added to the pool, but no one takes him seriously. Classic Cyborg is the favorite again to win—tied with you."

"What does that mean?"

"Either he'll be the last man standing or you will. If you are, then you'll be getting another pay-out, much bigger though."

"This is sick."

"Yes, Mr. Cruz, it is. That's why it's extremely illegal, but so much fun."

ROBO-STEIN, NEW CRAZY MANIAC #3

The briefcase was filled with so much money that it took nearly thirty minutes for PJ and me to count, sort, and bind it all up to deposit in the bank. I learned a long time ago that the larger the total amount of money, the smaller the bills criminals liked to have. In the criminal world smaller bills were always the safest currency.

"Crime pays," PJ remarked.

"It sure does, but they can keep the life," I said as we put the stacks of money back into the briefcase on my desk.

"But we can keep the money?"

"We can keep the money."

She smiled. "I was making sure you hadn't gone crazy."

"If we have to constantly defend against crazy maniacs, why should we have to pay for it. I'm happy to have *them* pay for it."

"What now?"

"Get the cleaners up here. Sanitize the whole outside area thoroughly. Dirty people carry all kinds of dirtiness with them. I don't want any of it on Liquid Cool's furniture, carpets, or in the air."

PJ laughed. The phone began ringing.

"I'll get it," I said and walked to my desk to sit. I pushed the button of my desk vid-phone. "Liquid Cool—Detective Trendy."

He grinned when he saw me answering the line, but he was much more serious this time.

"Can't stay away from me, detective?"

"Cruz, I thought you should know that the Franken-gang is dead."

"What? Franken-gang? What do you mean?"

"Franken-borg, like all gangsters, had his own gang. It was called the Franken-gang. 'Was' being the key word because someone wiped out every last member of the gang within the hour. Robo-Stein is all that's left. I thought you should know."

"He wouldn't."

"If I'm him, I'd definitely be coming for you."

"Detective, how can Metro PD allow these criminals to run wild? You can at least bring them in for questioning. Five people are dead."

"Seven now."

"Seven? How seven?"

"When you were battling Franken-borg to death he either fired his arm cannons at the buildings on the way up or on the way down. Either way, he blasted a whole crowd on one of the floors—the smoking area. Two dead, three seriously wounded, another half dozen wounded."

"Detective! These maniacs need to be brought in!"

"Cruz, I'm going to ignore you because you more than most know the limitations of the police department. We need solid leads, not outrage. Metropolis isn't a dictatorship any more than planet Earth. It's a free and open society of over fifty million people. We're looking for these criminal cyborgs, but they're all in hiding. In Robo-Stein's case, hiding or not, I'd bet you'll come across him long before we do."

"Thanks, detective, for letting me know."

"I told you to walk away from the case." He hung up on his end.

PJ was staring at me. "Wiped out?"

"Yeah. Didn't you say this Robo-Stein was a genius?"

"Yes, that's what I was told."

"Then why is all of his gang dead? You know what that means, right?"

"No."

"Stake-out time, PJ. Robo-Stein's already here in the building."

"What?" PJ said with a surprised look.

PJ saw to the cleaners; the building had an exclusive contract with one company that, for a fee, would thoroughly wash and clean every inch of your office. The guys they sent we had used before so there was no fear of plants from Robo-Stein or any of the other gangs.

I cloned the feeds of our security cameras to my desk computer. Then I transferred them to the wall display screen in the lounge area of my office. There I sat, staring at the different monitors—the main entrance, the elevators, the hallway outside, and the parking bay level where we parked. The cameras didn't show many people. So few people came into work, it was like a national holiday. Everyone was afraid of the impending storm. In my book, it was the best case of a bad situation. Few people in the hallways, streets, and parking area meant fewer potential victims and fewer opportunities for the new gang leader to exploit. He may or may not have known he had no gang left, but I felt he was very much like his late brother. He would want to handle any revenge job personally.

The Storm of the Century still had not let go its full fury. It was almost as if it wanted to help me out in my battle with Franken-borg and then go back to its holding pattern. The rain had already stopped when I got back to my office. What remained was the occasional thunderclap and bolt of lightning. As I stared at the wall viewscreen, I tried to imagine I was Robo-Stein. But I'd never met him, had no profile on him, and didn't know his background. He was a genius, so how would he avenge his brother and get me. Where would he lay in wait? I needed data.

"PJ! Don't forget to call Classic and have him come down here!"

"He called us!" I heard her yell back from the main area. "He'll be in first thing tomorrow morning. He can't get out of his anti-gang workshop at one of the schools."

Funny. I wondered if that was true or a perfect excuse to wait a day to see if I made it to tomorrow alive. If I were a betting man, I'd bet everything that Robo-Stein was in the building waiting. I could feel it. So where was he?

There was nothing about Robo-Stein in the police files. Or maybe there was plenty, but people didn't realize it. I moved my mobile computer from my desk to my lap, sitting in my lounge area. I watched the security cameras as I opened up Frankenborg's file on my computer and started reading the rumor reports on him again. The report was massive, chronicling even second- and third-hand accounts of the killer cyborg over his decade-long rise to power.

"Do you want them to clean in here?" PJ asked me, opening my door. Outside my private office, I heard the cleaners working away, starting to vacuum.

"No, I had it cleaned over the weekend, and Dead Pool Dax didn't come in here."

"See any suspicious people yet?"

"Nothing. There's no one working today."

"I told you, it's going to be bad. People don't mind getting wet, but they don't want to get washed away. But we came into work and got a big briefcase. Workers getting paid! Lazy people getting nothing."

"Yeah, PJ. Have you picked out what you're going to buy yet?"

"It's going to be an early Christmas for me."

"I'll celebrate after we find this Robo-Stein character."

"He can't be in the building. There are cops right on the streets next door. That wouldn't be smart; it would be dumb."

"I thought you said he was a genius."

"I was told he was a genius. But they're criminals, so what do they know about smarts. If they were so smart, they wouldn't have been in jail."

"Listen to this rumor about the late Franken-borg. He killed an entire crew trying to muscle into his territory. They had a safe house that had every security sensor known to exist, but Franken-borg somehow still got in and killed them. In fact, part of the fear with Franken-borg was how he could just show up in your place from nowhere without tripping any alarms, despite having a bulky, hulk body of bionics. Franken-borg was raw violence. He didn't do subtle. I doubt he ever turned off security cameras or sensors in his life. I think that's what the brother was for."

"Oh, no."

"PJ, send those office cleaners home please."

"Yes. *Toute suite.*"

I placed my computer on the couch from my lap, stood up, and pulled my omega-gun from inside my jacket. I flipped the switch, thought a moment, then flipped it again.

I heard PJ sending the guys home in the main area. She peeked back in. "What are you doing?" PJ was standing at the open doorway.

"I'm going shooting."

"Shooting? You're not going to do what I think you're going to do? If he's in the building already, then that's not smart."

"Why not? Genius-head wouldn't expect that."

"But you don't know what he looks like."

"Doesn't matter."

"You can't walk through the hallways shooting at random people."

"PJ, I don't think I'll have to walk very far."

"What?"

"I think he was with his brother when he and the gang attacked me. I think he's been here all this time."

"In the building?"

"Yes."

"All this time?"

"Yes."

"I need my shotguns, both of them."

Once the cleaning guys left with their equipment, we locked the main door. PJ kept all kinds of weapons at her desk, which was behind a metal barrier but decorated with all kinds of French monument and movie posters to look "hip." Her French music—always punk rock—played in the background all day, was off, so that meant she was in serious mode. There she was at her fancy glass desk with see-through glass drawers, and a boom box on top along with her own mobile computer. However, underneath it were all her shotguns. She had the laser one in the left hand and the pulse blaster in the right hand.

"PJ, remember the police are right outside the building."

"They're too busy with their crime scene to mind what we're doing in here."

"Unless we have a full-scale shootout," I said.

"We'll have plenty of time to hide our illegal weapons if that happens." I looked at her with a smile. "I know what you're going to say. We're not criminals and shouldn't be talking like that. I say, the good guys need illegal weapons too. What are you doing?"

I walked to the main door. I went out into the main hallway and stood there. This hallway in front of my Liquid Cool office had been quite a busy place with my past cases—all kinds of shootouts. I was glad so many people had decided to stay home. If there was any violence on the floor today, we wouldn't disturb my tenant neighbors. I looked both ways. Robo-Stein was here. I could feel it. I stepped back into my office and closed the door.

I came back out, followed by PJ with a shotgun in each hand.

"We'll stage it so it looks like we had the shootout right in front of the office."

"We'll need lots of gunshots, like in the walls." PJ was such a natural at ad-libbing.

"We'll add that later. I'll call the police now and tell them that Robo-Stein is here on this floor."

"Say that you think he killed a bunch of people too. You have to sound hysterical, though."

"I don't do hysterical."

"I should make the call then.

"I can make an emotional call."

"It has to sound real."

"It will. And they're already on scene so they'll be here and have this whole building locked down in minutes. They also have all that scanning gear with them—the best in the world."

When I lifted my mobile phone to my mouth, we heard a noise not too far from us. A figure seemed to appear out of thin air—he was wearing an Up-Top cloaking suit. He looked like some kind of super ninja, all in black from head to toe. PJ let loose with her shotguns, almost grazing me. I wanted to yell at her, but ignored it and started firing too. She was hitting the body, but all along the wall too. I shot at his head only, but it was if he had an invisible force field in front of his body as he ran.

"Why isn't he going down?" PJ yelled.

I switched the setting on my omega-gun and fired at his head again. The shot hit but a strange thing happened—his head started spinning around wildly. We ran after him, but he was much faster. Around the corner he went. We heard a loud, almost crashing sound. The hallway lights dimmed and the red emergency lights began flashing as the tower's alarms screeched. When we reached the end of the hall and ran around the corner, there was a huge hole in the wall. Robo-Stein had crashed through, probably head first, from a hundred stories up. He had escaped.

CLASSIC CYBORG

"**Y**ou can't do that!" I yelled at the Metro building inspectors.

"Sir, you need to get back and evacuate the building."

A team of building inspectors in gray uniforms had taken over the entire floor outside my office in addition to all the police officers milling around.

"You don't need to red-tag my building. The damage isn't that bad."

"It isn't?" the female inspector asked. "There's a giant hole straight through the building to the outside, a hundred stories up."

"Get some hover-building repair robots over here. I know you have them. I've seen them. My tax dollars have paid for them. I'm not independently wealthy like you. I need to work and so does everyone else in this building."

"I have four small mouths to feed," PJ chimed in. "How am I going to feed my small children if you put us out of business?" PJ looked like she was on the verge of tears.

The police officers were enjoying the show. The inspectors knew we were both liars—me about not knowing what caused the big hole in the side of the building and PJ having four small children. However, they couldn't take the chance that we'd tell our sob story to the press.

"Get out of the area and let us do our work," the male inspector said.

"Thanks, inspectors," I said. "You're life savers."

"Thanks, inspectors," PJ said. "My four small children will sing songs about how you saved their mommy's job."

"Miss, I don't believe you have any children at all," the female inspector said. "But if you do, I don't want any of them singing songs about me."

"Mr. Cruz," one of the officers began.

"Officer, I already gave a statement. My office is right down the hall. My secretary—"

"Client support and office manager," PJ corrected.

"And I heard a loud crashing sound and came out to see. Nothing more."

"That's it?"

"Yes."

The officers could have taken us down to Police Central, but they seemed more interested in leaving. They told us we could leave while they cordoned off that part of the hallway. We heard the inspectors on their mobile phones, so the repair robots were on their way.

PJ didn't start asking questions until we were safely back in the office and behind closed doors. We made sure to scan for any intruders or devices before we started to relax.

"How did you know he was right outside?"

"I guessed."

"He had a cloaking suit? They're *so* illegal."

"Illegal, but Metro PD can detect them."

"Did he really fly through the wall and crash through with his head?"

"He blasted his way through with some weapon, then jumped through the hole."

"Flew away like a bird. He must have had a real rocketpack on, not a normal jetpack, or he would have still fallen splat on the ground."

"PJ."

"Yes?"

"I don't want to do this case anymore."

She laughed. "That's why you get the big bucks, boss. You close the cases no one else can."

The first thing a person saw when they walked through my door was LIQUID COOL in large neon letters on one line and in smaller neon letters underneath DETECTIVE AGENCY on the wall outside my private office. The first thing I saw when I walked through the door early the next morning was Mr. Classic Cyborg. Well dressed and topless under his jacket as always, he strolled in on time, but this time without the smirk or smile.

"Good morning, Mr. Classic," PJ greeted from her seat behind her desk. PJ never greeted me with a good morning, but as the "client support and office manager," she must have felt it was an essential part of her duties.

"*Enchante*, Ms. PJ."

I was already waiting by the open doorway of my private office. He stopped in front of me and looked dead in my eyes. "Mr. Cruz, I've never been in the presence of someone able to do something I couldn't. Everyone told me that Franken-borg trained every day to kill me. That he built up his cybernetic implants for that purpose alone. He was my arch-nemesis and dark opposite. If I were still a gangster, we would have fought to the death, and only one us would be standing, most likely not me. Today, however, I am so different a man that I truly don't believe I could have ever defended myself against him. He was pure destruction."

"Come in," I said and led him into my office. I closed the door and we sat at my desk.

"Mr. Cruz, on the streets people who never knew you ever existed know of you now and are scared. I lied before when I made light of Franken-borg. He was a force of nature. Anyone who crossed him never lived to ever do it again. Everyone was scared of him, even me. Now you legitimately dealt with the scariest cyborg criminal on Earth. Keep that in mind, because you'll notice a dramatic change in how Pink Machete and Steel deal with you next time."

"What about Franken-borg's brother?"

"I read the police intel report yesterday. He paid you a visit. He's been paying people to spread lies on the streets about how great his intellect is, but that's all it is—lies. He's a coward who likes to attack people from the shadows. He can ram through a wall with his head, but that, of course, has very limited use on the street, short of bringing about laughter."

"He might be a bit more dangerous than that."

"Possibly, but not by much."

"Mr. Classic, I think this is where we part company."

"I know. It's been much more than you bargained for."

"That's one way to put it."

"I've gotten more than my money's worth. However, there is one matter left. I'll do just as I told you before and leave Metropolis. That would be best for you, and for me. Without Franken-borg on the streets, the only thing that'll happen next is a full-scale war between the three of them to control territory. But I need to find my daughter."

"She didn't seem the leave-the-city type."

"No, but leave that to me. Will you help me? It makes little sense to find another detective. All I need to know is where she is. I'll take it from there. I'll talk to her. Call it a missing persons case."

"What about our three friends?"

"Detective Trendy has assured me that finding them will be a top priority of the Cyborg Gang Unit. A cyborg who had the destructive capability to damage a standard mega-tower is something that can't be ignored. I didn't tell them that he was unique in his gang."

I was not about to tell him that there was no more Franken-gang, but why didn't Trendy tell him?

"So, find your daughter?"

"That's all. Nothing more."

If he was being truthful, I couldn't expect him to leave his daughter behind without trying to get her to leave too.

"I'll take the new case then. After all, she's in danger too."

"Yes, she is. If there's a gang war, Pink Machete and Robo-Stein will target her too. That can't happen."

"No, it can't. See PJ outside again."

He smiled. "Thanks, Mr. Cruz. I'm sure all this has not made me one of your favorite clients, but I'll make it up to you."

When Classic walked out into the main area to pay PJ, I heard the door open. I heard voices and got up from my desk. PJ was handing his credit card back to him, but that wasn't my primary focus.

"Mr. Cruz, meet the Boys," Classic said, gesturing to the half-dozen cyborg men standing at the door. He didn't have to tell me. I knew already—they were all ex-Metro PD. "I see Building Services is finishing the repairs on your office tower. The Boys will make sure no further damage happens. All of them are retired Metro Police. There's over three hundred years of experience standing in your office."

"Gentlemen." I nodded and they acknowledged me with nods or slight waves. Only one had bionics on his face, another had visibly bionic arms, but they were clearly all cyborgs.

"They'll be hanging around your office for the duration of the case. Detective Trendy will also have a patrol in the area at all times."

"That must have taken some doing," I said.

"After yesterday, he didn't have to ask. The police higher-ups insisted." He was absolutely right. The fact that someone had the means to laser through the solid reinforced wall of an office tower was something that would never make it into the press for public consumption. Instead, it would be classified and a cover-story would be given to the public. However, the police would put every resource they could on the streets to find the perpetrator and the weapon. "I told you I would make it up to you," he said. "One more thing though."

"What's that?"

"Follow me."

He gave PJ a wave and turned to the door. He led me out with our cyborg ex-police security detail.

Maybe I needed to become a fiction writer because I knew what I was going to see the moment we came out of the elevator on the ground floor of the parking bay. There was my Ford Pony in all its red splendor.

"Compliments of Detective Trendy." Classic threw me the keys.

I walked to it and slowly walked around it to give it a quick inspection.

"I'm sure you'll give it a proper washing, but they did one, exterior only."

I nodded. "Thanks, Classic."

"You're welcome."

"Now I can do some work."

"Let me know if you need anything else." Classic gave a wave and led his cyborg friends the other way.

My attention returned to the Pony as I touched the hood. There was no way I was driving my vehicle anywhere in Metropolis with those three crazy maniacs out there. My Pony was going into storage for the duration.

LA FAMILIA

The real reason I was able to dedicate so much time to cases and spend all my time at the office was because the family was out of town. I could have gone, but since I didn't speak Mandarin and everyone at my wife's grandparent's place would—and every other language that wasn't English—I made up the excuse to "hold down the fort" in Metropolis. Everyone wanted to see Cruz Jr.—all his relatives on his mother's side and mine. The thing of it was not even Dot and I knew we had so many relatives around the world. It was mind-numbing.

But I was glad they were out of any possible harm's way in Metropolis. The added bonus was that she took her parents with her, who I aptly nicknamed the Hellspawn. They had threatened to poison or cut me before I married their daughter, but now that Cruz Jr. was here that plan was gone. However, violence was not out of bounds. My parents-in-law made their fortune in retail and food, but they had more guns than PJ and I combined, and I was a detective and PJ was an ex-felon. They probably had more weapons than the gangsters I had to deal with. Good! They could use them to keep my wife and son safe.

"The case got you down?" Dot asked, her face on the display screen of the Pony's dashboard.

My wife went by the name of China Doll—women who knew her called her China; men called her Doll. Only her family and I called her by her real name.

As the chief executive at Metropolis's premiere Eye Candy Image Salon, she was the consummate fashionista with every piece of clothing, accessory, and jewelry being the trendiest and the most stylish around. Obviously, I couldn't see her whole outfit, but I knew she'd be looking like a movie star like always.

"Let's just say that I have one of those cases that can't be resolved fast enough."

"Not a save-the-world case?"

"No, not one of those anymore, though I'd gladly switch for one of those. I'll tell you about it when you get back. How's Mother China?"

"Cruz, you think hovertraffic is bad in Metropolis, you haven't seen bad hovertraffic until you've seen it here. There's no end to it and seems like people can fly anywhere they like. It's crazy."

"I've seen the video. I'd never drive the Pony there. I'm not that brave."

"Not me, either. Oh, here's Junior."

There was a brief flash of Dot's mother on the screen—Mrs. Wan (Hellspawn #1) handing my son to Dot. I could hear Mr. Wan (Hellspawn #2) in the background.

"They better not be doing anything to my son," I said.

"Say hello to daddy," Dot said.

There was my son. I knew better than to question the purple mess that he was dressed in, lest I find out that it was his mother's doing.

"Hey, Cruzie," I said. "I got some yummy chocolate cake waiting for you and mommy when you get back."

He smiled and giggled. Twice he tapped the screen, which he found personally hilarious. Thousands of miles away and I could still spend time with the family. We talked for almost two hours. It would be the only time I would smile or laugh in my Classic Cyborg case, which would begin anew the following day.

HUNTING HARDER

I strolled down the streets in a steady drizzle and the occasional rumble of thunder. This was shoe-leather detective work. No riding in hovercars or sitting behind the vid-phone in an office. It was all about the streets, walking through the crowds in their dark slickers and colored, visual-enhanced shades. My hands were in my pockets, my fedora tilted strategically down a bit. If I wanted to find the Electric Lady, I had to find Harder Steel. To do that, I had to find his gang.

My go-to guy for information on the streets was my friend Phishy. He was a slider, doing the small street hustles—including legal gun-dealing on the side—and he was popular among the sidewalk johnny crowd. Like me, he was part of the streets, but not the mean streets. Phishy didn't do danger. I dealt with it because I had to, but that didn't mean I'd jump into it willingly. I'd been shot more than once—one time put me in the hospital. I didn't want an encore. Information was what I needed, and like most things on the street—mean or otherwise—it could be had with the exchange of currency.

All day, I'd been bouncing from one lead to another. Phishy had given me the first. I wasn't in Classic's home district, but close by. My best bet was the juvenile street hustlers who loitered around one establishment or another looking for their next victim. I approached a group of four that looked semi-respectable. They made eye contact the second I saw them.

"I'm not a copper, so don't panic," I said. "I need some street intel."

"Like what, copper?" one asked. The others grinned. All of them were wearing different colored slickers and bluish-white neon shades.

"The Harder Steel Gang."

"What about them?"

"Where do they hang out?"

"We don't know, copper. You tell us."

"Mobiles."

"What?"

"Take out your mobiles and search for Liquid Cool. Do it. What are you waiting for? I don't have all day."

One of them pulled out his mobile and searched with one hand. "It's that Cruz guy," he declared and showed my pictures to his friends.

"You're the private detective?"

"I am and I'm looking for the Harder Steel Gang."

"What do we get?"

"Money, of course."

"How much?"

"Let's negotiate. If your info is reliable, we could make this a regular thing."

"Regular?"

"Yeah. A good detective always needs access to quality intel from the streets."

The hustlers looked at each other, nodding. "Step into our office and we can discuss the terms," one of them said in a professional tone. His friends laughed as he led the way into one of the establishments—another no-name bar.

Inside one could barely make out the patrons because the lights were so dim. I noted the neon letters on the wall: BEER, WINE, HARD LIQUOR, SMOKES, ACTION. There were a million conversations going on, very few in English. The men were leading me down an aisle to the back.

"Wait here," one of them said, then they all walked away.

I had put on my night shades, so I could see a nice, empty corner calling my name. I put my back against the wall and waited.

The men soon reappeared and walked to me.

"You don't trust us?"

"You really think I'm going to let you lead me into an unknown bar to the back."

"You're not a dummy then."

"No, I'm not. Are we discussing terms or not?"

"Yeah."

I held up a bill in my hand. "This is all I'm paying. Tell me where to go to find them."

"That's nothing. You have to pay more for info here."

"This is what I'm paying, or I'll ask someone else."

"You can ask anybody you want. Doesn't mean what they'll tell you is accurate."

"I want to know where the Harder Steel Gang is right this second."

One of the men was still looking at his mobile when his demeanor turned shaky. He looked up at the one who did most of the talking and showed him. They all looked at it.

"I don't believe it," the main man said.

"Believe it," I said.

"You don't even know what we're talking about."

"I'm the one who killed Franken-borg."

They stared at me.

"You're a liar," the main guy said, finally. "There's no way the likes of you could kill him. I say you're a liar. Hey, everyone!" he yelled out loud. "This guy says he killed Franken-borg! I say he's a liar."

The entire bar turned silent. Everyone was looking at me.

"You don't know what bar this is, do you?" the man asked.

"No, but I'm sure you're going to tell me."

"No, I'm not going to tell you."

I shot his knee out and blasted his three friends before they could react. The men were on the floor, groaning and crying.

"Hey, everyone," I said to the bar's onlookers. They all acted like shootouts in front of them was something that happened every day. "I was going to pay them to tell me where the Harder Steel Gang hangs out, but they're not interested. Anyone in here interested in taking the money that was going to them before they annoyed me?"

A few hands rose. I walked to the one who did so first. I put the bill in his hand—his metal hand—and then reached into my pocket for a few more.

"Here you go," I said. "Youth. They have no respect these days. You try to help them out, they act up."

"The Harder Steel Gang aren't as easy as them to take out," he said.

"I know. I've already met Mr. Harder Steel. This time I want to visit with his gang."

"Go out the door, turn right, ten miles down, neon hovercar street race."

"I did some hovercar racing in my day. Maybe I'll watch a few."

"You know what happened to Franken-borg's gang? Harder Steel claims he offed them, but no one believes him."

"And they shouldn't because he didn't. Thanks for the info."

"You really going to walk there by yourself."

"I am."

When I left the establishment, I did turn right, but then I ran as fast as I could. I ducked into an alleyway and watched. As I suspected, the guy who gave me the info came out with five other guys. He was on his mobile talking to someone. They were too far away for me to hear. Even if I could, it probably wasn't English. I needed to invest in a translator ear-piece because I wasn't going to learn any other languages. They knew I was close by but still didn't see me peering around the corner.

One of the men I shot hobbled out and stood next to them. Then more people joined them. It was like most of the establishment was outside staring down the street looking for me. The man who gave me the info yelled something and then started leading the crowd down the street in the direction he had given me. I ducked into the alley and crouched down, as they passed. There were more than enough pedestrians around. Off came my fedora, out came a compact black slicker. In ten seconds, I stood with my hood over my head and my entire body to blend into the crowd and followed them.

I heard crying near me. One of the men I had shot in the leg, hobbled past me to catch up to the others. I noticed that he had a gun in his left hand. He reached them quickly, and as they moved down the street, I noticed that his group was growing—all armed.

My double-crossing bar informant with the metal hand had told me the truth though. Ten miles later we arrived at a loud neon hovercar street show. However, it was the large silver hovercar off to the side that caught my attention. No one was near it and no one seemed to be inside. I studied the men around the neon hovercars. All of them were large, beefy cyborgs— visibly I saw their bionic hands and much of their heads were cybernetic. It seemed silver was their gang color. Each gang member was with one or two women. There were plenty of hangers-on admiring their hovercars. To me, a real classic hovervehicle restorer, they were pieces of junk not even worth the time to look at. Fancy flashing neon trim on a hovercar does not a classic vehicle make.

The man with the metal hand stood near the show, looking around. He was looking for me, and so was everyone else. He must have realized that I might have been following him all the time. I was crouched close to the ground in the dark shadow between two neon signs on two bar clubs. For a second, I thought he had seen me, but he started looking around again. I wasn't about to take any chances, so I bolted as soon as his head turned away.

He told me it was a race, but it was a street show. He actually didn't see me. I came around the other side and walked up to one of the Harder Steel gang members.

"Where's your boss?" I asked, as I touched my shades and the rearview attachment popped up. I could see the man with the metal hand clearly. Now, he saw me.

"Why?"

"Before I answer that question," I turned around, "do you know that man?" I pointed at him. "I think he's up to something." The man's face went from anger to concern.

"Why?"

"He's one of Franken-borg's men. I think they're planning a hit on either your boss or your gang."

The cyborg gang member literally started flashing red. I watched as the man with the metal hand and his entire crew, including the hobbling men, ran back the way they had come. This time, however, two of the Harder Steel gang members were running after them.

"You all get a lot of excitement in this neighborhood," I said.

"We know who you are," the cyborg said to me.

"Of course, you do. You're not an idiot."

He laughed. "What do really want?"

"I need your boss to talk to the Electric Lady. I need to deliver a message, and then I'm gone."

"Message? From her father?"

"Yes."

"She doesn't talk to her father."

"She's not talking to him. It'll be me. I'll deliver it and go. Are you a father?"

He looked at me for a moment. "Yes."

"Then you know how it is. A father wants to have a message delivered to his daughter. You get that. Doesn't mean she has to do anything with it, but he has the right to at least get the message to her."

By now, I was surrounded by a lot more of the Harder Steel cyborg gang. They were listening closely, and my tone kept them from turning vicious, which was their reputation.

"I'll call the boss, but he may not show."

"Why wouldn't he? He's not afraid of me. And Electric Lady already threw me across a room before, so she's not afraid of me either."

"Yeah, she likes doing that. You wait here."

"I'm waiting."

He walked away with the two women to one of the neon hovercars, and got in on the driver side. I imagined he was making a call. I looked around and counted ten cyborg gang members in silver around me. Behind them were their girlfriends, gang groupies, and spectators.

"Anyone know where Robo-Stein is?" I asked.

No one answered me. They all kept their eyes on me with what seemed to be slight nervousness.

"You killed Franken-borg?" one asked. "I don't see it."

"That's what he thought too. Then city maintenance had to sweep up all his pieces, blood and guts from the pavement. Robo-Stein tried a revenge play just yesterday, but it didn't work out for him."

"No one is fooled by you," another gang member said. "You got lucky is all."

"Believe whatever you want to keep your tough guy nerve."

"I bet I could rip your head off right here."

There was no hesitation on my part. The Harder Steel Gang was known for its depravity, just like Pink Machete and the late Franken-borg's gang. With these gangs, once the verbal threats began, it was only a matter of moments before they would act on making their threats a violent reality. I blew a hole in his forehead, and he dropped back to the ground.

The entire gang reached for their guns, as girlfriends, groupies, and spectators ran for cover. I'd already flipped the switch in my hand, activating the EMP bomb on my wrist device. I had used the device on killer robots. It was my first time using it on a group of killer cyborgs.

One screamed out. The others fell to the ground with thuds. The one who screamed looked like he was dead—cybernetic heart? I noticed that the girlfriends and most of the groupies were also incapacitated on the ground.

"Is everyone here a cyborg except for me?" I asked.

I walked to the nearby neon hovercar as I kept my eye on the group. On the ground was a gang member girlfriend looking up at me. Inside the neon hovercar was the gang member sitting in the driver's seat like a mannequin, glaring at me. All the hovercar's electrics were fried.

"Where's the Electric Lady?" I asked.

"You're a dead man."

"You're threatening me? Okay. I'll call the police and have them scoop all of you up and separate you from all your illegal bionics. I'll find a working mobile somewhere I can use outside the blast area."

"No!"

"No, what?"

"No, don't call the cops. I'll tell you what you want to know."

"Then talk!"

"They're at her factory. Her place is right in the same building. No one knows it, but that's where they are."

"That wasn't so hard, was it?"

"I was on the vid-phone with him, so he'll know you're coming."

"Good. That means I won't have to waste any time talking."

"He's going to kill you!"

"Are you threatening me again?"

"No! I'm just telling you. Don't call the cops."

"I'll leave you and your girlfriend here to sit or lie quietly and ponder the state of your evil lives."

"I'll be seeing you again."

"You're still threatening me. Once I leave, how long do you think it'll take for the local gangs to arrive and clean up the trash like you on the street? No one has to call the police here."

The hovercab dropped me off one block away. I wore my bullet-proof/laser-resistant vest underneath my tan slicker with the light-weight black slicker over it. My fedora was back on my head. I could hear much better without the hood, especially if it really began to rain.

As I approached the glass factory building, I'd scanned every inch. There were no windows, but there were plenty of security cameras. Actually, the structure was covered with more security cameras than I'd ever seen, which meant that not all were cameras—probably sensors and anti-personnel weapons of some kind.

There was no sound inside the building I could hear, no machinery at work. Factories such as these never shut down, but there wasn't a robot stirring anywhere. An entire multi-million dollar factory with its gigantic robotic arms and hoverbots shut down so its president could hide out with her gang boyfriend on the upper levels. It meant she was further gone than I wanted to believe, and that all the danger I faced in my message delivery duties was for no reason at all. The Electric Lady would never leave Metropolis, no matter how sincere Classic was in reuniting with his daughter.

All of the ground floor entrances would be firmly locked and barricaded. I stared up to the upper floors of the building. Was she watching me even now? I hoped she was, because I walked away, as if I'd given up seeing that the business was closed. Actually, I wasn't going anywhere. Knowing she was inside, I was going to be on stakeout. I already knew where I'd post myself to watch the building.

I didn't have to wait long. Several silver hovercars appeared and landed on the roof of the building. From my post nearby, I watched on my portable viewscreen. Harder Steel exited one of the hovercars. My mini-hoverbot had been circling the factory when they arrived, and they hadn't seen it.

The men were laughing.

"Dead!" Harder yelled. "Dead!" He continued to laugh with his men. "Franken-borg's men dead. Pink's men are dead. No one can stop us now."

Pink Machete's men dead?

I had expected them to go inside the factory, but it looked like they were having their own impromptu celebration party on the roof. They brought their own bottles of booze, passed around cigarettes, and the celebrating commenced. They told stories of how they ripped this rival gang member apart, pounded another to pulp, beat others to death. Lots of violence, but none of them said that any of their victims had been Pink Machete himself.

"I run it all now!" Harder declared. "The Steel Gang takes it all."

"But who killed Franken-borg's gang?" a gang member asked.

"We did."

"Seriously. We still don't know who."

"Which is why we say, we did. That's it."

"Don't you want to know who?"

"It must have been Pink's gang. But now they're gone too."

"What about Pink Machete?"

"What about him? He has no gang, and neither does Robo-Stein."

"They'll get more men."

"They'll try to get more men, but we'll be waiting for them. Wipe out the rest of their gangster wannabes. That'll send a message. Then start taking their territories. I want our presence felt everywhere. Also, increase the bounty on the streets for Pink and Robo. Double it. I want them both. Get it done. By the end of the week, I want them dead and buried."

"What about Classic?"

"Then him."

"What about Electric Lady?"

"I'll take care of that."

I didn't like what I heard. I had no idea what exactly he meant. Electric Lady had to be warned, but the gang still hadn't taken their party indoors, and it looked like they had no intention of doing so. I was starting to wonder if Electric Lady was inside at all.

"Hey, Cruz." The voice sent a chill down my spine. One of Harder's henchmen was standing a few feet away pointing a laser gun at me. "We were watching you before and followed you right to your little hiding place here. If you had seen me coming, you would have been ready."

"I did."

I blasted the gun right out of his hand, then fired two more shots before he charged me like a bull. He screamed because I shot his eyes out. The Harder Steel Gang was known for their bullet and laser-proof cyborg shell. Everyone always wanted to test that claim, but I wasn't one of them. Shooting out his eyes was good enough for me as I ran from my alleyway hiding spot. Unfortunately, as I turned the corner, I saw that I wasn't alone. Harder Steel was waiting for me. I looked behind and at least a dozen other cyborgs running to me.

"Stop!" Harder yelled. "In case he has another EMP on him." His men stopped in their tracks. "Hello, Mr. Cruz."

"Where's Electric Lady?"

"Do you want to talk to her again?"

"Where is she?"

"She's in the factory. Let's walk back."

"No, she isn't. I want to talk to her. Where is she?"

He started to laugh. I knew he was planning something. I threw one object toward him and another behind me. His gang scattered, and he flew away into the sky. I watched him hovering, staring back. He assumed I had thrown another grenade at him, but I hadn't. He wouldn't find it amusing when he learned it was just a rock.

I looked back to see his gang coming out of the shadows and running at me, pulling their weapons out from their jackets and waists. Harder Steel seemed to float in the air to a point above me.

"Where is she?" I asked again.

He began to descend slowly. His men had almost reached me.

"You should have brought another EMP bomb with you," one of them said. "Too bad you won't be able to say you'll know for next time, because there won't be a next time."

I flipped the switch in my hand, activating the EMP bomb on my other wrist device. They fell to the ground like rocks. I dove for cover and Harder Steel crashed to the ground. It was close. If he had fallen on me, the weight could have killed me.

I stepped over to him. He looked up at me, trembling from the shock.

"I'm going to ask you one more time. Where is she?"

"Cruz, I'm going to—"

"I've had it! I'll find her on my own. But while I do, since you've gotten on my bad side, I'll decide if I should call the police or put the word on the street for Pink Machete. I like choice number two better. Let him know that you're here lying helpless just waiting for him, since you'll be here for hours."

"She's at my club."

"Dark Metal?"

"Yeah."

"See, that wasn't so hard after all. If you had just answered the question the first time, without all this violence, I'd be doing what I'm doing now. Going away."

When I arrived at Dark Metal, I stood from afar and watched. My hovertaxi driver wouldn't even drop me off in front of it, and I could see why. It was a ten-story monstrosity of a club, and it looked like everyone partying, inside and outside were cyborgs—mean-looking cyborgs. Earth EMP devices were illegal, but Earth cyborgs had developed systems to protect their bionics from many of them. But they weren't protected from Up-Top, which is where mine came from. I had used them twice and only had one left. I was not about to waste it. I had to figure out how to get into the club to see Electric Lady or get her to come out.

Then all of a sudden, Electric Lady bolted out the main entrance. She wasn't provocatively dressed, as when I had seen her with Harder Steel before but the nodes on her body were blinking from beneath her hooded slicker. She ran down the steps, past all the party-goers in front.

Another man came out of the club yelling at her. She turned and shot him in the chest with a pulse gun. The man fell forward, dead. Like most hardcore criminal establishments, the crowd didn't seem to care all that much. She ran, but I went after her.

"Justyna!" I yelled.

Big mistake. She turned and fired twice at me. I managed to hit the ground.

"Stop shooting! It's me, Cruz."

She stopped shooting, but ran again. I jumped to my feet to watch her disappear in the distance, carried away by those bionic legs of hers. Even if I was in a hovercab, she probably would have gotten away.

I sensed something behind me and spun around, gun in hand. Another Harder Steel gang member was about to bludgeon me with a metal baseball bat. I fired, hitting him in the face. He yelled out, and I noticed he wasn't alone—far from it. What made things worse was that people, male and female, started to flow out of Dark Metal to surround me.

"You can't shoot all of us," a man said.

I shot him in the face, and he dropped to the ground. In unison, everyone drew a weapon on me. Guns, rifles, machine-guns, and pulse cannons were all pointed at me.

"Why don't you try that again?" another man yelled.

"Why did Electric Lady run away?" I asked.

"Too bad you won't be able to ask her," a woman said.

Everyone was looking at someone behind me. I turned. It was a Harder Steel gangster on his mobile. "Yeah, boss." It disconnected. "People, we've been hit. Two of our teams are dead." The man's eyes were tearing up. "This one here was behind it."

"Wait a minute," I said. "What are you talking about?"

"You killed our men."

"I killed a few men who tried to kill me. The rest I left behind, including your boss."

"Someone killed all of them, at the street show and at the factory. The boss barely got away."

"How could I do that if I was here trying to talk to Electric Lady?"

"You're dead."

"Did you think I came to this madhouse alone?"

"Yeah, we did. We hear you like to bluff people."

"You all don't learn."

"This is the police! Drop your weapons! Put your hands up or be fired upon and killed!"

The gang members had no idea what to do—freeze, run, or shoot it out. Dozens of silver-and-black police "PEACE" officers appeared from above. They descended from the sky like wingless black angels via their silent jetpacks with accompanying boot rocket nozzles. The police were clad in advanced body armor, visors concealing the top half of their faces, and long guns in hand. All around them, hovercruisers were in the air, their red and blue siren lights flashing.

"Drop your weapons!"

This time everyone complied. No one—*no one*—ever beat the police in a shootout.

Police units kept arriving. Not only the gang members who had surrounded me were arrested, but every single patron of Dark Metal. Detective Trendy and his partner appeared from one hovercruiser.

"You were cutting it close, weren't you?" I said.

"You had it under control, Cruz," Trendy said.

"This should be a big haul for you. All of Harder Steel's men off the street. I recorded their entire conversation on the factory roof, so you'll also be able to get them for the murder of Pink's gang." Their expressions were not ones of satisfaction. "What?" I asked.

"Harder Steel's gang didn't kill Pink Machete's gang."

"What? But we have them confessing too it."

"They didn't do it."

"Why do you say that?"

"Pink Machete's gang was already dead when they got there. Harder Steel's men lied to him. They went into their turf to kill them, but they were already dead."

"Franken-borg's gang dead. Pink Machete's gang dead. Detective, what are you saying?"

"You know what I'm saying, Cruz. There's a fourth player out there taking advantage of all this by wiping out the top cyborg gangs in Metropolis."

"Harder Steel's men thought that Pink Machete's gang killed Franken-borg's."

"They didn't."

"A fourth player?"

"Yes."

"How do you know? They could have each hired an outside crew to do the work."

"They could have, but we don't think so. That's not how things work. If you have to hire others to do your work, then you don't get the credit. You don't get the respect. No, it's someone else."

"Where's Harder Steel now?"

"We don't know. All we know is that he was not at the factory, alive or dead."

"All his men at the factory were dead."

"All of them."

"How?"

"Beaten to death."

"What about Franken-borg's?"

"Same way. Quick, vicious, and thorough. Beaten to death."

"Another cyborg gang?"

"Yeah."

"They're hunting Classic, but some secret cyborg gang is hunting them."

"That's how it looks. One more thing, Cruz. You can't use any more of your illegal EMP devices."

"But I got authorization for three uses. I got one left."

They were not happy with my answer.

"Detective, I'm the one standing next to these crazy maniacs in harm's way. No hovercars fell from the sky, so what's the complaint? Oh, did you see Electric Lady run out of there?"

"We saw her."

"Did you track her?"

"We tried, but she got away."

"How could you let her get away?"

"Cruz, did you want us to track one fleeing female cyborg or did you want us to keep the army of cyborgs around you from killing you?"

"I'm sorry. Thanks."

"You're welcome."

"What's your plan?" Trendy asked

"I have to find her, but I have no idea where to look."

"That's why you get the big bucks for being a detective."

"I better get to it then."

"Cruz, you need to realize this whole thing is becoming more dangerous, not less. Three gang leaders don't have their gangs anymore. That makes them even more dangerous than normal."

"Yes, detective. Remember, I've seen up close how dangerous they can be. I'll be careful. In fact, I'm more than happy to call you if I find any of them, so you can take them down. I'm supposed to be a private detective, not an anti-cyborg urban commando."

Whenever I took a case, I always had to factor in whether I was being used. Was I being hired because the client thought I was the best detective for the job, or because they could say to their friends at some cocktail party that they hired the "famous" detective? I always had to wonder if there was another angle being played or if I was intentionally being drawn into a case for ulterior motives.

Someone was wiping out the top three cyborg gangs in Metropolis. And it was all because of me. I killed Franken-borg—something that no one in the world thought was possible—and someone was taking advantage of the incredible void his death left in the cyborg gangster world. When Trendy revealed that Pink Machete's gang hadn't been killed by Harder Steel as he had claimed, I had that wave of paranoia come over me. Was it the same someone who opened the Dead Pool too?

I had to put that out of my mind because I had to find Electric Lady. I still had no idea why she ran from Dark Metal? She was scared, but why? I thought Harder Steel was going to kill her, having used her to get to her father, but he said he killed Pink

Machete's gang and that wasn't true. I needed to talk to her. Not only to find out what frightened her, but maybe she could give me the insight I needed on the whole mess. Someone was using me for their own purposes, and I didn't like it.

"The King of all Cyborgs," PJ said to me.

PJ never said good morning. But that's what she said to me when I first arrived at the Liquid Cool office.

"What does that mean?" I asked her.

"Dead Pool Dax. I found out how we can monitor the Dead Pool."

"That's a brilliant idea, PJ. I didn't even think to ask."

"You can't access it from your personal mobile computer or even a public one."

"You have to go to their computer access?"

"Yes, and I did that last night. I wanted to see. I went with some guy friends to one of those betting places. It's scary what criminals bet on. I looked you up and—"

"What?"

"The main betting in the Dead Pool is to find out who will be the 'King of All Cyborgs.'"

"Who's favored to win?"

"It was Franken-borg, then it became Harder Steel, but now Classic Cyborg is favored."

"Classic? What changed?"

"Everyone knows Harder Steel doesn't have his gang anymore, same as Pink Machete."

"Robo-Stein was never favored. How does it work? Who would make more money if they won—Robo-Stein or Classic?"

"Classic."

"Even though the odds would be long that, say Robo-Stein would win."

"Cruz, this is criminal betting. It's the reverse. The favored gets the most money. The least favored only gets a little money."

"When the Dead Pool first started, who was favored? Franken-borg or Classic?"

"I don't know. I think it would have been Franken-borg."

"Find out for certain and let me know."

"What are you thinking?"

"I don't know, but the police say there's someone else out there."

"Who?"

"Someone killing off the cyborg gangs, and succeeding."

"A secret cyborg gang?"

"I don't like surprises. Find out about the original Dead Pool. I can't say that I exactly trust what Dead Pool Dax told us either, so verify what he said. Why can't I get normal, boring cases like every other detective?"

"This is Liquid Cool. We don't do boring."

That wasn't true. We did plenty of boring cases. The big, high-profile cases were what everyone talked about and remembered, but it was the standard investigations, the boring cases, that paid the bills month after month. If we waited for exciting cases, our office would have closed a long time ago. I'd be still restoring hovercars and PJ would be hanging out on the steps of the Concrete Mama.

She was busy on the vid-phone. I heard her bionic fingers flying as she did her Net research. I could do better searches than her, but she could do far more searches in a shorter period than I'd ever be able to do.

While she did that, I reviewed everything about Electric Lady and her company. I tried to put a profile together on her. She became a gangster's girlfriend to hurt her father. However, this conversion was a recent occurrence, within the last couple of years. What happened? She was well on the road to becoming a Who's Who in the Metropolis world. Now, she was mixed up with killer cyborg gangs. Her story would end up the way these stories always did—with her dead or in jail.

"Boss, line one." PJ's voice came from my desk intercom. We actually did have more than one line now, but when we first opened, we only had the one line. She just liked saying "line one."

I turned on my vid-phone and there he was—Harder Steel.

"Mr. Harder Steel, how are you?"

"I heard you had my entire gang picked up from my club."

"They were about to shoot me at the time."

"Too bad."

"Too bad for them. All those illegal bionics of theirs become the property of the City of Metropolis."

"I was on the top of the world yesterday, and now I'm hiding out for my life."

"The police said your entire gang was hit."

"I only got away because an ex-girlfriend groupie of mine came by and dragged me out of there along with a couple of my men. Everyone else you left there is dead."

"Me? Don't blame me. If you hadn't come after me, I wouldn't have had to EMP you. You have only yourselves to blame for that."

"I thought Classic Cyborg was the jinx, but it's actually you. All this started happening when you showed up on the scene."

"All this started happening after Franken-borg got himself dead."

"Yeah, you're right. Someone's taking advantage of all of us."

"I can't say that I like that. Since it's unlikely you're going to be the King of all Cyborgs anymore, where's Electric Lady?"

"Why ask me? I heard she was running from you and you were shooting at her."

"She was running away before she saw me. When she did, she took shots at me. I never returned fire. Why was she running? Did she realize you only had her at your club to know where she was until you came to put her in the morgue."

"Do you always make things up? I'd never hurt Electric Lady. She knows that."

"Whatever. Why did you call me?"

"For you to go get her. Because of you, I can't have my face on the streets. The cops and whoever killed my men are looking for me. Maybe the cops did it."

"Oh, stop. You know the cops didn't do it. You know it was the same person or persons who did away with Franken-borg's men."

"And Pink Machete's."

"Exactly. So, where is she?"

"Pink Machete has her."

"What? Why would he have her?"

"How would I know detective? That's the word on the street. He has her, so go rescue her. You're the cause of all this."

"I'm the cause of your gang war?"

"He thinks I killed his men, so this is payback. Tell him that I didn't do it and he'll let her go."

"Do you honestly think I'm going to go looking for Pink Machete?"

"For me, no. But for Classic, you will. Go fetch his daughter, doggie. That's what you should do."

"I'm glad your men are dead. Where's Pink then?"

"Where's *Pink Machete*? I wouldn't forget the machete part if I were you. I have a bionic exo-shell, so I can make fun of him, not a weak normal like you. Will you go fetch if I do?"

"I'm about to hang up on you."

"He has a club too, detective. I'm sure you can figure out which one on your own. When this is all over, I will be the King of all Cyborgs, then I'm coming for you, Cruz."

"I won't be losing any sleep over your stupid threats. I suspect whoever wiped out Franken-borg's gang, Pink Machete's, and yours will be coming after the leaders next—not me. You have a good day, Mr. Harder Steel." I slapped the button and hung up the vid-phone on him.

HUNTING PINK

When Metro PD, led by its Cyborg Gang Unit, had as its priority taking down the three biggest cyborg gangs in the supercity and possibly preventing a full gang war, Trendy was easily able to arrange for me to have my own personal aerial surveillance. I walked those streets in search of Harder Steel knowing the full force of the most powerful law enforcement division on the planet was literally over my shoulder.

But now they had succeeded in pulling off one of the biggest gang busts in a decade, and two different gang crews were dead. The cyborg gang threat was over. Yes, their three leaders were on the loose, but for Metro PD they were no longer a concern—there were too many other criminals and gangs to take their place on their priority list. Going forward, I was on my own again.

Would I really go to Pink Machete's club alone? Hell, no. I wouldn't go there even if I had an army. Harder Steel could have been setting me up, hoping his rival would kill me for him, or working with his former rival to get me. Such things happened in the crime world all the time. Also, these cyborg gang leaders were adept at hiding, anything to keep their illegal bionics.

From my days as a sometime hovercar racer, I knew how to get into the civilian satellite feeds to survey the Blood Pink Club and everything around it. There was little difference between it and Dark Metal, other than the building was white with pink lighting to make it look like it was pink. I wish I could've stayed in the safety of my office to solve the case, but for now, as I stared at the viewscreen on my desk, it was all about recon.

When Harder's gang and groupies had me surrounded, weapons aimed and ready to cut me to pieces, they all hesitated because they didn't see it. They saw no hint of fear in my eyes, because there was none. As savvy criminal maniacs, they knew that meant I knew something they didn't know. So true. I knew that they were all in the sniper sights of the Metro PD. I also knew that surrounding me in a circle meant they couldn't shoot me without shooting each other—the dummies.

Attitude was what got me through that situation. Smarts was what would see me through the upcoming gambit with Pink Machete. I still hadn't seen his machete. As others had said before: When you did, you were dead.

There was something else that I had to take into account. That I was being followed, and not by one party, but many. I'd assumed that Pink was still one of them. Time to go to work.

I blasted out of the Liquid Cool mega-tower in my loaner hovercar like a rocket. I quickly did an illegal U-turn and was flying the other way. I saw at least three hovercars attempt to follow, but they were all blocked by oncoming sky-traffic. It was a maneuver I'd used many times before and would continue to do so in the future. I was always being followed. I was certain that one of the hovercars was an undercover Gang Unit team. They weren't protecting me anymore, but they were not about to let me out of their sight completely.

The entrance looked like a giant laughing mouth, and it was manned by huge cyborgs, each wearing a pink tie. VIP members were waved through, known on sight by the bouncers; everyone else had to wait in line. A man in a trench coat slicker walked right up to them.

"The line is back there," one of the bouncers said, pointing.

"Metro Health and Safety," he responded, holding up a badge. "The manager, please."

"Health and Safety? Why tonight? Who put you up to this?" one of the bouncers asked.

"Are you going to take me to the manager or do I need to call this in?"

"Call it in, because we're not letting you in."

He grabbed his mobile from his pocket and started to dial.

"Okay. We're joking. I'll take you in."

The cyborg led the inspector into the noisy, packed club. All the strobe lights, ceiling lights, and floor lights were pink. The music was so loud the inspector had to cover his ears with his hands. The bouncer glanced back at him and grinned. They went up a flight of stairs near the middle of the establishment, three different dance floors encircling it. The bouncer pointed the inspector to a man in a pink suit.

The inspector was almost in pain, rubbing his ears. The manager led him to an office with the bouncer and another man followed. They entered and the manager closed the door.

"Is that better?" the manager asked.

"How do you work in that every night?" the inspector asked. "You must have hearing damage."

"I'm sorry, I didn't hear you." The manager and his men laughed.

"Very funny. I'm with the—"

"Health and Safety. Yeah?"

"We have some complaints from credible sources that you are serving tainted food."

"That's a lie. No one eats any food here. We are a booze and dance joint. You want burgers, go someplace else."

"Good, so my inspection of the kitchen should take no time at all."

"This is harassment."

"Shall we go to the kitchen?"

"We paid your bag man last week."

"Sir, you should know that Metropolis Health and Safety inspectors in the field are under the same body-cam rigging as Metro PD. Say hello to my little friend." He showed them the vid-cam attached to the lapel of his slicker.

The manager and the men glared at him.

"I still say this is harassment. We are a legitimate business!" the manager yelled and pointed at the inspector's vid-cam.

"Are you the manager or the owner?"

"The manager."

"Where's the owner?"

"He has the night off."

"Shall we go to the kitchen?"

The manager threw open the door and led the inspector back the way he came. The manager's men followed. Suddenly, sirens blared.

"What's that?" the inspector yelled, as all the lights changed to flashing red.

"This is an automated recording," a computer voice boomed overhead. "Fire alarms have sounded. Please evacuate the establishment."

"Damn!" the manager yelled. "Find out if there's really a fire!"

"We have to go!" The inspector didn't wait. He ran back down the stairs as every person on the dance floors, at the bars, and everywhere else in the Blood Pink Club got out as fast as they could.

When the inspector got outside, everyone was gathered in front of the club. There was smoke coming from some place inside, but there was no fire. From above a red hoverfiretruck descended with sirens flashing. Soon, a police hovercruiser appeared for crowd control. Police in silver-and-black began to move people back. Firemen in red-and-black gear with the word "FIRE" on the chests and backs of their uniforms ran into the club.

Pink Machete stood in the crowd and began to scan the onlookers with a grin. The six-foot-six, bleach blond-haired cyborg strolled ahead, wearing a black slicker instead of pink and pink shades instead of dark ones. He saw who he was looking for.

"Mr. Cruz," Pink Machete said when he reached me. "Who are your friends?"

I wasn't alone. "These are the local district's neighborhood anti-crime watch groups. They've been trying to get the Blood Pink Club shut down for years. Says it emits a daily stench that's harmful to families, children and the overall feng-shui of the community."

Pink Machete began laughing hard. The neighborhood watch members were not amused by him at all. They were of all ethnicities, most of them forty-something and above. Every district had such community groups, who, though small, were a thorn in the side of local crime.

"Cruz, I like you. No one thinks like you do. I didn't think you had the guts to show up at my club."

"I didn't. That's why I brought four armies with me: police, fire, health and safety, and community watch." A policeman walked to us. "Officer, he's the one."

"Sir, do you mind submitting to a scan?" the officer asked Pink Machete.

"Officer, I'm a law-abiding citizen despite what these people may have told you. I'm happy to comply."

"Over here, sir." The officer led the cyborg gangster to his police cruiser, where another officer fully scanned him.

I knew he wasn't stupid enough to come to his club with his illegal bionics, but sometimes one got lucky. Tonight, however, wasn't one of those times. He strutted back to us, smiling wide.

"Cruz, I have to hand it to you. I still won't get to show you my machete."

"Yeah, not tonight. Where's Electric Lady?"

"That's why you're here? Why ask me? I'm not dating her."

"Harder Steel said you kidnapped her."

"Kidnapped her? Why would I do that? He's lying, or you are. I wouldn't trust anything he says. Why should you? He's the one holding her? I heard he tried to have her hit right in his own club."

"You're the liar now."

"Takes one to know one, Cruz. I hope you didn't damage my establishment with your fake fire ruse."

"I'm sure you can afford any repairs. Give it another coat of pink paint. I'm going to ask you again. Where's Electric Lady?"

"I answered your question."

"So he says you have her. You say he does. I really don't understand you guys. I find her and I'm done with this case, but you won't play ball. You've lost all your men, so has he. It's only a matter of time before other gangs move in on you. If I were a criminal, I'd give me what I wanted just to make me go away."

"You'll go away, all right. You'll go away permanently."

"Are you threatening him?" one of the neighborhood watch residents asked.

"Oh, no, sir," Pink Machete replied. "I'm stating the inevitable. Mr. Cruz here is making a lot of enemies."

It happened so fast. Someone smacked Pink Machete with a hand, and the nearly six-foot cyborg was on his back, rubbing his chest.

"Yes, he's making enemies, but he has lots of friends too." Classic Cyborg stood there. For the first time, I saw true fear in Pink Machete's eyes.

Pink Machete jumped up from the ground and sprinted away, disappearing into the crowd. Classic patted me on the shoulder, walked the other way to one of the police cruisers, and got into the passenger side. I could see Trendy through the driver's window, which went from clear to dark tint as the hovercruiser rose into the sky.

We weren't lucky with Pink Machete, but we were with many of his club management and security. Most had unregistered weapons, so all of them were arrested. Like any good city health inspector, this one had no trouble finding something in the kitchen that gave him grounds to shut down the entire establishment. The community watch groups couldn't have been happier. Neither Harder Steel nor Pink Machete had their club fronts anymore. However, that meant that three cyborg gangsters were all in the wind, which made them even more dangerous than before.

And where was Electric Lady?

PHISHY, SLIDER EXTRAORDINAIRE

As I flew into Buzz Town, I kept thinking about Pink Machete's reaction to Classic Cyborg—genuine fear. Classic had been out of the gangster biz for a quarter of a century, yet his reputation remained on the mean streets to a level that gangs who'd never personally met him before or saw his violent handiwork were still scared of him. That stuck in my mind. To the Average Joe like me, if you left a business, in a couple of years everyone forgot you ever existed. In the crime world, reputation truly trumped everything. In that world, it was as if Classic had never left, and that's how he was treated.

When I walked into the office, PJ was still working on finding out who started the "King of all Cyborgs" Dead Pool. However, she'd run into one roadblock after another in her research. The reality was that neither one of us was criminal enough to get the right answers from the right people.

"We have to pay," she told me.

"Pay to play, PJ. You say that all the time to our potential clients. Now the tables are turned."

"Only we'll pay and still won't get the truth. How would we know what they're telling is the truth?"

"We need a real criminal to find out for us."

"Yeah, but who?"

"I know someone who could find a safe criminal for us to deal with."

"Oh, no. Not stupid man. I could find a safe criminal."

"PJ, let him do it. You have other things to concentrate on."

"Like what?"

"Three crazy maniacs are out there, and no one knows where they are."

"Yes, that's true."

"That makes me nervous. They tried twice already to whack me here in my own building."

"Cruz, nobody says *whack* anymore."

"What do they say then?"

"Kill. The same word we all use."

"I like whack better. So, three desperate cyborg gang leaders are out there, and they know where we work. They tried before; they'll try again. You have double duty: let the clients in, keep the criminals out."

"Except if the criminals are paying clients."

"And they don't work for our three cyborg gang leader 'friends.'"

"They come in here, I'll punch them out the window."

"PJ, I don't even want them in the building. They're too dangerous. And no punching. Blast them."

PJ pulled out her pulse shotgun from underneath her desk. I stared at it.

"PJ, why do you have a deadly shotgun painted purple?"

"I'm wearing purple. It has to match my clothes."

I shook my head as I walked to my private office.

I really wanted to ensure that there was no way that any criminal out there saw any of my friends coming to or leaving the office. The best way to do that was to keep them all away from the office.

My vid-call to Phishy was the first thing I did when I sat down at my desk with my cup of silk coffee.

"Cruz!" he said, his face beaming over my vid-phone display.

"Phishy."

My wife referred to Phishy as a slider—moving from one street hustle to another. He wore off-white, long-sleeve shirts with colored fish all over them underneath a dark vest. Today, he had on a pink fishes shirt.

Whether you called Phishy a street hustler, front street freddy, or slider, he was on the street doing a little non-narcotic running here, a bit of courier work there—any scam to bring in some extra cash. Nothing illegal enough to get him a solid prison stint—always at the level where if he got caught, he'd get no more than a mere misdemeanor, pay the fine, and be on his way, not even a blot on his record. Metro PD would never bother with street hustlers working non-violent, low-money scams. In a vile world, you had to set your priorities properly.

With Phishy on the vid-phone, at least I would be spared his chicken dance, which is how he greeted me.

"I can't do my dance, Cruz."

"Next time, Phishy. I need some help."

"Sure, Cruz."

"Phishy, you and I stay away from the mean streets. Who do you know who we can trust, who can give us solid info on the mean streets?"

"For what?"

"I need to know if a woman's been kidnapped."

"Ransom?"

"I don't know. I just need to know what the word on the street is about her. She's one of those gangster groupies, gangster girlfriends."

"I think I know someone. Which gangs?"

"Cyborg gangs."

Phishy touched the display with a finger, activating the screen keyboard. I hated when people typed over me. "What are the gang boss's names?"

"Pink Machete, Harder Steel, Robo-Stein. If she's kidnapped and being held hostage, it would be one of them. She's dating Harder Steel."

At least Phishy could type fast so I didn't have to see his fat fingers type over me for too long. "Got it." He smiled. "I'll make a few calls."

"Calls only, Phishy. These are very dangerous gangsters, so don't take any chances at all. These are the kind of gang members who'll kill you just because they're in a bad mood."

"Oh, I'm always careful, Cruz."

"I'll be here at the office all day."

"I should have something for you in a couple of hours."

CY THE HOOD

My very first major case, the "Police Watch Conspiracy," was hatched in Whiskey Way. It was a district that was home to all kinds of criminal activities. It wasn't as violent or crazy as Mad City, but it was a place you were wise to avoid. Most of it was commercial properties, and every time I went there, no matter how much neon signage there was, it was a neighborhood of the shadows.

This was where Phishy had sent me to meet Cy the Hood. As far as street names went, his wasn't particularly inventive or scary, but the combination of meeting a real mean street criminal operator in some secluded eatery in Whiskey Way didn't instill me with confidence that I would come out of the encounter with the info I needed.

My Pony was in storage, so that was one worry dealt with, but I had a clunker of a hovercar that had none of the enhancements of my personal vehicle. I realized that at some point I had to stop viewing my hovervehicle as a classic that must be kept from any kind of damage at all costs. It was my work vehicle. Protecting my life was its primary purpose, not maintaining its mint-condition book value.

Again, any time an establishment didn't have any name signage meant it was shady. This time I parked next door and walked into the eatery with both hands in my slicker pockets. It was a diner and was quite full, but nowhere was there a waiter or waitress to be seen. I noticed someone waving me toward the back.

As I walked to the man, I realized that the diner was for business, not for eating; that was just pretense. People sat in booths, speaking in hushed tones, and watched me like a hawk as I passed by.

"Mr. Cruz," the man said, sitting with his back to the wall. He was fairly short, but heavyset and balding. There was nothing unique about him—a couple of silver necklaces, a mobile display wrapped around his left wrist, a cigarette in his right hand.

"Mr. Cy."

"Just Cy. Nobody is a mister or misses in this joint. You have to be upper-class for those kind of titles. Have a seat?"

I sat down. "Since my back is not to the wall, I'll trust you'll tell me if someone unfriendly is coming up behind us."

"Sure. You shoot it out. I'll sit and enjoy my smokes."

"My friend said you can help me with my case."

"Maybe."

"How much will this cost me?"

"We'll talk and I'll tell you."

"Electric Lady."

"I know her. Glass company CEO by day, gangster girlfriend by night. The progeny of the great Classic Cyborg."

I was talking to the right person. "She's disappeared. I need to know if she's been kidnapped and being held against her will."

"I don't see it, Mr. Cruz. You have a rep yourself, if you don't know. You killed Franken-borg." He shook his head. "How the hell did you do that? *I* could take you."

"Cy, as I often say to my slider friend, 'focus.' I'm here for solid info."

"I'm not aware of anything on the street that says Electric Lady is anybody's hostage. I'm aware of a few cyborg gangsters hiding out, but that's it."

"One of those gangsters said his rival was holding her hostage. Then that one told me the other one was holding her."

"Holding Classic Cyborg's daughter hostage? Why?"

"I don't know. Maybe you can help me with some theories."

"There's only one theory: to get Classic Cyborg to come after you. That's the only reason there could be."

"Do you think that's the reason?"

"Electric Lady isn't too bright when it comes to the men she dates, but she can defend herself fine. It's possible she's being held, but I think it's more likely she's hiding out too."

"Why?"

"War. Why else?"

"War?"

He laughed, and I knew it was at me. "The top three cyborg gangs in the city have been wiped out. What do you think, their territories will remain crime free? Others will move in. That means war."

"How many gangs?"

"In Metropolis, there's never a shortage of gangs. Many will try, lots will die. In the end, there will be a few left standing. Then I suppose the three cyborg gangsters will show up again and try to take them over, more killings. I'd say it'll be a year or two before it all settles down. The streets are like the stock market, Mr. Cruz—ups and downs."

"You believe she's hiding out?"

"Yeah."

As I replayed the event in my mind of her running away from Dark Metal, I wondered if what I saw in her face wasn't fear but frenzy. She wasn't running from someone trying to harm her; she was running to get out of the club before someone arrived.

"Can I ask you something else?"

"Sure."

"Do you know about something called the Dead Pool?"

"Who told you?"

"Dax."

"Dead Pool Dax is going to get his tongue cut out one day. He talks too much to outsiders. He likes to show off too much."

"Why shouldn't I know? I'm in it."

"You are, indeed. What do you want to know?"

"Who opened it?"

"Who created it? Why? Will it help you solve your case? What is your case, by the way?"

"My case is only to find Electric Lady."

"Then why do you care about the Pool?"

"Do you know or don't you?"

"I don't know and anyone who tells you that they know is lying."

"Dax knows."

"Yeah, you're right there. He knows and a few others who administer the Pool, but they can't say, and they won't. It would invalidate the entire Pool. There's a lot of money involved, so that won't happen. Dax would be betting too. That's why I'm sure he told you—to increase his chances."

"Okay, so I can't find out who started it. Can I find out who all the players are in the pool? Me, Classic, Pink, Harder, Robo."

"You need to be careful with the disrespect. Gangsters work a long time and do a lot of violence to gain their street names. Pink Machete, Harder Steel, Robo-Stein. And the legend, Classic Cyborg."

"Anyone else in the Pool?"

"Electric Lady isn't, if that's what you want to know."

"Anyone else?"

"No one. Only you fabulous five."

"The whole thing is deranged. Why should I be in the Pool?"

"Didn't they teach you that in kiddie school? Life's not fair."

"How do I find Electric Lady?"

"You don't."

"Can you find her?"

"I could, but I won't."

"Why?"

"Firstly, you wouldn't pay me the money I need to find her—"

"Classic might to find his daughter."

"Second, Classic Cyborg already has people out on the streets to find her. Save your money."

"Classic Cyborg has what people on the streets looking for her?"

"People. He knows a lot of people, good and bad."

"What would you advise I do?"

"You're the detective. I'm a street hood."

"Wait, or go looking?"

"I'd wait. But you won't have to wait too long."

"Meaning?"

"I told you already—war. Maybe you'll get lucky and a whole lot of people will get into the Pool and move you out of people's attention. Maybe they'll kill off the three gangsters for you and leave Classic Cyborg to regain his title."

"Regain his title? He doesn't want it."

"I know you don't get it, but a person's rep and the person are two different things. No one cares about Classic Cyborg anymore. He's been out of the racket forever. Everybody cares about his rep. That's what's driving the Dead Pool. That's why there's a ton of money in the pot."

"How much money?"

"A ton. Not Up-Top amounts, but close."

"And all that money is on Classic Cyborg."

"After you removed Franken-borg from the world of the living, yes."

"All the major money says that Classic Cyborg wins. What's the next most popular scenario?"

He squinted at me. "You ask a lot of questions."

"I'm a detective, and since you're not the sharing kind, I have to ask as many as I can."

"What made you ask that question?"

"Cy, that's a basic question. Who's the next favored person to survive—Pink Machete, Harder Steel, or Robo-Stein?"

"None of the above."

"What?"

"Not everyone's betting only on Classic Cyborg winning? I'm not a betting man myself, but someone always bets on the unlikely winner." He blew out a puff of smoke from his cigarette, grinning.

I froze. "That's ridiculous. How do they suppose such a scenario would be remotely possible?"

"Classic Cyborg kills them. He tries to kill you. You kill him. Cruz, the detective, wins the Dead Pool. The King of all Cyborgs turns out not to be a cyborg at all."

FERROUS METAL, CRAZY MANIAC #4

I had to admit that I was shocked. Did I think my client, Classic, would ever harm me? No. I'd been fooled a couple of times before, but I didn't believe I was wrong about him. However, a segment of the crazy criminal class with their deranged gambling game were putting down real money from their secret bank accounts that such a possibility was likely. I wasn't about to let their criminal minds affect me. I put aside what Cy the Hood told me about Classic, and focused on what was more important: a coming gang war.

I got back in my hovercar loaner and had to decide if I'd go back to the office and call Detective Trendy or make another visit to Metro PD. I heard what sounded like a rock hit the top of the hovercar roof, but when I looked to the passenger seat, I saw the long blade of metal from the roof through to the floor. I couldn't jump out of the driver's seat fast enough. I hit the ground hard on my back, but that's the position I wanted to be in. There were four guys twenty feet in the air with what looked like the largest hand cannons I had ever seen, but I was already firing my omega-gun.

My hovercar loaner had no modifications, but my weapon of choice had all kinds of accessories. It hit two of them right away and the rounds exploded in a blast that looked like fireworks. Their bodies fell as the others managed to fire their cannons at me. I rolled under the hovercar. One blade after another hit the ground so hard that they embedded themselves in the solid pavement. I already had their targets locked into my weapon and fired a volley of laser fire at the wall, watching the rounds curve up like homing missiles and hit their targets. One body, two bodies crashed to the ground. Another crashed on the hood of the hovercar. The last smashed to the ground ten feet away.

I jumped up to see who I expected. Cy the Hood stood at the entrance, fumbling with a gun. I shot him in the neck and he fell back. The safest place for me was back in the hovercar. Who knew how many other gunmen would be after me? The second I got back in, I started it up and ascended with a body still on the hood, as quickly as possible. I heard crackling from underneath the hovercar. I was being fired upon from the ground. I floored the accelerator and sped away.

Calling the police would have been pointless. In places like these, bodies would be disposed of, blood washed away, everything set the way it had been so there would be no trace of a shootout. But I smiled. I had one of the gunmen lying dead on the hood of my hovercar.

I was in a repeating time loop, that's what it felt like. Back at Metro PD waiting in the same white interview room, with an annoyed Trendy coming in, wearing the same undercover clothes as before.

"Which gang was he with?" I asked.

Trendy sat down at the table. "Cruz, you're the only civilian I know who doesn't think flying into Police One with a dead body on your hood is a big deal."

"He tried to kill me, and he's dead. Who was he with? I thought Pink Machete didn't have any men left."

"He doesn't. They weren't his."

"A new gang?"

"An old gang. They tried to move in on Pink Machete before, but it didn't work out the way they planned."

"Why would they be after me?" I sat there confused. It made no sense.

"You tell me, Cruz. You said there were four of them?"

"Four of them plus the guy who set me up. But why? It makes no sense."

"Too bad you didn't leave any of them alive for us to ask. You're quite dangerous, aren't you?"

"I don't want to be dangerous."

"I think you should stay home."

"Is there a gang war coming?"

"Yes, Cruz. There's always a gang war coming."

"Specific to our three mutual friends."

"Their gangs are dead, so other gangs will move in. That's how it works."

"Where could Electric Lady be?"

"You should drop this case, Cruz."

"He's your friend."

"Classic isn't my friend. He's a co-worker."

"You two were together yesterday."

"We needed to take down Pink Machete's gang before more innocent people were cut in half." He noticed I was staring off into space. "Cruz, are you still with us?"

"Who's the top guy?"

"What are you talking about?"

"With Pink Machete, Robo-Stein, and Harder Steel out of the picture, who'd most likely take over their territories?"

"A skell named Ferrous Metal. He's been waiting for his chance forever. Now's his chance. Why?"

"Then they were his men."

"Probably."

"Why me?"

"Cruz, as far as the street's concerned, you're the one who killed the unkillable Franken-borg. Someone takes you down, then they get that rep."

I shook my head. "No. These were henchmen, guns for hire. If they killed me, no one would get the rep. These henchmen weren't Ferrous Metal's men."

"Then who?"

"Someone else. I think I'm starting to see the big picture."

"Care to share?"

"Not really. But you're right, I need to stay off the streets."

"I said you need to stay home."

"My office is my home."

"I can still have your building red-tagged, then you'd have to go home."

"On what grounds? All the repair work is done. There's a lot of people in that building. More than a few offices have lawyers. All they'd have to do is call the Mayor. I'll stay in my office so I can work."

"What are you up to, Cruz?"

"Nothing."

"If people are after you, then your office is where they'll go."

"All the more reason for me to stay there. I can defend myself there. I don't want any of these crazy maniacs near my residence."

"There're criminals everywhere, Cruz—around your building and in the city. That's why we have a police force."

"I'll stay in my office. Easier for people to find me. I want people to be able to find me."

"Do you?" Trendy watched me with squinted eyes.

"I do." I squinted my eyes too to mock him.

Phishy stared at me from my desk vid-phone.

It was after hours and I sat in my private office with my door locked. I didn't just intend to work through the night, but sleep in my office too.

"What? Dead?" Phishy was truly shocked. "Cruz—"

"Phishy, no one is blaming you. You didn't do anything wrong. Cy set us up." I had to reassure Phishy because he always wanted to do right by me.

"I'm really sorry, Cruz."

"Don't worry, Phishy. Not your fault. He set us up, but he won't be doing it again."

"But why? I thought we'd be working with him again."

"It would've been nice to have someone we could go to, but we'll find someone else, someone we can trust. Don't worry about it, Phishy. He might have set me up, but I believe everything he told me was true. It's probably the only reason he was telling me the truth. So you did help me after all."

"I did?"

"Yeah, Phishy. You keep all our sidewalk johnnies away from all this. There's a gang war coming."

As soon as I hung up with Phishy, a call came through. It was from an unknown number, which meant I wasn't going to answer. As soon as the answering machine began, it disconnected. It was the fourth time a call came in from an unknown line since I returned to my Liquid Cool office. I didn't like it.

I had the security camera monitors feeding to my big wall viewscreen in my private office lounge area. The arrangement was plush chairs around a glass table, all set up on a dark blue rug. Other than the viewscreen illumination, all the lights were off and all the lights in the main area outside my door were off. There was a creepiness to the fact that I was all alone. However, I did have company—my omega-gun and an assortment of heavy weapons laid out on my main desk, and a few photo-stun grenades too.

It was hard to concentrate with my paranoia running wild. But as the old adage says: just because you're paranoid, doesn't mean no one is after you. In my case, four people were after me, possibly a fifth—the three gangster leaders, this Ferrous Metal, and another party who I believed was watching all of us from the shadows. This unknown party was the one who killed all three of the gangster's gangs. But why come after me? Or was I drawing the wrong conclusions?

The main line rang again from that same unknown number. This time I was very tempted to answer it, but not all calls were traceable if you weren't Metro PD. If I did, they'd know I was here for certain. Then what?

The bay windows of the entire mega-tower were tinted. Additionally, PJ and I made the windows impenetrable by infrared or night-sight vision devices, and reflective against any sonic means. I had the shades drawn and a new metal barrier engaged that covered the complete length of the room adjacent to the windows.

The main line rang again. This time it wasn't unknown, it was from my favorite local diner, the Wet Cabeza. Why would my local diner be calling me in my office at one in the morning?

"Yeah," I answered.

The man on the vid display looked like a kid with an oversized body, metal teeth, and silver shades covering his eyes.

"You made me come to your crummy diner. I've been calling you all night."

"Mr. Ferrous Metal."

"Yeah, that's me." He chuckled. "You are a detective."

"What do you want?"

"I hear you killed four of my men."

"Why would you send four men to kill me? That's not very friendly."

"I didn't send them to kill you, or you would be. I sent them to get your attention."

"They did that."

"And you killed Cy too. Why you do that?"

"I don't like getting set up, and he was reaching for his weapon."

"Because he thought you'd shoot him."

"And I did. What do you want?"

"There's a new sheriff in town, bro."

"I'm not your bro. What do you want?"

"I plan to be the King of all Cyborgs."

"You? Are you also a stand-up comedian?"

"I can see the future, and in the near-future, I kill you and get into the Dead Pool."

"Are you on drugs? You? All I have to do is put the word out on the street to Pink Machete, Harder Steel, and Robo-Stein that you're the one trying to take their territories and disrespecting them and they'll come out of hiding just to put you in the morgue."

"I've already taken their territories. I'm running everything now."

"That's why you called me?"

"Everyone knows you and Classic Cyborg are pals. Tell your pal I know his weakness, and I'm ready for him."

"Classic has no weaknesses."

"Yes, he does."

"Where is she?"

"What?" he asked. "Where's who? Oh, you mean Electric Lady. You'll have to find out."

"You called me to waste my time."

"I called you to tell you that when I'm the King of the Cyborg, I'm going to look to expand, maybe into Rabbit City."

"Ferrous?"

"The name's Ferrous Metal, punk."

"You shouldn't have done that."

"Done what?"

I hung up on him. Immediately, I called another number at the Wet Cabeza. It wasn't just a diner. It had a business department that rented meeting rooms on its second level. After a few moments, someone finally answered.

"Mr. Cruz." The young man recognized me right away.

"Are you okay over there?"

"We had to call the police. This strange man came in and took over our main phones. He ran out of here and sped away in a waiting hovercar."

"Okay. Tell the police to contact the Cyborg Gang Unit and tell them that the man's name is Ferrous Metal."

"Ferrous Metal?"

"Yes. Repeat it."

"Ferrous Metal."

"If you tell them that, they'll make your case a priority."

"Thanks, Mr. Cruz. Was he dangerous?"

"Very, but there'll be a lot more people looking for him now. I doubt you'll ever see him again."

"I hope not."

We both disconnected. I stood from my chair in the near dark, keeping my eyes on the security cameras. Ferrous Metal was talking a lot of nonsense. He wanted to verify that I was in the building and he had.

I found out why Ferrous Metal was so formidable. He didn't have scary illegal bionics like the three gang leaders he wanted to destroy. He had an army of men in his gang who did; he wasn't even the best fighter among them, but he controlled them. If you fought one, you had to fight all of them. It was actually Frankenborg who had destroyed the gang time after time. The late unkillable cyborg relished in killing Ferrous Metal gang members, but he was dead now. Pink Machete and Harder Steel were not as effective, but managed, through their gangs, to keep Ferrous Metal out of their territories and in hiding most of the time. However, they didn't have their gangs anymore. Ferrous Metal would take over everything. All because I killed Frankenborg and some unknown party had wiped out all three cyborg gangs. Trendy was right, there's no such thing as a permanent void in the crime world. Someone would inevitably step up to fill the power vacuum, or try to.

I found myself off-track with his threat about my home, Rabbit City. The threat meant the potential for more innocent people to die, and I wouldn't be able to concentrate until something was done. The crazy maniac knew my favorite diner and had strolled right in. The only reason he didn't kill an employee or customer was because he was scared I was calling the police after him.

Three a.m., four a.m., five a.m. I didn't sleep. My eyes were fixed on the security camera feed on the viewscreen until PJ arrived in the office at eight a.m. When she walked into the office, I was standing at my open door.

"Look at you," she said. "Did you sleep here?"

"I didn't sleep. Did you see any strange people around the Concrete Mama?"

"Strange people? They know where we live."

"They were at my favorite diner early this morning."

"They know about the Wet Cabeza? No, I didn't see any strange people."

"Hold down the fort."

"What? You have clients today."

"Reschedule them. I left a project for you on your desk. I'm going driving."

"Driving?"

"I'm going to take Pony for some routine flying around Metropolis. I don't do enough of that."

"Are you about to do illegal stuff?" She held up her hands. "I don't want to know."

I was supposed to be finding Electric Lady, so I could get off this miserable case, but it would have to wait. Any other detective would have simply put it out of their mind, but I wasn't any other detective. I lived in this city and even if Ferrous Metal hadn't threatened my own neighborhood, I would've done what I was preparing to do.

I sat in my Pony, fresh out of storage, with the faces of the three neighborhood watch leaders on my dashboard viewscreen, along with two others. They were just like my wife and me, famous or not—making a living, raising families, living life. With billions and billions of humans on Earth, on space stations, on the moon, and Mars, it was easy to get lost in this universe. However, us Average Joes and Janes had to stick together. The police could take down any criminal maniacs that existed, but they couldn't and would never be everywhere. The neighborhood watch leaders confirmed what I already knew: the gang war had already arrived. Ferrous Metal's gang was on the streets.

"All I need to know is where they hang out," I said to them.

Thanks to Ferrous Metal's call, I knew what he looked like and I knew what his gang looked like. Every gang had something unique about them; his gang had metal teeth and wore silver shades. They had begun to spread slowly like a virus on the streets, intimidating residents, pedestrians, sidewalk johnnies, store owners, tourists, everyone.

Thanks to the neighborhood watch leaders, I had a complete map of every street corner Ferrous Metal's gang claimed as their turf. When I was on the amateur (and illegal) hovercar racing scene, there were all kinds of driving exercises that you had to master in order to have any chance of getting accepted. If you couldn't fly perfectly backwards at eighty mph down a course without breaking a sweat, if you couldn't fly up the side of a mega-tower, if you couldn't stop on a dime, you had no business being in the race game. I dove from fifty stories, racing from behind a building. There was another exercise you had to master called "Don't Hit the Pedestrian" where mannequins were set up on either side of a course with barely enough room for your hovercar to pass between them. You had to complete the course at no less than one hundred mph, and you couldn't hit one of the mannequins. I modified the exercise to "Hit the Dummies." They never saw me.

There were twenty Ferrous Metal gangsters on the corner. After I sideswiped, all of them were scattered across the street in different states of unconsciousness. I set the Pony down and got out, omega-gun in hand. The police called it fish-wire—a fibrous wire used to handcuff crowds. I had a line attached to my belt and wrapped it around the wrist of the first gang member, locked it, moved to the next one, wrapped his ankle, locked it and moved on. When I was done, there was just a tangled mess of wire and people. They weren't going anywhere.

I gave the signal, and hovercars began to land. People got out with smiles.

"Did you call them?" I asked one of the neighborhood watch members.

"We did. Thanks, Mr. Cruz."

"Good. Go through their pockets and get all their weapons and mobiles. We don't want them shooting anyone or warning any of their other crews."

I left the community residents in charge and got back into the Pony. I repeated the exact same thing against five other crews. Each time, the gang members didn't know what hit them—my Pony flew at them with enough force to send them flying ten feet or more in the air before crashing to the ground. It was good they were cyborgs, or they'd be dead.

I knew it would start easy, but it wouldn't remain that way. Criminal gangs somehow had a way of knowing. Two miles away, I peered through my binoculars from a mega-tower rooftop; my next Ferrous Metal target was ready for me. It was another crew of about twenty men, much larger than most gangs, and all of them were looking into the sky—looking for a red vehicle. All of them had their hands in their jackets.

There was an alleyway only a quarter mile from them. That's where I set the Pony—only it wasn't red anymore. They had their illegal bionics; I had my illegal changeling cloak on my vehicle. Now it was a common gray.

"Where is he?" I heard one of them say. They were all focused on the sky, so focused that none of them saw me stroll up behind them.

"Gentlemen, I want you all to take your hands out of your pockets, raise them in the air, and slowly lie flat on the ground." I didn't yell, but I said it in a loud tone.

One of the gangsters turned, and I shot him in the chest. He fell to the ground.

"Gentlemen, I'm not playing games."

"You can't shoot all of us," another said, and I shot him in the back. Down he went.

"I can do this all day," I said. "Hands out of your pockets, in the air, lie down flat on your stomach."

"You're so dead, copper," another said, and I shot him in the back too.

"I'm not a copper, and no talking. You all must be the dumbest gang I've ever met."

"You'll see how smart we are—" I shot the gang member in the chest.

"You're not going to behave, are you?" I said.

"No!" another said. At that point, I let loose with my omega-gun and shot all of them.

Again, I gestured in the air and hovercars approached. When the residents exited, all I heard were laughs and applause.

"The police are on their way, Mr. Cruz," one of the female residents said to me.

I kept the Pony's exterior color on gray as I flew to the next crew, but by this time they had gotten off the streets. It wasn't even noon yet and three-fourths of Ferrous Metals gang were already in police custody.

"I'm here," I said to a couple of neighborhood watch residents on my dashboard vid-call display.

"They're in the convenience store," the man said, with a panicked look.

"This isn't going to be a clean takedown. Call the police now. Tell them shots are being fired."

"You hear shots?" the woman asked me.

"I will when I start shooting, but don't tell the police that."

The gang members had simply walked from their street corner post to the nearby convenience store and took it over. But for them, that meant hanging out in the back of the store smoking, joking, and eating food from the shelves. None of them were watching the front or the back, so they didn't even see me when I walked through the door and stood there watching them with my hands on my waist. They didn't see me motion to the convenience store attendants to get up from behind the counter and get out.

Finally, one of them noticed me. All of them stopped joking and stared at me.

"Where's Ferrous Metal?" I asked. "I see why he runs the gang even when he's not the strongest. He's the only one who has any brains in your crew. I tell you what I told all your gang friends: you are the dumbest gang members I have ever met. Pink Machete, Harder Steel, and even Robo-Stein don't need gangs to deal with the likes of you. Where's Ferrous Metal? Because you are all in need of serious adult guidance."

None of them said anything, but I saw their fingers getting very itchy.

"Put your hands in the air and then slowly lie on the ground on your bellies. Do it now, please. I don't have all day."

"And if we don't?" one of them asked.

With my omega-gun, I locked in on multiple targets and fired. I dropped all of them in a few seconds.

One of the attendants peeked back into the store. "You shot them?"

"The police have already been called."

The man stepped inside and his colleague followed.

"We need a gun like yours."

"Did these maniacs eat the food off your shelves without paying?"

"Yes! Kids around here are always doing this!" I had obviously hit a nerve with the clerks.

"I'd say that gives you the right to go through their pockets and take all the cash on them for the food they stole and for all the pain and distress they caused you today."

The clerks looked at each other and then me. "Can we?"

"Tick-tock. The police will be here soon."

For a second, I thought the two clerks were cyborgs too, because they moved so fast, rifling through all the unconscious gang members with lightning speed. They ignored the weapons, but all the cash went right into their pockets.

No one had been killed. Lots of shooting, but no one dead—yet. I wanted all of them in an interrogation room with Trendy and Cyborg Gang Unit officers. The "geniuses" probably had tons of intel that could be used to get other gangsters off the street and end all kinds of criminal operations. However, I had a feeling that the Grim Reaper was going to get some kind of payment today from all this, one way or another.

Now that Ferrous Metal's gangs had been removed from the streets, I took down another one at the convenience store, the police took down another three—one at a restaurant, another at a diner, and another at a high school parking lot of all places. Again, the gang members were dummies, but Ferrous Metal couldn't get where he had gotten if all of them were like that. *Where were his enforcers?*

By noon, all the remaining gang members had disappeared. I had the neighborhood watch groups, as well as my Sidewalk Johnny Brigade, keep them under surveillance. Before I was a detective, I had a less than positive view of the harmless, street hustlers of Metropolis. Today, they were a vital resource—my eyes and ears on the streets. Sidewalk johnnies spent their time hanging around, watching trouble, causing trouble, hustling, looking for a hustle, but doing little of anything meaningful. They congregated, watched, chatted it up, sat around, smoked, joked, disappeared to the bathrooms when needed, or disappeared to their sleep shack for a few hours. All of them had their "turf" too—a street, corner, or alleyway. My Sidewalk Johnny Brigade were much more than that.

When they called me on my mobile, what they told me didn't surprise me at all. The Ferrous Metal gang was doing what I would have done if I were a crazy maniac. The crew had decided to visit the Concrete Mama.

The Concrete Mama in Rabbit City was home to my family and me. I always described it, architecturally, as a chunk of granite set down on Earth from space. It was a no-frills monolith tower of legacy housing. If there was ever a planetary shockwave from a nuclear blast or an asteroid crash, you could bet the Concrete Mama would still be standing. It was ugly, but it would be here until the end of time in its ugliness. It was also my home for fifteen years before I was married. Today it was home with my wife and Cruz Jr.

I had told Ferrous Metal that threatening my home was a mistake. He obviously didn't get the message, even though most of his gang was gone, courtesy of the local neighborhood watch groups and me.

Mr. Post, the Concrete Mama's daytime doorman, had called me. He had locked the main entrance so none of them would be running inside to take cover. When I dove from the sky at five of them, I was not interested in sideswiping anyone. This time, no one would be surviving—and they didn't. I hit them straight on. Their bodies sailed twenty feet away.

I did a combat stop, hopped out and the shootout began. Even a dummy can have a flash of genius. As I traded gunfire with the remaining dozen or so crew, I saw a black hovercar slowly trying to sneak up behind me. I was wearing my clear shades, which had all those fancy optics, including a rearview mode.

Unfortunately, I saw something else too. Mr. Post was about to come through the main entrance of the Concrete Mama, with a laser rifle in his hands. Who knew what kind of firepower was going to emerge from the black hovercar coasting up from behind like a shark with its fin cutting the surface of the water.

I swung around and flicked my pop-gun at the approaching black hovercar. It sped at me like a rocket. The round shattered the vehicle's completely black windshield to pieces, and the vehicle shot up into the sky. I turned again, aimed my omega-gun, then let it auto-fire at the gang members as I ran back the other way to my Pony.

It was not pretty, as the gang members had two choices: get shot in the front by me or in the back by Mr. Post. Soon Mr. Post was joined by some other guy I had never seen before (I later learned it was his teenage nephew, who was in the military). I heard Mr. Post yelling to someone in Spanish (or was it Portuguese) and the local hover-ice cream truck man appeared, firing a laser gun at them too. (Yes, the hover-ice cream truck man) Now, it was really over.

It took me seconds to get back into the air when I got back into the Pony and gave chase after the black hovercar. They were fast, but I was faster. Someone in their hovercar stuck a hand out of the passenger window with a gun, thinking he could shoot at me, but with the wind there was no possible way. The gun blew out of his hand, and the vehicle started slowing down because it had lost its aerodynamics. I sharply turned to the right, roaring past and strafing the side of the vehicle with gunfire. When the windows were shot out, I saw that there were a lot more than two in the back seat, more like double that—maybe they were sitting in each other's laps. It was like a clown car that performed for children, where the tiny hovercar landed and fifty clowns piled out. Well, they were clowns to come after me. The vehicle dropped like a rock.

As it fell to the surface, someone managed to grab the wheel, but stabilizing isn't stopping descent. The vehicle crashed to the ground and exploded. Two of them jumped from the vehicle seconds before, as if that would save their lives. It didn't.

"Boss." PJ's face appeared on my dashboard display when I answered.

"Yeah."

"I'm connecting Detective Trendy."

"He has my number."

"He called you here at the office. I can't tell him to hang up and redial you there. I'll connect him. We're a premier customer service business, Cruz. That's what Liquid Cool is."

I laughed. "Okay."

"Here he is." Her face disappeared and his appeared.

"Mr. Cruz."

"Detective."

"I'm not sure I can think of a time when an entire gang was taken down in one day by one detective and an army of retired folks in community neighborhood watch groups. I think you're in the wrong business, Cruz. I think your true calling is gang suppression. How much would we have to pay you?"

"I'm flattered, but I like my job fine now."

"I'm not complaining, but this seems far removed from private investigation work."

"Ah, but detective, it's all part of the master plan. Where's Ferrous Metal?"

"No one has seen him. He's disappeared. Not like we haven't seen that before."

"Seems like he disappeared before we started the clean-up operations. Too bad we don't know where he is."

"No, but I suspect you'll find him. He has no gang."

"Find him. Maybe. Have you heard anything on the streets about Electric Lady?"

"Not a word. Nothing on the three friends either. What is this master plan you mentioned?"

"Let's see how the day goes. Maybe, I'm wrong."

"Okay. Thanks again, Cruz. This was a real good day for the good guys. A lot of bad guys off the streets. A lot of happy and relieved residents. I still say this is your true calling. I'll figure out ways to entice you."

"You do that, detective. Tell me if you hear anything about Electric Lady."

"I will."

I was back at the Liquid Cool office. PJ had rescheduled all my appointments so we could work in peace. I gave her a project, and I had my own project to work. My posthumous mentor Wilford G. said in his book, *How to be a Great Detective with 100 Rules*, that sometimes the street detective had to go right back to the beginning and verify or reverify everything they thought they knew. A good detective uses assumptions to fill in blanks and solve the case, but sometimes that skill can backfire and send the detective down the wrong path. Stop and go back to the beginning. That's what I was doing.

The vid-phone rang.

"Boss!" PJ yelled from outside my office.

I touched the vid-phone button. It was Detective Trendy.

"Cruz."

"Detective, it's been ages."

"Becoming quite a habit. We found Ferrous Metal."

"Dead."

"You knew already."

"I guessed. How was it done?"

"Riddled with gunfire. Him and three of his top guys."

"But that's not how they were killed."

"If you keep this up, Cruz, I'll begin to think you did it."

"Beaten to death."

"Yes."

"Just like the Franken-borg gang, Harder Steel's gang, and Pink Machete's."

"What's going on, Cruz?"

"Someone is clearing the field, so only the most important pieces remain."

"Do you know who?"

"I have a few theories, but that's all."

"Are you in danger?"

"Not from this unknown party."

"Maybe I can get both of you to work for gang suppression. We'd have Metropolis gang free in no time."

"That would be a nice fairy tale ending, wouldn't it?"

"Yep, which is why we know that's exactly how it's not going to end."

DR. SILVER-ROSE

When Dr. Silver-Rose saw me waiting for her in the lobby area of Cyborg Psych, her expression was one of shock.

"Are you waiting for me, Mr. Cruz?" she asked, briefcase in hand and about to walk through to her office.

"Yes, I am, doctor."

"Okay. You can follow."

We were back in her office and consulting room. She gestured to the chair in front of her desk. I sat before she did.

"I'm sorry, Mr. Cruz, but why would you want to see me again?"

"My appearance seems to have upset you."

"Not at all, but I've heard that your life has become quite busy lately. You seem to be very adept at shooting criminals. I hear you could hold your own against the top marksmen in Metro PD. To what do you attribute your talent?"

"Video games."

"I know many people who play shooting games in virtual reality and in virtual life, but few, I doubt, come close to your proficiency. You should have joined law enforcement."

"I might have if not for the body cams."

"Yes, body cams and Police Watch over your shoulder. You might have to follow the law all the time."

"Exactly."

"What can I help you with this time, Mr. Cruz?"

"I have a general request. I know you've said that everyone in Cyborg Psych works for you, but that you aren't their boss. It's just one big happy family. However, in terms of employment files, including psych evals, that would be under your supervision and control."

"That's correct, Mr. Cruz."

"Good, I was hoping I came to the right person. I'd like to know about the psych and medical files of all your staff."

"Excuse me, Mr. Cruz."

"Could you provide me information on any staff members who would have a psych or medical issue?"

"Certainly not, Mr. Cruz. That's privileged and confidential information. Mr. Cruz, I do know something about you and your methods. Why don't you ask your real question rather than play your games?"

"Because you'll say no."

"I already said no, so why continue this conversation?"

"Does Classic Cyborg have any psych or medical condition that would make him susceptible to weakness—physically, psychologically, financially, or in any other way?"

"Mr. Cruz, you can leave right now."

"Doctor, this is important."

"So is patient privacy."

"It'll take me time, but I'll get the info I need."

"Not with my help."

"Why don't you tell me and I'll go away?"

"You will go away, Mr. Cruz. I'll also make sure you're not allowed back into the division ever again."

I stared at her, then smiled.

"Thank you."

"Why are you thanking me?"

"You answered my question. I'll go away."

"I didn't answer any question."

"Yes, you did. You do this thing when you're trying to hide something."

"I don't do any 'thing' when I'm hiding something, and I'm not hiding anything. Privacy is an important thing in society, Mr. Cruz. As a health care profession, we guard that knowledge."

"If you say so. What's the penalty for releasing a person's mental and psych file?"

"Termination, prosecution, fines, imprisonment, and permanent revocation of their medical health license."

"So the bribe would have to be rather large."

"Bribe?"

"Yeah, I'm going to have to find someone to bribe to get the information I need."

"You do that. I doubt you'll have any luck whatsoever. In fact, I'm going to take extra precautions to safeguard his file and everyone else's."

"Thank you, doctor. I knew I came to the right place."

I stood from my chair and walked back into the hall, closing the door behind me.

I didn't leave immediately. Dr. Silver-Rose never came out of her office, but I took the elevators to Personnel. The staffers there knew me well, as I visited many times before while working government cases. My detective agency didn't work on only civilian cases, but corporate and government too. With any client, the first rule was to do a full background check. If that client was a government client, that included any information from their employment file. I would never see the details of the client, but I could view general summary information about them: tickets, arrests, fines, credit scores, city liens, complaints, etc. The average citizen of Metropolis had no idea that the city maintained millions of points of data on government workers. And to anyone who could read the codes, an entire detailed profile could be created. I literally sat at a computer screen for an hour jotting down the codes of interest in my mobile.

When I was finished, I cleared the screen with the flip of a switch, thanked the staffer who had helped me log in, and I was on my way. I walked to the elevator and stopped, smiling. In the lobby area was Dr. Silver-Rose. She stood from her chair and walked to me.

"Doctor, what a coincidence to bump into you again."

"I have to admit that you are annoyingly good at your job. You couldn't have lasted this long if it were all show and no substance. Did you find what you wanted?"

"I found enough of it."

"Is this the life of a detective in Metropolis? Sneaking around and the like."

"Shooting people, too, don't forget. No, doctor, I'm simply doing my job. Solve my case, give my client his or her money's worth in results, then move on to the next case. I shouldn't need to explain this to you. In my business, lack of knowledge can get you killed."

"Does your client know you're illegally digging into his personnel file?"

"I didn't illegally dig into anything. I made up a story to observe your behavior. You left your office, followed me almost fifty flights up, sat in a lobby for an hour without doing your job, and confronted me. Who's the one playing games? You are personally invested in my client. Why?"

She glared at me.

"Doctor, you're doing that 'thing' again. The expression."

She brushed past me in a huff.

"Are we taking the same elevator down, Doctor?"

"I'll catch the next one."

"Are you going to tell me why you're interested in my client and his case? Before you stonewall me, ask yourself do you want me to go away or to keep digging? I'll give you a snapshot of my medical and psych file. Former patient with severe OCD tendencies. That means I'm that dog with the bone that never, ever let's go."

"Leave me alone." She had gone from calm and cool to simmering rage. Now she was almost crying as she rushed into the elevator and pounded the button to close. Her abrupt change of behavior startled me.

I returned to the Cyborg Psych reception area, and they told me that she had left the building for an appointment. I was supposed to be solving the mysteries of this case, not finding new ones.

HUNTING ROBO-STEIN

Dr. Silver-Rose was the typical mental health professional—intelligent, intuitive, well-read, well-informed, well-spoken, well-organized to the last detail, logical. No one with traits any less than that could have achieved her position within the supercity. However, my last encounter with her was plain weird. It didn't mean she was a schizo. I'd met many people who lived such an ordered and sheltered life that they truly didn't know how to respond to even the most minor of out-of-the-ordinary situations. I wonder if she too had disappeared, out of reach to me and anyone else. I hated loose ends and unanswered questions, but it was part of the detective life.

I had started from the beginning, re-evaluating all my assumptions and what I thought I knew. Now, I had to start that all over again, because I'd have to include the doctor in my list of players. However, all I really had to do was find Electric Lady, so I had to stay focused if I was to ever get out of this case.

Franken-borg was dead, but his presence lived on. Things were happening because I had permanently, and unexpectedly, removed him from the world of the living.

I returned to my Liquid Cool office, and PJ pointed to a nicely-dressed man waiting in the lobby area. He saw me and stood.

"Phishy sent me, Mr. Cruz," he said.

I walked to him. "What do you have?"

"They say the back alleys of Metropolis are the real 'final frontier.' I believe it." He handed me a slip of paper. "He said you like paper."

I took the slip from him. "Robo-Stein?"

"Robo-Stein," he confirmed.

The scariest part of Metropolis that I had ever been to was Mad Heights, colloquially known as Mad City. If I even drove anywhere near the district, my chest tightened. I was adaptive, but I wasn't different from Dr. Silver-Rose, I liked routine and boring. The street hustler that Phishy sent to the office had info that took me to a section of Metropolis that reminded me a lot of Mad City. It looked like most neighborhoods I was accustomed to, with its mega-towers and neon signage. However, they didn't have sidewalk johnnies, they had street thugs who stood with their backs against the walls in cheap suits.

I never made eye contact with any of them, but I was watching them as they watched me. My hands never left my pockets as I walked to the back alley entrance of a no-name establishment. The second I walked through the door, I saw exactly what Phishy's street hustler informant meant—heads! On the walls were lifelike heads of all types.

"Can I help you, sir?" I heard the voice, but couldn't see him. In front of me were mannequins, all facing the door, for as far back as the eye could see. The man could have been standing right in front of me, and I wouldn't have been able to pick him out.

"You'll have to give me a moment."

"Yes, it can be a bit unnerving for first-time visitors. What can I help you with, sir?"

"I'll be happy to answer you, when I'm able to tell who's a mannequin and who's human."

"I'll help you out." The man raised his hand. I was glad that he did so. My eyes could finally pick him out, but once I did focus in on him, three rows of mannequins back, he still looked like a mannequin with his cheap clothes, shiny skin, and slicked back hair. He approached with a smile.

"Is this better, sir?"

"Yes, thank you."

"I'm Mr. Vale, sir. You must be here for someone else."

"Yes."

"Friend, loved one, colleague?"

"Friend. I'm sorry. I'm a bit overwhelmed. Head prosthetics?"

"Twenty percent of cyborgs have some type of cranial or facial cybernetic part, much higher than most people think. Our specialty is to make it look so real that no one ever knows otherwise."

My eyes scanned the heads on the walls, then the mannequins.

"Any size, any ethnicity, any gender. We can make any modifications needed."

"What's that in the back?" I asked.

"Yes, sir, the specialty section."

He led me to the back of the store. This section of the store had red paint instead of white. Each of the heads on the wall was surrounded by a lit neon circle. I laughed at the displays: one head had ram horns, another a unicorn horn—of course—a horned devil head, and more.

"For custom parties?"

"Very good, sir. Yes. Cyborgs have a healthy sense of humor too."

"I'm going to ask a question, but it's not to offend you or cause you any trouble. I have cyborgs in my life, so I don't make jokes about it."

"What type?"

"Both arms and another had a decapitation at the neck."

"The latter was very serious."

"It was, but full and quick recovery as a child."

"You're going to ask about the criminal element."

"Yes."

"Of course, that's a big part of my clientele. But this a strictly legal business. I sell legal products only. However, if they are further modified after their purchase, that's beyond my control or concern."

"How many of your clients have full cybernetic heads?"

"I had two, but you killed one."

I smiled. "You know who I am?"

"I do, sir."

"Red Rabbit."

"Yes. I was one of the ones who helped put him back together after the unfortunate accident caused by former business partners."

"Then you know who I'm looking for."

He gestured me to follow, as he walked to the counter. "The only reason I'll help is because I know you're not a cop, and Mr. Robo-Stein has an outstanding bill that he hasn't paid. I have no way of reaching him, but maybe a detective can."

He lifted the partition and moved back behind the counter to a desk computer. "What information do you need, sir?"

"When was his last purchase?"

He typed. "Two months ago."

"What did he buy?"

"Twelve custom pieces."

"Twelve? You let him go that long without paying?"

"He had a brother at the time, so I was not about to confront him about his delinquency if I intended to stay in business, and alive. If I didn't know your full history, I'd say you didn't like cyborgs all that much."

He typed on the flat keyboard, then turned the screen so I could see. "The twelve pieces."

I stared at the twelve custom heads. "How long does it take for you to make pieces like these?"

"I've been doing this for a long time. I can do most in a couple of days. Detail work can take me a week to a month. These took about five weeks for the whole set."

"Can I take a picture of the screen with my mobile?"

"By all means."

That's what I did. A dozen heads: Franken-borg, Harder Steel, Pink Machete, Electric Lady, Classic Cyborg, Ferrous Metal, Harder Steel's #2 guy, Pink Machete's #2 and #3 guys, one unknown woman, and two unknown men.

I pointed to the unknown woman and the unknown men. "Do you know who they are?"

"The woman? Her name is...Rose. Rose Silver. She's a cyborg doctor, or the doctor that the criminal cyborg class calls when they need a doctor. That man is Copper Copper and the other is Blitzkrieg."

"Nice names."

"Street names always are. He did want me to make more, but I said he had to pay me for the last ones."

"Make more? When did you speak with him last?"

"Couple of days ago." He pulled the screen back, typed something, then turned it again so I could see. Three heads: me, PJ, and our local hover-ice cream truck guy.

"That's how you know me."

"Yes."

"Do the others know he's planning on impersonating them?"

"I told them the moment I found out Franken-borg was dead. But not these three new ones."

"I'll take care of the notifications of the other two. Did you speak to the original twelve directly?"

"No one talks to anyone directly in the criminal world. Messages left all around."

"I wish I could stay and chat more."

"You have a lot of work of an urgent nature to attend to."

"Yes. But before I go, can you tell me about previous orders?"

"That I can't divulge in any way. He paid for those in full."

"I had to try."

"Of course, sir, as you should have."

"I'll be on my way then."

"Stop by anytime, sir. Maybe send your cyborg friends over."

"But you do head prosthetics."

He tapped a button. The entire store changed. The walls flipped around and the floor descended into the floor and returned. Now I was looking at bionic arms, legs, and chest pieces—male and female.

"Mr. Cruz, I do it all."

Hover-ice cream trucks, like the hover-food truck industry in general, were very popular. Ice cold ice cream in one of a million flavors, not to mention the million and one toppings. Kids loved them, and so did the parents. Like drug dealers, hover-food trucks worked their turf, which they guarded mercilessly. No one could encroach into another person's territory. The guy who worked the streets around the Concrete Mama was known by everyone, the son of the previous hover-ice cream guy of twenty years. The son took over the business five years ago. He was also a Concrete Mama resident and dating our new doorman's sister.

I surveyed the area and found a nice safe place to set down the Pony—a public parking structure not too far away. I walked down one level from the roof and could see him clearly by looking over the edge. The hover-ice cream truck guy was on a very strict schedule that never changed. A couple of hours on one street, then the next couple of hours some place else, four hours of lunchtime some place else, and so on until night.

My mobile was already in my hand as I dialed the number Mr. Vale had given me. Yes, criminals didn't have a direct line for outsiders. You had to leave a message. So, I left one as I took the elevator to the top of the parking structure.

"Hey Robo-Stein, you crazy maniac. I'm here. What was I supposed to think? That I got a great tip and that you had replaced our hover-ice cream guy or was planning to? Then, I'd show up and investigate. You have a long way to go before you even move in the direction of a criminal mastermind. I have some questions before I play another one of your dumb games. Call me back you cheapskate criminal who doesn't pay his bills. You're going to be the King of all Cyborgs? In your dreams. Call me back so I can get my questions answered."

I hung up and waited. It was a trap and I knew it from the start. He tried to get me at the Liquid Cool building, escaped, and set it all up. Phishy and I had been fooled once with Cy the Hood, but we weren't about to let it happen again. If someone from the mean streets showed up with good info for us for a fee, then it was a setup. Mr. Vale wasn't directly part of it; he was an unwitting pawn in Robo-Stein's game. I hated games.

All of these cyborg maniacs were too dangerous and unpredictable to leave out on the streets. I didn't want innocent people to start getting killed again. I'd already verified that our hover-ice cream truck guy was not an impostor. He seemed fine. That meant Robo-Stein's plot was to get me on the way to the hover-ice cream truck. It was the same strategy that the late Franken-borg used—lie in wait for your victim.

My mobile rang, audio-only, from an unknown number. I had hurled enough insults at him. He probably worked himself into a huge cursing fit but had calmed down to call.

"Hey, criminal mastermind wannabe," I answered.

There was silence for a bit, but I heard the breathing. "I can see you."

"No, you can't. Where's Electric Lady?"

"I don't know and don't care. Are you attempting to trace this call?"

"Why? I don't care where you are. You're nothing without your brother, and someone's already out there looking for you. They killed your gang. I'll simply wait for them to catch up with you. So, you have no idea where she is?"

"I heard she's being held for ransom."

"By whom?"

"Maybe me, maybe someone else."

"One of you has her. That much I know. It couldn't be you now that I'm talking to you. You don't have the balls to do this and get on the wrong side of Classic Cyborg. Not without your brother to fight your battles."

"I have the balls and the brains to do this!"

"You kidnapped Electric Lady? She'd beat you up and stuff your body in your cyborg head, then kick you down the street like a football."

"No, she wouldn't! I could take her! I can take you!"

"You ran from me. You'd run from her. I'm sorry I wasted my time. You're nothing without your brother."

"That's not true! That's not true! I was the brains of the gang! I'll show you all! All of you!"

He hung up on me. Well, I got the answer to my question: he didn't have her. I felt a vibration underneath me. It was like there was an earthquake happening. I knew what that meant.

Robo-Stein's metal head punched through the ground. I realized how he was able to move through solid concrete now. His bionic heads rotated at incredible speed and emitted some kind of ray, probably similar to his brother's arm cannons that could vaporize walls.

His head stopped to look at me. My omega-gun had its special attachment on just for him. I blew his head off with an explosive charge so massive that I was thrown back a few feet myself. When I got back up and ran to the crater-sized hole in the thirty-first floor, I peeked through to see his body still falling through a series of holes in the ground.

When the walls of any modern mega-tower were breached, it meant blast doors came down or rose. Did I have time to get away? I bolted for the stairway, but the doors locked shut. The tower's alarms sounded. The lights started flashing red. Once again, I was trapped in a building with severe structural damage until Metro PD arrived.

SINISTER BETTY

I was so mad. It took almost two hours for those of us trapped in the parking structure by the emergency structure protocols to be released—there were nine of us. Nine unlucky Metropolis residents trapped in a one hundred fifty-story parking structure. I had hoped to find the pancaked body of Robo-Stein on the ground floor, but there was no body to be found.

When the ground floor barriers lowered, a virtual army of police came in and detained all us. We could protest and grunt all we wanted. We'd be in custody for hours until they completed their investigation. One of the officers saw me and stopped. He stared at me with his arms folded. His partner did the same and then all the police officers did. The other eight residents looked at them, then glared at me.

"It wasn't my fault," I said.

"Mr. Cruz," the lead officer said.

"It wasn't me. It was one of those crazy maniacs, but he got away."

Once they knew I was involved, they let everyone else go. But not me! This time I was the *lucky* one, as I was loaded into the back of a police hovercruiser to wait until the detectives arrived. I lost an entire day being questioned by officers. Police cleared the building and repair crews had already begun their work when I was finally allowed to go. I was in too much of a foul mood to do anything but go home.

While the late Wilford G. was my posthumous mentor, Compstat Connie, the human computer who ran Metro PDs Crime Information Center (CIC), was my current one. She would retire one of these days, but I was so impressed by her when I was a police intern in high school that I never forgot her. For the last year or so, I had taken it upon myself to learn as much from her fifty-plus-year career as I could. She knew criminals, knew criminal patterns, and, more amazingly, could predict crime patterns. Computers could predict things fifty percent of the time. She could do so eighty percent of the time, but the City was too stupid to take advantage of her skill. So, I would be her successor in a way, no other detective, large or small, was going to be able to.

I found out that Connie was off that day, so I couldn't even visit her. The multi-hundred million dollar CIC division wasn't in a prominent place in the main city towers but in what could only be called the basement levels. With her not being in, I was forced to go to the upper levels to do my research. The CIC public research area was used by data research companies, the media, and large, high-end detective firms. The latter two were why I never used it. Everyone wanted to know your business, and I was never in a sharing mood.

I returned to the Pony so I could at least change from my tan fedora and slicker into something more inconspicuous, which meant a black hoodie. Back to the elevators I went to go to the dreaded public CIC research room. It was filled with endless cubicles of city computer terminals for one or two people. The setup was awful. All the terminals faced the main door, so everyone could glance up and see what new person arrived. My "disguise" fooled no one. Most people didn't glance up; they stared.

"Hi, Mr. Cruz," someone said as I walked down an aisle.

"Hey, Mr. Cruz," another said.

"Working on anything interesting, Mr. Cruz?" another asked.

This was the gauntlet I had to go through to find an empty cubicle. If it were Up-Top, with their digital tech, you could've accessed the confidential city files from the comfort of your home or office. However, this wasn't the space colonies, Lunar Colony, or Mars. You wanted to access the files; you had to come in person. Earth didn't do digital. Up-Top could say anything it wanted. Earthers viewed digital tech as inherently non-securable.

In addition to spending the next several hours doing my research, I had to make sure no one snuck up behind me to peek at what I was doing. Which really wasn't a problem, because I brought my own security screen to place in front of the computer viewscreen. I plugged it into a pair of glasses for optimum private viewing. A person could be sitting right next to me and all they would see is black.

"That's not very sporting," a voice said from behind me.

I turned around to see one of Metro's many vulture reporters. "Get out of here." Now, I could do some work.

My task was simple: start from the beginning and read every scrap of data about my three cyborg gang leaders at large, their main lieutenants, Ferrous Metal, and the other two cyborg gang leaders that Mr. Vale revealed to me. Only people with legitimate reasons could get police approval to access the public criminal files, which actually contained almost all the information the police had that was "fact" (reports and notes weren't included as they were considered rumor). However, for real bad gangs like these, most "rumors" were treated as fact.

In addition to my tech toys, I brought a ton of notebooks. No digital pads of any kind. They could be hacked, and I was sitting in a room full of people who knew how. As I filled the pages with notes, scrolling from screen to screen, I saw the full, ugly picture of the people I was dealing with. Trendy had given me their profiles after they had established themselves as hardened criminals. I wanted to know how they got there and who they were before they started the dark journey. I arrived around nine in the morning and I was still there at eight that night.

The research room closed at midnight, and I knew I'd be there right up until the cleaning crews threw me out. I was plugged into my security screen shades, but I left a tiny corner on my view to show me a panoramic view of anyone behind me. Over the hours, lots of people walked by trying to see what I was doing but soon moved on. This time I saw Detective Trendy walking to me. I took my shades off and turned.

"Mr. Cruz, they told me you were in here."

"Detective."

"I'd ask what you're working on, but I already know."

I stood up a bit to see who was around. Surprisingly, most of the cubicles around me were empty.

"Cruz, reporters and fancy megacorp detectives don't work as hard as you. They left a long time ago."

"Any news on Electric Lady?"

"She's still in the wind."

"Like our friends."

"Yep."

"Copper Copper and Blitzkrieg?"

"The names never get old. What about them?"

"Are those two dead?"

"Yeah. Months ago. The first one was an ex-cop, kicked off the force for drug involvement. Both of them were nipping at Ferrous Metal's heels to take his territory."

"Three levels of cyborg gangs have been neutralized."

"Yeah."

"Exactly, how long ago were they killed?"

"You didn't get to their files yet?"

"Not yet."

"Three months ago."

"Lot of coincidences, don't you think. All this started happening around the same time."

"Yeah, and none of us believes in coincidences."

"Are you and Classic still on good terms?"

"Why would you ask that? Of course we are. I work with him every day."

"Why didn't you tell him that Franken-borg's gang had been wiped out? You knew, I knew, but he didn't at the time."

"Cruz, sometimes people forget. There's no secret agenda. No one cared about Franken-borg's gang. Everyone was scared to death of Franken-borg."

"I didn't mean to suggest anything by the question. I'm doing my detective due diligence. Checking all the boxes."

Trendy grinned. "Yeah, Cruz, whatever you say."

"Anything I should know? You did come to visit me."

"No, just visiting. I was off and decided to swing by, see how civilian detectives work. Or how you do. I also heard you had another encounter with Robo-Stein and another mega-tower has been damaged. This time it's red-tagged."

"They do like destroying buildings."

"I hope you're being careful. They may be hiding, but they can appear at any time. Or they can hire other people to do their dirty work."

"It's all about reputation with these gangs. If they want to get me, they have to do it personally."

"Listen to you. Do you think you're able to think like them now?"

"Give me 'til midnight."

Trendy laughed. "Yeah, they told me you're working with Compstat Connie, memorizing the faces of Metro's criminal population. I thought they were joking, but if anyone can do it, it's you. Everyone already thinks Connie is an android with that brain of hers. Did she ever do that playing card memory game with you?"

"Over fifteen years ago, when I was a police intern."

"Flash fifty-two cards in a row in front of her, and she'd recite each one back to you in order without hesitation."

"Tell me about Dr. Silver-Rose?"

"What about her?"

"Anything I should know? Fact or rumor."

"Why are you asking?"

"Why are you stalling?"

"The doctor is above board."

"Well, she isn't."

"Why do you say that?"

"She isn't. She has a connection to Classic that isn't boss or employee. And she's also...in the wind."

I could see in Trendy's face that my revelation caught him off guard. "What did you say to her?"

"Detective, I'll find out. I don't know why people continue trying to hide things from me when I'm working a case. I always find out because I never stop digging."

"Okay. The doctor has worked in the underground medic world for years."

"Underground meaning illegal."

"Yes."

"Why would this be allowed?"

"Cruz, she got permission from the Metro brass themselves."

"Why?"

"I don't know. But what I do know is that she has given us detailed reports over the years that have allowed the Gang Unit to take so many cyborg gang members and dangerous cyborgs with mental issues off the streets that I can't even count. Who knows how many innocent people she's saved?"

"Trendy, I need you to find out why. It's very important. Have you ever seen Dr. Silver-Rose emotional?"

"No, she's as professional as they come. Why?"

"She was frantic and crying because I was looking into Classic's medical file."

"Frantic and crying," Trendy repeated.

"I need to know. Dr. Silver-Rose by day, Dr. Rose Silver by night?"

"So you know already?"

"I only knew the name, but anyone could have figured out that it was her. Seriously, I need to know. We have a gang war delayed, not averted."

"Classic is not a bad guy."

"I don't care. We need to know everything about the people connected with him. You do remember that someone is personally wiping out all the top cyborg gangs in Metropolis. We need to piece this all together to know what we're dealing with. I don't like surprises."

Trendy sighed. "Neither do I."

Trendy got permission for me to stay in the CIC research room by myself until one in the morning. He had gone home, but I knew it wouldn't take long for him to get back to me regarding the doctor.

The reason I was pushing forward to reexamine all the players in this case so hard was because I knew a cosmic clock was ticking in the background. The Dead Pool was opened at the beginning of the year, but then they waited. They waited until everything was in place. Then it started. Robo-Stein had gone after me twice. And though the three cyborg crime leaders were in hiding, they wouldn't be for long. My fear was when they emerged, the violence would explode. All of this was like an ancient gladiator fight with Metropolis as their arena. I didn't want to see any more innocent victims, and my killing Franken-borg had only heightened the stakes. I needed to get ahead of it and fast. This was a case that the longer it went on literally could kill me, and some other unlucky souls.

I did go home to the Concrete Mama for at least five hours sleep after a long super shower. I walked through the Liquid Cool doors at ten a.m. for my first visitor. PJ had lined them up the day before.

PJ led my first visitor to my private office. I had met her before at the glass factory, but this time she wasn't in a yellow jumpsuit with a red hard hat. She was dressed normally in a buttoned slicker and a scarf on her head rather than a hoodie. It was a classy look that I had to remind my wife about, who was always on the lookout for the latest fashion trend.

"Have a seat, Ms. Astra. You look much better without the safety gear."

She came in and sat. PJ closed the door. "What is it that you want, Mr. Cruz? I was surprised to get your woman's call."

"Well, PJ isn't my woman, but I know what you mean. I was glad to hear that the glass factory was back open despite your boss being away."

"Business goes on whether she's in or not, I'm in or not."

"Do you know where she is?"

"I don't keep tabs on my boss. She's the employer. I'm the employee."

"But you were friends in school, grew up together—"

"Here we go. The deep background check on my life. Yes, she's my friend but she's also my boss. I know where the lines are drawn."

"She wasn't always into the gangster life, was she?"

"No."

"When did things change?"

"I told her not to do it, but she wanted to know more about her mother. She didn't like what she found. Over the years, she started to change and become more and more like her mother. Wilder parties. Dangerous men. Dangerous *gangster* men."

"That's all it was? She randomly found out about her deceased mother, then started to become her so she could end up like her or worse?"

"Mr. Cruz, Justyna was always a gangster girl at heart. Her grandmother kept her straight, but once she turned eighteen, I knew she'd change. It was inevitable. She hates the glass business. She says she started it. She didn't. Her grandparents did and turned it over to her. She was a natural businesswoman, but she...she acts like she hates him, but she wants to be him, always has."

"Tragic, I'd say. To have all those opportunities handed to you and let it slip from your hands."

"She never saw it that way. She saw it as an obligation that she never wanted or asked for."

"These dangerous men and this dangerous life are going to get her killed or sent to prison for life."

"She doesn't care. They all always think they're so much smarter than the police, so much tougher than the other gangsters."

"You talk like you have first-hand experience."

"One brother in prison; one in the morgue. I do know about it. Every other person in our neighborhood knows about that life personally. You can't save them. We all try, but they'll do what they want to do."

"Can Electric Lady be saved?"

"Personally, I wouldn't waste my time."

"That's very harsh to say for a friend."

"I'm an honest person. That's why she hired me. I don't sugarcoat things or lie. I tell you to your face. Once she started dating that Harder Steel character, it was the end. I told her that. She told me that she was going to turn the 'stupid factory' over to me. I said I couldn't wait. Then I could run it properly and take it national."

"But she hates her father. Did he ever reach out to her?"

"On her birthdays. Sometimes she took his call. Sometimes she hung up on him. He was never involved in raising her. He said he left the gang life, but he also left his daughter. She always felt he had another family somewhere. She felt abandoned by him."

"Who raised her?"

"We were raised by nuns in a well-to-do prep school, elementary to pre-college. Nuns, if you can believe it. The money came from him. At home, she lived with her grandparents."

"Her father must have thought that the prep school was the best thing for her, the furthest thing from gangster life."

"It was a good plan. Most girls turned out well in that school. I turned out well. She didn't. She needed a father. Her grandparents did what they could, but they were too naive and sweet to handle her. At eighteen, she was out of there."

"Maybe you should have raised her. Seems like you'd have the firm hand she needed."

"I have four boys and not one will ever raise a voice to me. They know better."

"Do you know she's in hiding now?"

"I heard that."

"Why would she be hiding?"

"I have no idea. I hear her boyfriend is too."

"Well, I know why *he's* hiding. Do you know how I can find her? She was hiding out at her boyfriend's bar, but she ran out of there like a rocket at warp speed."

"No idea. She has lots of gangster girlfriends. You'll never find her. There's too many of them."

"That's what I learned. Is there a way to get a message to her? These gangsters all seem to have message lines. Does she have one, since she's a gangster in training?"

"I never thought of that. Maybe she does. I'll have to check around and get back to you."

"Good. If you can help me find her, I'll be a step closer to wrapping up my case and you'll be a step closer to being the new owner of Piorun Glass."

"I'm liking you much better this meeting than last. So, we have an alliance?"

She extended a hand, and we shook on it.

Astra was not the only friend, acquaintance or employee of the Electric Lady. There were dozens, and I talked to as many of them as I could. PJ had lined up the most promising leads to come into the Liquid Cool office, but Astra was by far the most helpful. Everyone else gave bits and pieces confirming the full profile of Classic's daughter. I sure hoped Astra found a number for Electric Lady, because the only way I was going to find her was if she came out of hiding and walked through the Liquid Cool door.

Trendy called me later in the day, as I knew he would. I took his vid-call from my desk. From his expression, I knew it was not good news.

"Mr. Cruz."

"Bad news, huh?"

"Apparently I have stepped into an intelligence issue."

"The Intelligence Agency?"

"Yes."

"Trendy, Dr. Silver-Rose works for Intelligence?"

"I had no idea until they refused my request for information on grounds of classified information."

"Is anything in the case just straight and simple? What do you think she was doing?"

"I checked around and we think, maybe, they might have been doing experiments in the field."

"Experiments? On cyborgs?"

"I'm simply throwing out a theory."

"The doctor struck me as someone who'd never experiment on people. It has to be something else. It couldn't be hurting people. It would be something to help people."

"I agree, but what?"

"Who at Police One would have the clearance to find out what she was doing in her Rose Silver persona."

"The Chief of the Metropolis Police. I hear he likes you, Cruz."

"He only tolerates me."

"You saved his life once."

"A fact he doesn't ever want to be reminded of, but he's returned the favor. He wouldn't tell me. This case isn't big enough for him to care, especially now that most of these three gangs are dead or in custody."

"Imagine that, Cruz. This case isn't high-profile enough for the supercity to care. Seems plenty big enough to me and you."

"We know how the world works, Trendy."

"We do, indeed."

"You tried. That's all I can ask. I might have another angle to try."

"If you do find out, let me know. I'd like to know for sure that she's not some kind of mad scientist experimenting on cyborg mental patients in dark alleys."

"I don't think it's in her DNA to do something like that. We'll find out."

"While we're talking, do you know a Sinister Betty?"

"Do I want to know a person named Sinister Betty? Because I don't think so."

He laughed. "Everyone spells it Betty, but it's actually B-E-T then hyphen double E."

"What about her?"

"She may be coming to visit you."

"Why would she do that, and how do you know?"

"She's a parolee, and a condition of her parole is that she has to get prior approval for anyone she meets with. She got approval to meet you."

Astra came through. She found an emergency number for Electric Lady. I knew it was the only way I'd have a way to reach her, and that I'd only get one shot at it. I set up everything then sat at my desk with my private office door closed. I dialed the number.

"You know who this is. I have to say I'm a little hurt by you shooting at me and then running away like that before I could even speak. I still need to talk to you and it's urgent. I won't leave a number because I don't have to. If you're nervous, call after hours and leave a message. We need to meet and it's not about him, though he has a message. It's about you. You're in serious danger. But you probably already know that too. We need to talk, and immediately."

I hung up my audio-only call. That's all I could do. Leave a message and wait.

It wasn't even a minute later when there was a knock at my door. PJ opened it and came in.

"She left a message."

"Who?"

"Electric Lady."

"How? I literally just left her a message. She couldn't have responded that quickly."

"Listen to the message. I'll forward it."

I was right. She wasn't responding to my message. She was responding to Astra's message. Astra gave me her number, but not before leaving one of her own to tell Electric Lady I needed to talk to her and she'd better call me. I smiled. "Thanks, Astra," I said to myself.

Electric Lady's message was that she was all right and she wanted to meet right away.

Before I left the office, I had one more person to meet. I waited until one of our sidewalk johnnies came in through the door. I'd put Phishy in charge of the multiple projects our Sidewalk Johnnie Brigade were involved in. I never liked it, but most of them wore fedoras (as long as they weren't tan) and often Liquid Cool T-shirts underneath. I hated those T-shirts, but PJ said as a businessman I had to have multiple revenue streams for my business.

"What do you have for me?" I was anxious to get on the road so I was waiting for him in our main lobby.

"I think we found something interesting, Mr. Cruz," he said as he handed me a bundle of papers.

"Tell Phishy and the guys thanks."

"No problem, Mr. Cruz."

We shook hands and he was on his way out the door. I glanced at the papers, then ran back to the elevators and back into the office. I bolted in and gave them to PJ.

"With your bionic fingers, you can type faster than me."

"What is it?" she asked.

"Maybe the answer to what our Dr. Silver-Rose has been doing moonlighting as an underground medic. I have to go. If a Sinister Bet-ee calls, put her on the schedule."

"Sinister Betty? Who is that?"

"She's coming to see me after a nice vacation at Metro Prison. Find out why."

"Something sinister," PJ said.

"And it's not Betty, but B-E-T-E-E."

"Oh, I get it. Gambling."

"Yeah."

"More Dead Pool stuff."

"Probably."

"Oh, before you leave, I think there's a mistake in her background file, the doctor's."

"Mistake?"

"She's been a shrink forever, but she also has an advanced degree in oncology."

"Oh."

"Oncology is cancer. No one gets cancer anymore."

I smiled. "Yes."

"Why would she get a degree in a medical field that doesn't exist anymore? I see you smiling, so you know something."

"I only know what you tell me."

"She studies cancer when there's no more cancer in the world. Cruz, what's the answer to the riddle?"

I laughed. "PJ, I gotta go."

"Oh, yes, Electric Lady. Go!"

I had to be careful. Every time I flew out in my bright red Pony I had to assume someone spotted me. If Electric Lady had taken the chance to reach out to me from her secret hiding place, the least I could do was not lead anyone back to her.

Buzz Town's Circuit Circle was the perfect place to spot a tail, if you knew proper defensive driving tactics. The sky lane went around in a circular path in wide lanes and numerous exit routes. By hopping into one level up or down, swerving to a lane on either the left or right, at the right moment, one could force anyone following to move prematurely.

The reality was for the most part, in most areas, it was impossible to spot a tail. Even if my vehicle wasn't red, someone could hide behind me in any lane and I wouldn't know. Randomly and recklessly changing lanes was one tactic that could help, but there was only one foolproof method.

For the next forty minutes, all I did was drive. I drove around and around on the Circle, constantly moving between lanes and levels of traffic. Then I floored it, cutting down another street and into a parking structure. The lasting benefits of being a former, sometime-illegal hovercar racer was I knew all the secret routes in the supercity. There was a way to drive, mostly in central Metropolis, from structure to structure so one could even avoid any satellite. Illegal hovercar racers always believed that the police used satellites to track them, but it wasn't true. Police could care less about a bunch of kids racing for kicks; they were focused on the hardcore criminals.

I slammed on the airbrakes!

The hovercar in front of me dropped down out of nowhere and was coasting ahead slower than if a person were walking. I was so mad. Classic hovervehicle drivers like me didn't slam on their brakes—ever. I hopped out of the Pony and walked to the hovercar in front of me, it was moving that slow. Inside, all I saw were hands on the steering wheel and barely the top of a head, the elderly woman was that low in her seat. I tapped on the driver's-side window. I had to get her out of the way—it was a single lane. She turned, and her eyes widened to the size of donuts. She blasted away. I expected to hear a crash when she whipped around a corner without looking, but I heard none. I guess she didn't like my hat.

I continued on until I was satisfied that no one was tailing me. When I got to another parking structure, I ascended to the top level, came out, and dove. It was so illegal, but with how the surrounding towers were built, a nearby bridge, and the sky-traffic around the corner, it was a nice blind spot. No one, not even the best, could have followed me. I slowed down and slipped into the bottom level of the sky traffic. In a couple of minutes, I was in the upper fast lane.

This was a stroke of luck for me. If I hadn't been able to get in touch with Electric Lady, the case would have been at a standstill. These were criminals and wannabe criminals—and a doctor—who knew how to hide. If they didn't want to be found, I wasn't going to find them. They had to come to me, which was what I was afraid of. Robo-Stein had "visited" me twice already. I'm sure Harder Steel and Pink Machete planned to join in too. I had to get this case closed.

I arrived at my location—a diner in Metal-Ville. As soon as I walked in, the counter guy said, "Are you Cruz?"

"Yeah."

He gave me a note scribbled on a napkin, and I was back in the Pony to another location. After a string of convenience stores, I was on the way to a public park. I understood her caution, but I still wasn't pleased. The last time I was at a park I had to shoot someone. I hoped it wasn't an omen of things to come.

In Metropolis, parks were on the roofs of buildings. In the old days, they were on the ground, but I don't think any were left, except for the huge official Metropolis Public Park. I got to the two hundredth floor for public park access and immediately noticed the sky. It was night but there was an almost black cloud cover. In the distance was the occasional sound of thunder. So the Storm of the Century was still coming. We just didn't know when and I had no desire to be washed off a two hundredth-story mega-tower.

The park was surprisingly filled with a lot of people. It was designed with tables and benches arranged to encircle small gated lakes that dotted the grounds of faux-green grass. Most of the people were playing cards, chess, or obscure board games. There was only one jogger I could see running down a path, which went around the entire perimeter of the roof park.

I saw her in the distance. This time she wasn't a walking neon light show, but I recognized her on a bench by herself and started walking. She was in a hooded slicker, her hands in her pockets. I had my hands in my pockets too, so it was fine. I stopped my approach when I was several feet from her.

"Thanks for meeting me."

"What did you call me for?"

"Your father wanted to talk with you. He wants you to leave Metropolis."

She laughed. "With him?"

"I don't know, but he seems more interested that you leave the city."

"I'm not doing that. He should leave."

"You do know you're in danger."

"If I am, it's because of him."

"Why did you run out of your boyfriend's place like that? Shooting at me, by the way."

"It's not important."

"It is important. You ran away and now you're in hiding."

"It's none of your concern, so don't pretend that you care."

"Actually, I don't care, but that doesn't stop me from trying to talk some sense into your thick skull. Are you shacked up with your boyfriend again?"

"Is that why you're really here? You delivered your message for my father, so you can go."

"I really don't understand you. The first time we met I told you I saw your boyfriend kill some innocent people and you called me a liar. How do you think one becomes the leader of a killer criminal cyborg gang? It's not by helping little old ladies with their shopping."

"I'm a big girl. I don't need to be lectured by you."

"Can I put you on the phone with your father? I have my mobile. No need for me to be the middle man. You can disrespect him directly."

"Sure, errand boy. Dial him up. I'll curse him out and you can listen. Everyone around me is using me. Astra wants my business. You want your juicy bonus from my father. He wants to alleviate his own guilt."

"Guilt about what?"

"Dial him up! I want to get this over with."

I pulled out my mobile. "Does this mean Mr. Harder Steel is your ex-boyfriend?"

"I didn't know you were my father too. Yeah, we're not a couple anymore, Mr. Mind-Your-Own-Business."

"For someone with the name of Electric Lady you should have a personality that's far more positive and—"

I jinxed it. I said that the next time I was on a rooftop park, I'd probably have to shoot someone. My fingers were about to dial, but my eyes never stopped scanning the surroundings. The only hovercars that should've been so high up were police or emergency. The one I spotted was neither.

"Electric Lady," I yelled. "We might need some of your bionic kung fu."

"What?" She gave me a weird look.

"Get up from that bench. For a wannabe criminal, you're not too observant. There's a dark hovercar behind you."

She stood up and turned. "How do you know I know kung-fu?"

"It's called being a detective."

My mind was focused, but then I noticed a couple of children about to walk in front of us.

"Move away from the people!" I yelled and ran toward the black hovercar that was descending on a path to us.

I ran past the Electric Lady. The hovercar had lift-up doors. Three doors rose and out flew three figures dressed in black. One man flew one way, the other two disappeared out of sight. I yelled out as a high-pitch sound rang in my ears. That's all I needed. I fired my omega-gun at the black hovercar in a hail of bullets. When the bullets were out, the gun automatically switched to laser mode. There was pandemonium from everywhere on the roof. People screaming and running for the exits. I was about to deliver my kill shot to the hovercar when I crashed to the ground face first.

The heat of the hovercar passed over me. I was groggy but lucky that the blow to the back of my head hadn't knocked me unconscious. I slowly rolled over in time to see the three men with jetpacks lifting and throwing an unconscious Electric Lady into the hovercar. They got in, closed the doors, and blasted away.

I got back to Liquid Cool and staggered through the door, an icepack pressed firmly to the base of my skull.

"What happened?" PJ asked, jumping up from her seat behind her desk. "Are you okay?"

"I need to call—"

PJ immediately put a finger over her mouth to gesture for me to be quiet. She pointed. In the lobby was a woman in a crimson slicker and dress with a large, stylish crimson hat. She wasn't alone. Two rent-a-thugs were on either side.

"Mr. Cruz," she said.

"Sinister Bet-ee?"

"In the flesh."

"Do we have an appointment?"

"She does," PJ chimed in. "But she's very early."

"No need for me to wait out there. That storm is supposed to drop any minute," she said.

"They've been saying that for a week," I said, removing my ice pack. "You'd think in a region of Earth where it rains all the time they'd be able to predict these things by now."

Sinister Bet-ee laughed. "Never trust the weather service."

"Only bet on a sure thing."

She laughed again as she stood. "I wanted to see you in person, Mr. Cruz. You've created quite a bit of excitement in the illegal gambling world."

"Should you be using words like 'illegal' with your status?" I asked.

"I can say any word I want, Mr. Cruz. I can't commit a crime on parole, unless I want to go back. I haven't decided yet if I want to go back yet. The best gambling action is in Metro Prison."

"Why did you want to meet me? I have a lot of work to do and you're early."

"You should have met me sooner. I could have saved you a lot of time, maybe even that blow to the back of the head. Does it have to do with Electric Lady?"

She had my full attention now. "What about her? What do you know?"

"If you had met me earlier, I would have told you that people wanted to move things along. Decisions were made, and it was decided that she should be kidnapped."

"What?"

"Yes, Mr. Cruz. It's been decided that we need to wrap up the Dead Pool."

"Why are you telling me this?"

"Because, Mr. Cruz, all my money is riding on you."

"I'm not going to pretend I know the criminal betting world, but I can figure out most things. I have no idea why you'd bet on me in your sick cyborg gladiator match in the streets. I did think Metro's criminal class had a bit more intelligence than that."

"No, Mr. Cruz, it involves a lot more than little ol' Earth."

"Are you telling me that the betting involves the crime-betting world Up-Top?"

"Yes, it does. In fact, quite a few of us are eagerly anticipating three new players to enter from Up-Top itself."

"Which players?"

"When you hear their names, and you will, you'll know."

"Cyborg gangsters?"

"And more. Things will get very interesting when they arrive."

"But you're betting on me?"

She smiled. "Yes, I am."

"How rich will the winner become?"

"Rich enough to live Up-Top themselves, if that's what they want."

"Which means the winners of the Dead Pool would make far more money."

"The largest Dead Pool in history, Mr. Cruz. All because of how you handled the late Franken-borg—permanently."

"Why bet on me? You're that confident that I'll kill Classic Cyborg? Well, I'm not. In the end, there will be Classic and me as the last standing, and that will be it."

"No, Mr. Cruz. That won't be it. It will only be over when one of you are dead. If you don't kill him or if he doesn't kill you, every criminal from here to Mars will jump into the pool for the chance to be the last one standing. My money is on you, Mr. Cruz. Classic Cyborg couldn't kill Franken-borg, but you did. You're the smartest, so I know you'll do what's required in the end. Make us rich. Win, Mr. Cruz. You win, I win. I'm counting on it, Mr. Cruz."

GETTING ELECTRIC LADY

I was so disturbed that I forgot what I was doing. *Every criminal from here to Mars will jump into the Dead Pool?* She had already left, but I was still standing there dazed. The case was going from bad to worse. I snapped out of it.

"PJ! Go after her and give her your mobile number," I said.

"Why? I don't want a criminal having my mobile."

"PJ, she has instant access to the Dead Pool. If others jump in, she'll know. We need her to tell us and get us their photo."

"Oh, yes, that's smart."

She was out the door. I could focus on the other crisis—I didn't know which was the biggest one yet, but I did know which would consume all my time going forward.

I called Classic's office. The general receptionist answered at Cyborg Psych, and I told them it was extremely urgent.

"I'll try to reach him, sir, but he's not available," the receptionist said, staring back at me on the vid-phone.

"If he's in a meeting, get him out. If he's giving a class to some kids, get him out. Tell him it's his private detective, Cruz, and it can't wait. I'll hold."

"Okay, sir. Hold." The screen went black, but we were still connected. I could tell because the elevator music began playing. She returned. "Sir, the calls are going to his voicemail."

"Where is his next appointment?"

"Sir, I can't disclose that. I can connect you with his voicemail."

"I can do that on my own. I need to reach him urgently. What about his boss?"

"Dr. Silver-Rose is also unavailable."

"Is there any human being in your department who can directly contact him? This is an emergency."

"Hold, sir." She disappeared.

A man's face appeared on the screen. "Hello, sir. I understand you're trying to reach Mr. Classic."

"Yes, it's an emergency. I need to reach him immediately."

"Sir, Mr. Classic is not law enforcement or a first responder. He's not required to have direct-connect. We can't reach him. You'll have to reach him by leaving a message, and he'll call you back when he's available."

"I'm not a child, and you don't have to talk to me like I'm an idiot. You said the exact same thing your flunky colleague said. The man's daughter has been kidnapped. Why won't you help me?"

"Hold on, sir." This time he disappeared from the viewscreen.

Frustration didn't begin to describe what I was feeling.

Another woman appeared. "Hello, sir. I understand you're trying to reach Mr. Classic."

"Can you connect me!?" I yelled.

"Sir, we can connect you to his voicemail—"

I hung up. The only option was to get to Metro PD and call Trendy en-route. PJ hadn't returned yet, so I had to wait. She ran through the door, smiling.

"I got it," she said.

"I have to get to Metro PD."

"You have more appointments."

"Classic's daughter was kidnapped."

"What! Electric Lady? You saw it? They hit you on the back of the head?"

"Someone hit me and I didn't enjoy it. Handle any clients that have to be rescheduled. You know how kidnappings go."

"Nothing else for the next forty-eight to seventy-two hours."

"If I have to, I can call clients in my downtime—whenever that is. But first I have to reach Classic."

"I'll try the phone too."

"Don't waste your time with his division."

"Oh, I know people who I can call. I'm a cyborg too, you know. I have contacts."

"If Bet-ee sends you a photo—"

"You'll have it one second after I do."

I checked my pockets. I had what I needed. "Hold down the fort," I finally said, and was out the door.

We had forty-eight to seventy-two hours to move quickly, and I had to make up time by finding Classic fast. Why wasn't he answering his phone?

With all of our security measures, Liquid Cool was a virtual fortress. However, the mega-tower parking bay was still public. It was monitored by security cameras, but access wasn't completely restricted. I was always careful and my reserved parking spot was in a prime location. No one could hide in wait without me or someone else seeing them.

My theory was flawed. I came out of the elevators, and three suspicious characters were simply standing in the middle of the lot, watching and waiting. They were wearing colored shades, but I noticed the change in their body language right away—they recognized me. They had been standing with their hands clasped in front. But as I approached the Pony, their hands moved to their sides. PJ and I had seen them before on the security monitors, but they were walking to a hovercar. Somehow, they figured out how to show up when someone left the Liquid Cool office, walk to any vehicle, walk back in sight of the elevators, wait a bit, then go back to where they were really hiding out of camera view. Criminals always found a way.

As I approached, I noticed that all three were cyborgs, most likely criminals. I could see their metallic hands.

"Mr. Cruz, I'm a big fan," one of them said.

I had been to this kind of party before. I drew first and blasted his right hand off as he began to raise it. Guns popped out of the palms of the other two and the shootout began. I was already running for cover, but managed one last shot before dodging the laser fire of the two gunmen.

The explosive charge blew all three of them several feet back onto their backs. They would never get another chance to fire at me. I was on my feet and standing over them while they were still dazed.

"Who are you three?" I asked. "I always like meeting my fans."

The man without his hand glared at me. "You are—"

Before he could finish his sentence, I sprayed the other two with laser fire. "Since you're doing all the talking," I said, "no need to keep the other two around."

He laughed. "This didn't work out the way we planned."

"For you, no. Who are you? What's this about?"

"If a nobody can put you in the ground, even if they can't get to the end, their gang gets instant cred."

"The Dead Pool? You volunteered for a suicide run for your gang to be known by a bunch of strangers you'll never meet. Did you ever wonder why you're a nobody gangster? Maybe 'cause you're not too smart and not too good at what you do."

"I did get to meet the man who defeated Franken-borg."

"Yeah, but still no autograph for you, you crazy maniac. Don't you have to buy into the Dead Pool? Where did you get the money?"

"We took out a loan."

"I don't believe you. Illegal gambling is about untraceable cash, not bank loans. Who gave you the money?"

"That's for me to know and you to find out."

"Honestly, whoever you are, you aren't worth my time. Off to the Metro PD you go. You're going to find out why cyborg gangs, no matter how powerful, would rather die than be arrested. They're going to strip every piece of illegal and legal bionics you have from your body. Let's see how well you do in the prison population with plastic mannequin hands."

The elevator beeped and I was already pointing the omega-gun.

"Cruz!" It was PJ's voice.

She ran to me with her mobile in one hand and her laser shotgun in the other.

"Oh," PJ said, noticing the bodies on the ground. "Sinister Bet-ee sent me photos of three new guys who jumped into the Dead Pool."

"These three?"

"*Exactemente.*"

"Thanks, PJ, for warning me."

"Anytime, boss," she said grinning.

In addition to my not-really-a-shootout in the Liquid Cool parking area, I got caught in extremely bad sky-traffic. I left PJ to take charge of the three wannabe hitmen and called the police as I raced in the Pony to Metro PD. Kidnapping cases were all about time, seconds couldn't be wasted. I had wasted plenty, but I kept dialing Classic's number. There was never an answer.

It wasn't too smart to run near, in, or around Metro PD, but I did.

"I need to see Detective Trendy in the Cyborg Gang Unit right away," I said when I reached the general intake counter. I already had my ID out and placed it so the police officer could see it.

"Cruz."

"Yes."

"I'll see if he's in."

"If not him, then his partner. It's a kidnapping."

"Kidnapping? That wouldn't be the Gang Unit, that'd be the Feds."

"Classic Cyborg's daughter."

She turned to another officer sitting at a desk behind. "Find Trendy, ASAP." The male officer nodded. "I know what you're doing, Cruz, but the Feds will get this one."

"They might, but we're here and they aren't—yet. If we move fast, maybe we can locate her before we have to call them."

"He said to send him back," the officer at the desk called out.

"You know the routine, Cruz. Come on back."

She buzzed me in, and I walked through the door behind the main counter to the inner waiting room. An officer in civilian clothes was already walking to me from an aisle within the bull pen of dual cubicles of the street police.

"Follow me, Cruz," he said.

We had barely started down the hall when Trendy appeared with his partner.

"Trendy, where's Classic? He's not picking up his mobile."

"What's this about a kidnapping?"

"Electric Lady was kidnapped."

"How do you know that?"

"I was there. I found a way to reach her and we were meeting. A bunch of ninja types came from the sky, knocked me to the ground, and snatched her."

No interview rooms this time. We would be working in a real tactical planning room with plenty of seating and a big whiteboard in the front of the room. First, it was Trendy and his partner, but in a short time an army of officers in civilian clothes joined us. Once again, I had to recount all the details of my meeting with Electric Lady and the kidnapping.

"She said she wasn't with Harder Steel anymore?" Trendy asked.

"Yes."

"You believe her?"

"I do. She ran out of his place like a rocket when I tried to meet with her that time. Something made her run and go into hiding."

"What?" one of the gang officers asked.

"I don't know. That's one of the reasons I was meeting with her. To get some answers."

"Who do you think the kidnappers are with?" Trendy asked.

"I would've said only our three main suspects, but it seems we have a lot of new gangsters out there anxious to involve themselves in all this."

"What does that mean?" Trendy asked. "What else happened?"

"Three thugs tried to gun me down in the Liquid Cool's building parking bay."

"And?"

"I shot them." The police officers gave me disapproving looks. "Don't look at me like that. It was clear self-defense and my employee called the police."

"You left the scene," an officer said.

"Yeah. I left the scene, raced to Metro PD, and am standing in a room full of police and telling you. This is a kidnapping. I couldn't wait on the scene. I had to get here so we could find Classic. Where is he?"

"We'll find him," Trendy's partner answered.

"What I want to know is why he's disappeared to begin with?"

"Don't worry about that, Cruz," Trendy said. "He'll be here. The real question is what we do now. How long can we go without calling the Feds?" he asked another officer.

"Technically, zero time, but we can stall," he answered.

"How long?" Trendy asked.

"Detective, you'll get one chance to do whatever you're going to do, and then that's it, so make it count."

"I don't know why we need to involve the Feds at all," Trendy said. "Metropolis is the largest city in the world. We can handle our own business."

"No, we can't and you know it," the Captain said. "It's exactly because we're the largest city in the world that kidnappings are under Federal jurisdiction. They have the expertise and I'm happy to turn the cases over to them, unless you want to work twenty-four hours a day."

"No, Cap," Trendy said. I realized that the short, but ripped man in civilian clothes too was their immediate boss.

"What's the plan?" the Captain asked Trendy.

"Cruz is right. We need Classic in the room. We need to know if he's been contacted with any ransom demands."

A uniformed officer peeked through the door as we all turned to look at him.

"What is it?" the Captain asked.

"Classic's here."

"Send him in right—"

The door opened wider and there was Classic Cyborg with tears in his eyes.

As a father myself, I don't know why it seemed strange to see Classic on the verge of tears. Maybe no matter how reformed he was, I still saw him as this larger-than-life, legendary cyborg gangster. Now, he sat in a corner with a glass of something a lot stronger than soda in his hand—the usual offered beverage at police stations.

The tactical planning room was in full swing with a big whiteboard at the front with the mugshots of Harder Steel and a lifelike drawing of Robo-Stein, with the head of a metallic skull. Uniformed officers and those in civilian attire were in and out of the room, with the Captain directing the madness. All of it brought on by a simple fact—there was now a ransom note.

We were ready to go. The Captain quieted down everyone who'd assembled, and they all turned their attention to Classic. I sat in a chair nearby.

"Classic, everyone's here," the Captain said to him. "We don't have much time. We have one chance to handle this or it'll become a Fed freak show."

Classic stood and moved closer to them. He nodded. The Captain gave the signal to another officer, and the ransom message played.

"Classic Cyborg, we have your daughter, Electric Lady. This will be your one and only ransom demand. To get her back all in one piece and alive, pay us two-hundred-fifty million dollars in untraceable digital currency to the number coded into this message. You have twenty-four hours to send the money—no negotiation. Non-compliance means a different piece of Electric Lady will be mailed to the Metro Police every hour until there's nothing left."

The electronic voice stopped and there was a loud click as it disconnected.

"We have the number," the Captain said. "Disposable and it's never been used before. Someone opened it up a few days ago. We have a team trying to find out who opened it."

"Classic, we have the audio-tech going over every nano-second of the message," another officer said.

"I got the message when I was coming out of a meeting," Classic said.

"Do you think they had you under surveillance," the Captain asked.

"Possibly, but I didn't see anyone. It could've been random. Is it a purely digitized voice or digital masking?"

"Computer-generated," an officer replied. "The program isn't unique; it's used by millions."

"That's a lot of money, Classic," Trendy added. "Do they really expect you to pay?"

Classic shook his head. "I couldn't put that much money together in twenty-four hours when I was in the game. How could I now?"

"Then what's their game?" the Captain asked.

"To make me suffer," Classic answered. "We have twenty-four hours to find her, and then that's it."

"Do you want the Feds?" the Captain asked.

"No," Classic said. "We need to handle this our way first. It's the only chance she has."

"We've gone over everything Cruz gave us," Trendy said. "Went over every external and internal surveillance camera of the hovercar of the kidnappers, nothing. We can't identify them or the hovercar. We have nothing."

"Then everything hangs on audio analysis. Or we have to pray they left some kind of clue to follow."

"Classic, if they did, we'll find it. Promise," the Captain said.

"Metro Audio Forensics is the best on the planet," Trendy said.

Classic forced a smile, but the situation was desperate. The only thing to do was wait. None of us wanted to wait for anything; we wanted to act.

A uniformed officer burst into the room. "We have a possible sighting of Harder Steel!"

Criminals did dumb things all the time. However, when we left Metro PD for a district near Metal-Ville, that made no sense at all. I kept my mouth shut as we piled into our mobile tactical command post—a giant hovercraft that had a large room equipped with every gadget and connected to every piece of technology needed to run a war if it had to. The vehicle was used for major terrorist events and massive riot threats, never to go after gangs or used for a single kidnapping. They were treating this as more than personal. Even I knew that this was an off-the-books operation. If it went wrong, every one of them, including the Captain, would find themselves on permanent desk duty. It was probably why they brought me along. They didn't want me walking around in public, even if it meant allowing me access to their classified police hovercraft.

All eyes were on multiple monitors on one side of the room. Some of the feeds were static, which meant they had patched into fixed cameras from exterior building security or from inside retail stores. Others were moving, which meant they were from drones or hovercar cameras.

Everyone had headphones and enhanced shades except for me. That didn't bother me in the least bit. All I cared about were the visual feeds. They were all focused on one specific residential tower, with all entrances and exits covered. Pedestrian traffic was relatively light. Maybe people were still concerned about the supposed Storm of the Century and were staying indoors. The people we could see were moving about their business, no sidewalk johnnies or sallies were around, no dope daddies on the corner. The district had sporadic street crime, but today it was as clear of crime as any well-to-do area.

"Has the suspect been spotted?" the Captain asked.

For me, without their headphones, any conversation I heard was one-way. I saw the camera of one screen move right and focus on a yellow hovercab landing, then other monitors changed to capture the hovercab from other angles.

"Keep calm, everyone," the Captain said. "We're waiting for confirmation."

The hovercab touched down and sat there. We all watched it. No one was talking; no one breathed. I had no idea how far away we were from the scene of interest.

A giant hovertruck coasted right in front of the view of the cameras.

"Where did he come from?" the Captain yelled. When it passed, the hovercab was rising in the air. "Did the suspect exit that cab? Did we get a visual on the suspect?"

I was watching Classic's body language. I could see the anxiety in his face as his bionic hands gripped his headphones and squeezed so hard that they were cracking. He let go.

"Send in someone!" he yelled.

"He's coming back out?" the Captain said.

Everyone focused on the monitors. I froze myself, quickly scanning each viewscreen for any sign of a person. There was a man that came into view, still within the shadows. He was waiting.

"Is it the suspect?" the Captain yelled again.

"What is he looking at?" an officer asked.

One of the monitors switched to across the street. Two men were standing outside the main entrance of a virtually empty diner. Both men seemed to be staring back at the man in the shadows.

"What's happening here?" the Captain asked. "Why isn't the suspect ID'd yet?"

The man was tall, muscular, but even I couldn't tell if it was Harder Steel or not. However, we all saw him reach into his jacket.

"Sniper one, do you have a clear shot?" the Captain asked.

Snipers, I thought. This was a major operation. The man suddenly ducked back into the shadows.

"Do you have visual?" the Captain asked. "Infrared? Night? What do you mean you don't have him in sight? Oh, my God."

I jumped as all the monitors switched back to the hovercab. The same one was still in the air, hovering.

"He's the driver, not the passenger!" Classic yelled.

"Eight through ten, back on the man on the ground. Fourteen and fifteen, back on the diner," the Captain commanded.

We had monitors on the hovercab in the air, the street where the man in the shadows disappeared, and on the two men hanging out in front of the diner. *Did we have three separate situations or were they all part of the same one?*

"Where is the suspect?" the Captain asked.

"We need to move in," Trendy said.

"No one on this squad is getting shot today. I want visuals on the suspects first."

Things happen in the blink of an eye. That's the phrase I often heard in class by police veteran instructors when I was a police intern, and I had already experienced it myself in my new career as a private detective.

The two men from the diner moved forward, firing laser guns at the hovercab in the sky. Instead of flying away, the hovercab turned and flew toward them. A blur came out of the shadows from across the street—running at the two men at a speed only possible with bionic legs. None of us could tell if it was Harder Steel or not. The figure was wearing a large, hooded slicker. We couldn't see his head at all.

"Move!" the Captain yelled.

For the first time, I felt that I was actually in a hovercraft. It blasted forwarded as we kept our eyes on the monitors. It was not a lucky day for the two men in front of the diner. The hovercab rammed one at full speed, tossing his body into the air. The other man tried to gun down the approaching cyborg but with no success. The suspect literally punched a hole in the man's chest.

As the man collapsed in front of the cyborg and his partner fell to the ground nearby, the "red-and-blue light show" began. Police hovercruisers appeared from everywhere. Before the cyborg suspect could even flinch, he was shot down from above. I could tell from the rounds that they were non-lethal. The hovercab was easily incapacitated with a pulse cannon from a hovercruiser. It quickly descended, hitting the ground with a loud crash. I watched as police swarmed the hovercab, blew out all the doors, and pulled one man from the driver's side. They were lucky—the police needed him alive.

Classic pulled off his headphones and was out the door. He had bionic legs, and I barely kept up with him. The hovercraft had landed at the scene. Classic was already at the main suspect, who was handcuffed, ankle-cuffed, and "flash frozen." It was a special weapon to render the bionics of any cyborg inactive. His hood was already off.

"Who's this?" Classic asked with disgust. "This isn't him!"

The kid looked very much like Harder Steel, but it wasn't the cyborg gang leader.

"Did you think I was Harder Steel?" the kid laughed, the sides of his head were covered with white cryo-particles. "Harder Steel is nothing. I'll be the one who takes over his whole territory."

"Where's my daughter?" Classic asked.

"What? I don't know anything about a daughter, copper."

"I'm not a copper. I'm Classic Cyborg. Where's my daughter?"

The kid wasn't laughing anymore. He swallowed hard. "I don't know anything about that."

"But you do know something."

"I don't know anything. All I know is Harder Steel and his rivals are gone. No one has seen them. People are moving in to take over their territories. Maybe those other two guys knew something. They were from another gang."

"You mean the two men that you killed."

The kid was sweating. "I didn't know you needed to talk to them. I'm sure someone out there knows something, Mr. Classic Cyborg."

"Like who?"

"Don't be mad at me. I didn't know. Gangs are moving in. One of them has to know something. The word on the street is that all three of them are putting together new crews."

"Who is?"

"Harder Steel, Pink Machete, and Robo-Stein."

"New crews? As of when?"

"As of now. Those two guys were part of Harder Steel's new crew."

"The two men you killed?" Classic yelled again.

"It doesn't matter. The next generation is here, and we're not going to wait until you all end up in the prison senior citizen system. We're making our move now. Why should any of you be the King of the Cyborgs? The new model is always better than the old. Youth over old."

Classic seemed very calm. "What youth never understands is that the fountain of youth is not about age. It's about the mind and discipline."

That's when Classic picked up the kid's body and threw him before the police could grab him. It was too late. That kid was yelling every second of the way as his body crashed through the bay windows of the diner across the street—way across the street.

The only thing that saved any of us was that the kid wasn't killed in his terrestrial flight through the diner's window and impact into the wall at the other end of the building. I hid as Chief of Police Hub arrived on the scene and verbally ripped the Captain and another officer to shreds. The entire area was cordoned off to keep the crowds and the media back, but it was a big mess.

"Do I have to get my own hovertaxi?" I asked Trendy as he walked over to me. Chief Hub was already gone in his hovercruiser.

"That would be best, since I'm suspended."

"Suspended? All of you?"

"All of us, including the Captain. The Feds have the case."

"Where's Classic?" I looked around and couldn't see him. I had been keeping an eye on him, but he was gone.

"He's on the way back to Police One."

"Don't we want to talk to the Feds?"

"Cruz, you're not a cop, and I'm a suspended cop. Classic is the only one they'll let in their tactical ops center. We're not invited."

"But I have information. I'm a primary witness of the kidnapping. They'll let me in."

"Cruz, why are you still working this case? You did your thing. You're done."

"I'm not done because none of this is done. When three cyborg gangster maniacs are dead or in custody, Electric Lady has been found, and Classic has relocated out of Metropolis, then it'll be done."

"How likely do you think all that will happen?"

"Very likely. We're in the final stretch, but unfortunately, that means a whole lot of bad things can still happen."

"You go bother the Feds if you think it'll help find Classic's daughter."

"What will you do?"

"I'm suspended. I'm going home."

"You know this isn't done, right?"

"I know." Trendy pointed to a hovercruiser landing from over my shoulder. I glanced back. "Looks like you don't have to call a hovertaxi after all."

"Mr. Cruz?" a police officer called out to me. I nodded, and he hopped out of the vehicle and opened the rear passenger door. "Your presence has been requested by the Feds."

"Back to the station then," I said and got in.

It didn't take long to get back to Downtown Metro—the Feds were in an adjacent building to Police One. The tactical ops room I sat in this time was twice as big and already had a team of agents on computer terminals working the phones and reviewing all the video surveillance at and around the kidnapping site. There was also a big whiteboard at the front, but instead of photos of suspects, agents were writing new leads in different colored markers in three different columns.

Then Classic entered the room and sat down in the chair next to me.

"Did you hear anything from the audio forensics guys?" I asked.

He shook his head. More Feds came in, dressed in dark suits. One of them walked to us.

"Mr. Classic, I'm Agent Chi. I'm in charge of this operation." Classic stood and shook his hand. "We reviewed your statement. Unfortunately, your eagerness to take matters in your own hands may have complicated matters."

"How so?" Classic asked.

"We appreciate you and your colleagues wanting to get a head start on the investigation, but all that's happened is we've added a double-homicide to everything, which has nothing to do with your daughter's kidnapping. But, I have to assign our scarce resources to run down leads and treat it as if it does. We could have used those resources more productively elsewhere."

"What's the plan then?"

"I need you to let us do our jobs. We'll update you when we have something concrete. Audio forensics is still analyzing the message. Other departments are working their ends. Nothing yet. We need to give them time."

"We don't have time."

"Mr. Classic, you know how this works. We have to run down our leads. That takes time."

"Do you have anything at all?"

"No, but we only just started. We would've started earlier if you and your colleagues followed procedure and called us immediately."

"All I'm hearing is a lot of excuses from you."

"You're hearing facts from me."

"I'll let you do your work then." Classic looked at me and gestured for me to follow him.

"Mr. Classic, where are you going?" Agent Chi asked as Classic stood and turned to walk away.

"Getting something to eat."

"Mr. Classic, you are on suspension too. Don't make matters any worse. Let us do our job."

"That's what I'm doing."

"I'm going to have to insist, Mr. Classic, that you remain in the building."

"We'll be in the cafeteria lounge."

The Feds couldn't stop Classic even if they had legal cause to do so. From what I saw, he was a cyborg every bit as powerful as when he was still back in the game. We left the tactical ops room for the elevators, but we didn't go to the cafeteria level. We went straight to the employee parking level.

"Where are we going?" I asked as I followed.

"You're a detective, so let's do some detecting."

My eyes light up as we approached his vehicle. "That's your vehicle?"

The large headlights flashed three times as the doors unlocked. It was a classic, silver hover-monster truck. Painted on its hood were lightning and flames. I had a smile a mile wide. I may not have been a classic hovercar restorer anymore, but I would always be a classic hovervehicle admirer.

"Get in."

He didn't have to tell me twice.

I hadn't been in a real hover-monster truck in ages. I loved everything about them—from the mini-stepladder to climb up, the super-elevated cab to peer over the roofs of most other vehicles in sky traffic, and the rumble of the hoverengine. It was a beautiful machine to fly. It was the only vehicle in existence that made you wish for the ancient days of wheels. I imagined running over scores of parked hovercars on the ground with mega-tires and crushing them to pieces. I had reverted to the age equivalent of Cruz Jr.

"Have you always had this vehicle?" I asked.

"Yes, it's seventy-five years old. It was my uncle's. He gave it to me as a birthday present."

"Seventy-five years old. It looks like it just came off the manufacturing line. I doubt my Pony will look this good after seventy-five years."

"It will. This truck only looks this good because I keep bringing it to people like you. Or people in your former vocation as a hovercar restorer."

I looked below, under the overcast sky.

"Where are we going?"

"Following a lead."

"Feds can't do it?"

"The Feds will waste hours going over work we've already done. We need to move quicker. Besides, where we're going, I'm uniquely qualified to handle."

"Where would that be?"

"A nest of vipers."

"Vipers? I dealt with them before in my Blade Gunner case. I didn't like it. The snake gang put real snakes in my super-shower."

Classic laughed. "The stories you must have. Don't worry about the vipers. I'll keep them away from you."

All the time Classic had been the exemplar of good driving. A hover-monster truck was basically a double-decker vehicle pretending to be a single-level one, but he drove in the sky as smoothly as one could.

"Cruz, you should hold on."

I never got a chance to ask what he meant. He dove the vehicle so suddenly my stomach was in my mouth. In front of us was the blinking storefront of some kind of establishment. Again, whenever there was no signage, it meant it was a place of illegality. I grabbed the upper handhold with my right hand and extended my left out to rest against the dashboard.

"Oh, snaps!" I yelled.

The hover-monster truck busted through the front of the establishment, and I swore it took the entire front wall with it. Then, with a flash, all I saw were people diving and jumping out of the way. The super quickness of their movements meant one thing—it was a crowd of cyborgs. Classic busted the vehicle right out the back wall, then stopped.

He opened the driver's door and stepped out. I climbed out of my side to follow. I almost started laughing. The front and back walls were gone, rubble scattered everywhere. The only things standing were the left and right walls, and a crowd of very angry, very scary looking people.

"Do you always park your vehicle by driving through businesses?" one of them said as an exiting crowd walked to us.

"Is this it?" Classic asked.

"Is what it?" the man asked.

"Is this the next generation of cyborg gangsters? None of you look tough enough to take on a stray dog."

The crowd had moved to us like a swarm. I saw lots of metal limbs, metallic plates, glowing eyes. Not one of them looked older than thirty.

"Who might you be, old man?"

"My name's Classic Cyborg."

The crowd stopped.

"You don't look that tough to me," another said. "Are you fit enough to fight anymore? Your doctor might have something to say about that. You might get a hernia or have a heart attack if you tangle with us."

Classic stopped and went back to his vehicle. I didn't follow but watched him like everyone else.

"What are you doing, old man?" the first cyborg thug asked. "Do you need a weapon to take us on? The great Classic Cyborg? You're a joke."

He disappeared behind the hover-monster truck. Again, I didn't see it coming. The vehicle whipped inches past me like a rocket. This time the cyborg crowd didn't have time to react as the vehicle knocked them away as if it were a game of human bowling. I turned to see Classic walking back.

"I'm not leaving here until I'm certain that none of you has any information about the kidnapping of my daughter. I'll gladly inflict whatever pain you need me to."

He grabbed the side of his hover-monster truck and effortlessly dragged it out of the establishment and to the side. His beautiful vehicle wasn't so beautiful anymore, but he didn't care. He stepped to the cyborg gangster lying on the ground who had done most of the talking and grabbed him by the neck. The kid's eyes opened wide in fear.

Classic didn't engage in any bodily violence. He went through the kid's pockets and tossed him to the ground. Most of the other cyborg gangster wannabes were unconscious. He went through all of their pockets too. I don't know what he was looking for, and he didn't interrogate anyone as he hunted. When he finished checking their pockets, he gestured to me as he walked back to the hover-monster truck. We got in and, despite its damage, blasted away.

We returned to Police One, parked, and made our way back to the Fed tactical ops room. Agent Chi was waiting at the main entrance with a few other agents.

"Mr. Classic," Agent Chi said. "I told you not to leave the building."

Classic lifted his hand and touched his palm—it was a circular data disk. "On this file is the DNA of multiple suspects on this case."

"What suspects?" Chi asked.

"Run the DNA and let's see."

Chi took the disk. "Do I want to know how you got this?"

"Do I want to waste my time telling you? No. Run the DNA."

Chi handed it to an agent. "Run it."

"What updates do you have for me?" Classic asked.

"We're working the case."

"So I should prepare myself to start receiving body parts?"

"We're doing our job, and we're very good at it."

Classic wasn't satisfied with his answer. "We'll be in the cafeteria."

This time Chi assigned an agent detail to us—one male, one female. They followed us onto the elevator, and when we got to the cafeteria, seated themselves at the main entrance to watch us clearly in the busy and noisy room.

"Will the Feds get anything from the disk?" I asked him. All I had was a cup of silk coffee. Not as good as my own office coffee, but it would do.

"It's a long shot that one of these other gangs kidnapped her, working contract. If so, we can find her in time. If not, there's not a chance."

We were summoned back to the tactical ops room by another agent. The kid looked like he'd slept in his black suit the night before. When we entered the room, it was filled with seated agents. Chi was at the front, saw us, and began.

"Our primary suspects, known on the street as Pink Machete, Harder Steel, and Robo-Stein, are still at large. However, based on street intel, the reports from the unauthorized Metro Cyborg Gang Unit operation that captured two rival gang members, and new information from another unauthorized operation, we believe that Mr. Classic's daughter may have been kidnapped not by the three prime suspects but by new gangs who are moving in to seize their territory.

"We've identified nearly a thousand individuals. There isn't time for us to slowly and deliberately investigate each suspect, so Operation Cyber Strike is hereby authorized. We'll work with Metro PD, and we move out in thirty minutes. All 997 suspects will be taken down hard and arrested in one strike. Ladies and gentlemen, move out."

The entire room stood and began to exit. Agent Chi walked up to us.

"Mr. Classic, you'll remain here. I don't want you playing detective and I don't want your detective on my case."

"I guess we'll return to the cafeteria then."

Classic turned and marched out of the room. I was about to follow. Chi grabbed me.

"Stay with him and please keep him out of trouble," he told me.

"I'll try."

"Do more than that. We'll let him know as soon as we have something concrete. He has to let us do our job."

"What do you think I'm going to do? The man can throw hovertrucks through buildings. I'm not going to stop him and neither are you. Agent, it might be helpful if instead of letting him sulk in a public cafeteria, you put him in the real tactical center for this case. Give him something to do. Let him watch the interrogations on the monitors. That's the only way to keep him calm."

Chi turned to his senior agents standing with him. "Take them to the room."

"We're going to give civilians access?" one of them asked.

"Yes. Make it happen."

"Yes, sir."

We were in the real command center for the case. I had been involved in kidnapping cases in Metropolis before. The sad fact was there were a lot, and law enforcement had to prioritize somehow with all the other crimes they had to deal with. Someone was going to get the full resources of Metro PD or the Feds; someone else would only get an officer, an agent or two, and that's it. For Classic, he had the full resources of the Federal Kidnap Recovery Division. I knew that everyone forgave and forgot his past, but it still struck me as too much. First the Gang Unit was breaking Metro PD procedures to work the case and now the Feds were giving his case the presidential treatment.

The command center setup was similar to the Metro Cyborg Gang Unit, only much bigger. Far more monitors on the walls—of not only field arrests off-site but interrogations of arrested gang members on-site. Nearly a thousand cyborg gang members were rounded up in fifteen minutes. Row after row of agents were working in cubicles at computers, and teams of behaviorists and profilers were watching the interrogations.

There was one thing that was purposely missing from the room—a clock. But it didn't matter. I knew Classic was well aware of the countdown of time. He quietly watched his personal monitor with headphones on. They had set us up in the back of the room. I had my own monitor too, but I was more interested in watching the agents in the room as a group.

Classic had put a lot of his hopes into the audio forensics team, but they had found nothing of use on the recorded ransom message. They came to tell us that around eleven pm. We only had until around ten a.m. the next day. So far, the Feds had come up with nothing.

It was one a.m. when Classic pulled the headphones from his head, got up from his seat, and stormed out of the room. I didn't follow, but I had a good feeling what he was about to do. So did Chi, who noticed him from the front of the room and immediately ran out the same door.

I heard a commotion. The room went quiet. Chi's body came crashing through the door. Well, I didn't have to guess anymore. Classic was going to pay the ransom.

I hated Whiskey Way—the low-end, high-crime town. The kidnappers had sent us here. I sat in the passenger seat scanning the street as Classic landed his hover-monster truck in a ground parking lot. There wasn't another vehicle of any kind around.

"Is this our smartest move?" I asked him.

"It's our only move," he replied.

It was six a.m. but it was as dark as midnight. I didn't like it at all. There wasn't a pedestrian anywhere to be seen, which was why the kidnappers had chosen the location.

"What are they going to say when they find out you don't have all the money?" I asked.

"They know I don't have that kind of money. It's about getting me to pay something."

"You're really going to hand them the money?"

"No, I'm going to tell them we'll do an even exchange."

"I'm not an expert on these kinds of things, but will that really work? They tell you to pay a set amount; you pay a tenth of it. They tell you to give them the money and wait for instructions; you tell them that you'll only do an even exchange. Won't they hurt Electric Lady anyway?"

"No, they won't. We know the kidnappers. It's either Harder Steel, Pink Machete or Robo-Stein. One of them is the kidnapper, so it's about me, not her. They'll play."

"I hope so. When are they meeting us?"

"They didn't say. They only told me to be here."

"They're watching us then. Did you tell them that you're bringing along your detective too?"

"No. They didn't ask."

"I don't do bodyguard work, by the way."

"Yes, you do."

"Well, I do bodyguard work, but only for kids, not adults."

"Isn't that practically the same thing?"

"If it's a kid, then it's protecting them at their home. That's okay. If it's an adult, they're running around the entire city, maybe sitting in a hover-monster truck in some secluded parking lot. No, that's dangerous."

"For someone as risk-averse as you, you've taken down a lot of bad guys."

"I don't like to get shot."

Classic chuckled. We waited for over an hour in his vehicle without seeing another person or hovercar. His dashboard phone beeped and he reached out to push the button.

"Yes," Classic answered.

"Why did you bring a cop?" We recognized the same computer generated voice from the first ransom message over the speakers.

"I'm not a cop and you know it," I quickly answered. "Stop playing games. You know it's only the two of us."

"Where's the money?" the voice asked.

"In the trunk of the vehicle in five suitcases," Classic replied.

"Mr. Classic Cyborg, we didn't think you'd get all that money together so fast."

"I called in all my favors, and I had some money tucked away."

"Look straight ahead," the voice said. "The tallest tower that you see. Drive and set down on the roof. We'll meet you there. Remember, we're watching your every move."

The call disconnected. Classic started up his vehicle and began ascending, then flew forward.

"Are the windows bulletproof?" I asked.

"Of course. And laser-resistant."

As we started to rise higher into the sky toward the mega-tower, it began to rain.

"Great," I said with annoyance.

"This could work to our advantage."

"Not if it's the beginning of this Storm of the Century. I don't mind if they're washed off the roof to their deaths, but I'd like that not to happen to us."

"We don't have to worry."

Distances were often deceiving in Metropolis. The mega-tower building looked like it was close, but actually, it was many miles away. When we reached it, Classic set the hover-monster truck in the center of the massive roof. It was an office tower and there were some vehicles already parked, but mostly it was empty. Two black hovercars dove from the sky in front of us. One hovered in front of my passenger side and the second remained in front of us. The doors lifted up on the first, and men in black attire and black ski-masks hopped out, pointing weapons.

"Put your hands on the dashboard!" one yelled.

Classic complied immediately. I put my left hand on the dashboard but lowered the passenger side window with my right, then placed it on the dashboard too. The gunman's hand came into our vehicle, his gun inches from my face.

"Pop the trunk!" he yelled at Classic.

"Where's my daughter?" he yelled back.

"We're not negotiating. Pop the trunk! We get the money, leave and you get a call about where she is."

"No," Classic said.

"No?"

"Even exchange."

"Are you mental?" The gunman moved his gun from my face to point at Classic. The two other gunmen took positions to get a better shot of him from the side.

"Tell your boss that's the deal," Classic added.

"We're the boss! She's going to die because of you."

"Tell your boss. We'll go and wait for his call."

"You're not going anywhere!"

I didn't like getting shot, so having a gun near my face wasn't on my favorites list. I punched his hand away as I flicked my left wrist. My pop-gun blasted him into his black hovercar. I kicked my passenger door open and the shootout began, or my shootout began. I didn't know if it was the same three that had kidnapped Electric Lady before, but all of them were dead on the ground.

In the nano-second Classic decided to change the ransom terms, violence of some kind was inevitable—either we were getting shot or they were. I made sure it wasn't us. However, it wasn't over.

The other black hovercar quickly rose in the air as an arm came out of the passenger side. There was a hail of laser-fire as they tried to make their getaway, but it's very hard to hit a target when firing from a rising and spinning hovercar. His shots hit the ground with lots of fury and fireworks, but they were nowhere close to Classic or me sitting in his vehicle. I fired back with my omega-gun, one round after another. Then it came—a blitz of laser fire. They had an illegal laser cannon mounted on their hovercar. I wasn't the fastest runner, but I was fast enough. However, I had no interest in finding out what other surprises they might have, as their hovercar would soon be out of range.

My omega-gun could rapid-fire lasers too, but that's not what I shot at them. I had to assume their vehicle was as well-armored as Classic's. When the device I fired hit their hovercar, it made a loud metallic thud. The omega-gun wasn't really a gun; it was a projectile delivery device made off-world. My device was delivered, and the kidnappers' second hovercar wouldn't be making any getaways today. It began to violently spin in a clockwise motion, increasing in speed. It was already breaking apart when it lurched and came crashing down. We didn't see the direct explosion, but we heard it and saw the brightness of the fireball.

I returned to the hover-monster truck. Classic hadn't moved an inch. It wasn't until I opened the passenger door that I stopped in shock. The entire vehicle was riddled with gunfire and the front glass was gone, shattered to pieces.

"What happened?"

"You didn't notice it with the rain, but they weren't only firing lasers."

"They had a machine-gun cannon too?"

"Bullets must have been moving at the speed of light."

"Were you hit?"

"No." Classic looked like he didn't have a care in the world. There wasn't a mark on him. He was Mr. Invincible. "You had everything under control."

"Did I?" I asked.

"You did. They're dead; we're alive."

"Now what? You knew this was how it would end the second you told them you were changing their plans."

"Their boss will call again. Kidnappers don't give up so easily when they're gangsters."

I closed my door and sat back. The rain was falling inside the vehicle. Classic started it up without a problem and we blasted off.

The plan was simple: I'd stay home until the kidnappers contacted him again. He'd call me and pick me up. I did agree with him; this wasn't over. The kidnappers might yell, curse, and threaten, but they weren't going to kill Electric Lady and walk away. They wanted the money, or more likely, a hold over Classic to trap him.

I hadn't been home at the Concrete Mama in over twenty-four hours myself. Classic dropped me off right at the front. He waited until I made it through the main entrance doors before blasting off in his vehicle. I so liked the "blast off" effect on its hoverengine. Maybe it would be a modification for the Pony in the future.

Mr. Post was not the first person I saw in the lobby. It was the "boys"—Classic's retired Metro PD cyborgs assigned to me as bodyguards. The six men stood at the elevators, waiting.

"Hello, gentlemen. I thought you were staking out the Liquid Cool office building."

"That building is well covered. This one, not so much."

"Are you expecting something? You're all assembled here in the lobby."

"Mr. Cruz, maybe you should go upstairs."

I didn't like how he said that and realized my back was to the entrance. I turned. I could see someone approaching.

"Mr. Cruz." I turned again and it was Mr. Post. "You need to evacuate the lobby."

"Evacuate? What's going on?"

"Follow me." He was already pushing me to the elevators.

The Boys looked as if it was High Noon at the O.K. Corral. They were standing in the lobby facing the entrance. I never did see what the six retired cyborg police veterans were waiting for.

Mr. Post got me into the first elevator that arrived and the doors closed.

"What's going on, Mr. Post?"

"We have it handled, Mr. Cruz. Police have already been called. A few suspicious characters have been watching the building since yesterday."

"You mean waiting for me."

"We're taking care of it."

"What do they look like? Anything distinct about them?"

"Yes, but I shouldn't tell you. Let us handle it, Mr. Cruz. The police are on the way, and you have the retired crew watching the lobby."

Mr. Post was ex-Metro police himself, which was why the tenants of the Concrete Mama hired him and why I had recommended him to them.

"What's the unique thing about these suspicious characters watching the Concrete Mama?"

"They're cyborgs, and their heads are tattooed to look like skulls."

"Skulls? I never knew there were so many cyborg gangs in Metropolis."

"They're not from Metropolis and they aren't gang members. They're from Up-Top. They're contract killers, and they haven't been waiting for you, they've been waiting for Mr. Classic."

I realized that I had had my mobile off the whole time. When I turned it on, I had messages from PJ. Three photos of the newest entrants to the Classic Cyborg Dead Pool complete with their skull head tattoos—they called themselves the

Exterminators! It was what Sinister Bet-ee had hinted at: the Up-Top "players" had arrived.

Cyborgs from Up-Top. I didn't like it. I didn't care if it was from the space station colonies, Lunar Colony, or Mars. I didn't like it all. Sinister Bet-ee did warn me beforehand in her excited, though cryptic, way. The Up-Top "players" had arrived. The Exterminators. Cute. It seemed that I'd have to deal with every major cyborg gangster there was.

I had other calls besides PJ's. Trendy, his Captain, an array of police brass, and the Feds had left me messages too. I didn't need to listen to their messages, though I did, because I knew what they wanted. All of them wanted me to talk Classic out of paying the ransom to the kidnappers. There wasn't a chance I'd ever do something so foolish. Being thrown around like a rag doll by a cyborg who could literally throw hovertrucks through buildings was something I wasn't going to experience—ever!

However, I did want to call Trendy back. Before I did, I made one other call—an Earth to space vid-call. It didn't last long, but if I hadn't, it probably would have been both Classic's and my last day alive.

I had my own home office in my residence, and I sat at a simple desk in front of the vid-phone to dial Trendy. He picked up on the first ring.

"There you are."

"Detective Trendy," I greeted.

"Cruz, I need you to talk some sense into Classic."

"How would that work exactly? You've known him a lot longer than me."

"He has to put the Feds back on this."

"Can I ask a question?"

"What?" His face had a suspicious expression.

"I've worked kidnapping cases before on behalf of clients."

"And?"

"I've never known the Feds to back off any of them on the say-so of a civilian. If I didn't know better, Trendy, I'd say Classic is getting special treatment. Why might that be?"

"He is getting special treatment. He's one of our own."

"If it were just Metro PD, I'd agree, but not the Feds. I've seen the Feds do whatever they wanted to despite what a family asked them to do. Here, Classic tells them what to do, throws the Agent-in-Charge through a door, tells them he's going to pay the ransom, and they say 'okay?' What's going on, Trendy? I've only seen this kind of deference paid to a civilian whose a Movie-Town celebrity, the Mayor or City Council, or some Up-Top gazillionaire looking to invest in Metropolis."

"Nothing's going on, Cruz. He's your client. Are you this suspicious of your clients?"

"No, I'm this suspicious of *everybody*, except my wife. Cruz Jr. is a teleporting ninja, so he's borderline."

"Nothing's going on, Cruz. Stop looking for conspiracies everywhere."

"Where's Dr. Silver-Rose?"

"Why are you asking me that?"

"Where is she?"

"How would I know that? Is she missing too?"

"No, she's hiding."

"Cruz, you need to talk to Classic and get him to get the Feds back on the case while there's still time."

"Okay, I'll talk to him," I said. I wouldn't.

"Good. Call me when you get him back on the program. The Cap and the rest of us are off suspension and back on the case. Tell him that. We're doing all we can, but he has to work with us."

"Okay."

"Call me." He hung up.

"We're on," Classic said to me from the viewscreen of my home vid-phone.

"I'll be ready," I said, "but not at my building."

"The Boys told me."

"I'll grab a hovertaxi and meet you at the place that criminal cyborgs fear more than death."

Classic smiled. "See you then."

The Boys still had the main lobby staked out. This time there was a police hovercruiser parked in front of the Concrete Mama as well. I smiled and walked to the cyborg police vets.

"Do you think I can get a favor? I'm meeting Classic."

That's all I had to say. Police might retire, but they remained connected. The police hovercruiser became my hovertaxi ride to Metro PD. We arrived in the main parking bay and there was Classic, waiting inside his hover-monster truck. It had a new front windshield and most of the bullet holes were patched up, but it was still a mess from the visual standpoint of a classic hovercar collector or restorer.

I saved all my questions for after I climbed in on the passenger side and closed the door. He started up the vehicle and coasted out, waving to the officers on guard.

"What did they say?" I asked.

"What didn't they say. We killed all their men, or you did."

"It wasn't personal. Well, it was personal, but all avoidable."

"I remember. You don't like to get shot."

"Us mere mortals aren't bulletproof like you. What's the plan?"

"Another drop. I show the money and they'll bring her to the scene. Then we make the exchange."

"Classic, I don't mean to be rude, but this is stupid. It's a setup. Why are we doing this? Even if you wanted to pay the money or a portion of the money, you should let the Feds run it. Two guys flying into an ambush in a hover-monster truck? We're good, but not that good."

"It'll be okay."

"How do you know?"

"They gave me their word."

"Are you serious? The kidnappers of your daughter gave you their word. That's it?"

"Yes."

I wasn't happy, but what was I going to do about it. Classic was playing by a rulebook that had been made obsolete over two decades ago. We were dealing with criminals who had no honor at all.

"I know you're not happy about this, Cruz. But we have to do it my way. I can't explain it. There's still a chance I can come out of this without having to jump back into the life. If she dies, that's what I'll do to track down every last one of them. I need to run this, not the Feds."

Where did we drive to? Whiskey Way again. That should have been my first sign that we should have stopped and gone back home. No criminal would use the same district a second time after a previously failed "business" transaction. Maybe it was reverse psychology on their part. We flew through a dark alleyway to another mega-tower.

"I picked the building. They picked the time," he said as we approached the rooftop.

Another no-name mega-tower in a seedy district. The parking lot wasn't empty. Two silver hovercars were already parked, one behind the other. All the windows were tinted black.

Classic didn't land but hovered right in front of the vehicles. He turned the hover-monster truck so his driver's side was facing them. He stared and did nothing else. The front passenger door opened, and a man in black with a black ski mask stepped out. He gestured for us to land and turn off the engine. Classic did so.

"Step out of the vehicle. Both of you!" he yelled.

Classic didn't hesitate. I reluctantly complied.

"Mr. Classic Cyborg, we don't want a repeat of the last encounter. Can't have you killing any more of our guys."

"I didn't kill them. He did," Classic answered, pointing to me.

The man moved his death glare from Classic to me. "Keep your hands where I can see them."

"Where's Electric Lady?" I asked.

"In the other hovercar," he answered. "Are we all going to play nice and do some business."

"Yes, we are," Classic answered. "But let me see her first."

"That's not what we agreed to," the man said. "Money first."

"The bags are in the trunk," Classic said.

"Get them."

Classic backed up slowly and waved his right hand. The trunk auto-opened. "I'm reaching in. Two big bags."

"Go ahead."

Classic reached and started walking back to the man with two huge duffel bags. "The money." He dropped the bags to the ground. "My daughter."

"I have to check the duffel bags. Make sure you're not trying a doublecross."

"Doublecross?" I asked. "Why did you use that word?"

"What?"

"Why did you use that word, doublecross? Is that what you're planning?"

"What? We're not planning anything."

"Tell your friends to have Electric Lady stick her arm out the window."

"What?"

"What? You like repeating that word a lot. You heard what I said."

"I'm checking the doublecross first, I mean the duffel bags."

I shot him so fast that I was spraying the driver's side of the first hovercar with laser fire before his body hit the ground. I hadn't moved my aim. The laser blasts punched through the black glass, and whoever sat in the driver's seat was riddled with more laser fire. The hovercar lurched forward and slammed into the hover-monster truck, but it wasn't going any further.

The other black hovercar quickly rose in the air as an arm (not Electric Lady's) reached out of the passenger side. I dodged a hail of laser fire as they tried to make their getaway. His shots hit the ground, missing me completely, as I fired back with my omega-gun, one round after another. Then I realized it. It wasn't a hovervehicle; it was a spacecraft.

I touched my ear to dial. "At my location. The black vehicle rising," I said. "Verify targets inside only."

Classic saw that I had stopped firing. "They're getting away," he called out.

"They're going nowhere," I replied.

A giant blast came from high above with a beam as wide as the craft itself. The hovercar stopped in mid-air, then exploded to pieces—all that was left was a fiery alloy frame. It began to fall and hit the roof with a sickening crash. It was only then that we saw them—two in the front and one in the back. The cyborgs stood in the remnants of the vehicle and marched toward me— three burning figures with skull heads. I fired at the Exterminators, taking a step back each time. They kept marching at me.

They screamed and bolted at me. I was dealing with a group of super-cyborgs (not to be confused with the Super-Cyborgs I'd met in my Blade Gunner case) and there would be no space station protocols to help me here. However, I had contacts in Up-Top law enforcement too. I had called Mr. Seraff of the Interspace Police.

Space calls always had an ultra-perfect quality. With their digital tech transmission, they almost looked better than if the person were actually in front of you. Too perfect for the average, analog, tech-loving Earther like me, but to each their own. A female officer answered, "Praetorian Space Command."

"My name's Cruz. I need to speak immediately to Chief Agent Seraff."

"Mr. Seraff is unavailable."

"It's important."

"He's on Mars and unavailable."

"Tell him we have a Priority Red situation. Three Asimovians are on Earth."

"Hold, please." She disappeared from my viewscreen.

Seraff was with me on the space station when we encountered those Super-Cyborgs. An entire space armada would have been authorized to kill them. I told them that three of them might be on Earth, that the Exterminators were Super-Cyborgs—capital "S" and "C." I lied; they were super-cyborgs— all lower case. But it was enough for him to send a military spacecraft to blast their illegal space vehicle from Metropolis airspace. Now, it was up to me. I had gotten all the help I was going to get.

I ran; they ran after me. I jumped off the roof; they followed. I watched, floating in the air via jetpack, as the three of them fell to the Earth. Unlike Franken-borg, their bodies didn't have built-in jetpacks. From one hundred-fifty stories up, no cyborg could survive the impact, especially with their added bionic weight. Even from my height, floating in mid-air, I heard the echo of the violent triple impact.

I returned to the roof. Classic hadn't moved from where he stood.

"She was never here," I said.

"I know," he replied. "I thought you couldn't jump and then activate a jetpack. You'd still fall."

"I had it activated already. Up-Top police sent me their files. They like to chase people, but they can't fly. I can't outrun them, so I thought I'd fly. They didn't see my feet weren't touching the ground."

"Clever. I didn't know you had friends in such high places."

"I do, but it was a one-time assist. What now?"

"The final play."

"Those cyborgs were from Up-Top. They called themselves the Exterminators."

"I know, Cruz. The Dead Pool. But again, the only one who did any eliminating was you. Let's go."

"How are you getting your daughter back?"

"There's only one way. Forget the ransom. Forget everything. In my day, we called it a parley, when no one could trust anyone. All of us in the same room for a meet. Everyone to negotiate what they want, and what they deserve. We'll bring it all to an end."

FRITZ, THE MEDIATOR

We were back in Downtown Metro in the parking bay of one of the main banks. The first ten stories had walls that appeared to be made of glass. I wasn't sure that I'd ever put my money in a bank with glass walls, and I knew my wife wouldn't let me even if I wanted to. Classic came out with a big bag, followed by two security guards. He stopped, said something to them, and they reluctantly walked back into the bank.

"For me?" I asked when he got back to the vehicle.

He reached in through my open window with the bag and set it on my lap. "'In for a penny, in for a pound,' I believe is the saying."

"I can't say I ever liked that saying. What's this for?"

"There's a person who's called the Mediator. His specialty is setting up meetings between parties in the criminal world. Find him, pay him, and get him to set up the parley."

"He can be trusted?"

"He can. He can't be bought. It's a matter of principle with him. It's what he's known for."

"This will find your daughter?"

"It will."

"Is this all working the way you intended?" I asked.

He hesitated, watching me. "Life never works out precisely the way you intend. Sometimes it just works."

"Or doesn't."

"I chose to be the optimist."

"I'll find the Mediator, then. Where does he live, work, or hang out?"

"I've heard he can be found at a place called the Check Point, but you might have a bit of trouble getting in. They don't like non-criminals."

"Why don't you contact him?"

"He doesn't deal with the principles of a meeting. Only intermediaries. That's how he works. You contact him. He'll contact me and the others. You're paying him to set it up. Get to him any way you can. I won't say how, because you're the detective. You can catch a hovercab from here. I'm sure you want to be back in the driver's seat of your own vehicle."

"But will I? Whether sitting here or in my own Pony, it seems I'm only along for the ride."

I opened the door, and Classic stepped to the side. "Take what you need from the bag for expenses," he said. "I'll await the call."

"Will you answer it this time?"

"I will."

"Good."

I closed the vehicle door and walked back to the bank, with bag in hand. It was best to call my hovertaxi from inside, even if it was a bank with glass walls. I didn't look back at Classic, but I knew he was watching me.

I had never seen them before. There were pop-up retail stands everywhere on the sidewalks selling heavy raincoats and life rafts. My personal stakeout had entered its second hour as I stood in the shadows across the street from another no-name establishment. The district was called Angel's Beach, but there was nothing angelic about the place. It was a filthy city; streets coated with oil from who-knew-where and littered with cigarette butts. Also, there was no beach! We were in Metropolis. The closest we came to a beach was the jagged death shore bordering the Great Oceans. The place was nothing but a giant casino—gambling everywhere. The police probably stayed away because where would you start? Illegal gambling and money changing hands were everywhere.

As usual, the dark bar had plenty of thugs hanging out in front of it. The particular thugs I had my eyes on were adorned with plenty of neon tattoos on their bodies. It was time to make my move. If the Storm of the Century came, I surely didn't want to be here, but it couldn't be helped.

I walked over to the front of the bar. Rather than go in, I stopped in front with the thugs. From what I had observed earlier, they were the bouncers and strictly regulated who entered. Only those who knew someone inside could enter, and even then only after they put some currency in one of their hands.

"Hi," I said.

The six men glanced at me, each with a raw cigarette in their mouth. None of them were especially interested in my existence, but they kept their eyes on me.

"Who might you be?" one of them asked.

"Johnny," I answered.

"Johnny?"

"Yeah, like sidewalk johnny."

"You a sidewalk johnny?"

"No."

"What do you want?"

"Can you spot me?"

"Spot you?" Now I had their attention. The sheer gall of my question. "For what?"

"I need to get in, but I don't have any money. Spot me a few bills, then I'll get some money from my guys inside and give it back with interest."

They all watched to see if I was joking. The first one started to laugh. "You have some big titanium steel balls to come up to us and ask something like that. We take money, we don't hand it out."

"What do I do?" I asked aloud. "The cops are scoping the place. I had to dump my money in a dumpster. I need to get off the street."

"Cops?" the man asked. "What are you talking about?"

"Cops," I said. "They're the next street over. That's why I have no money. I had to get rid of it."

Another man put a vise grip on my shoulder. "You need to stand still because you're making us nervous with the cop talk."

"Who're your guys inside?" the first man asked.

"Fritz."

"Fritz the Mediator?"

"Yeah."

The first man tossed his cigarette to the ground and pointed to the others. "Hold him until we get back. You two go and check the other street for these cops he's talking about. You two check the other street. If they're cops, they'll try to box us in. I'll go in and find Fritz to see if this guy's on the level. Hold him here, until I get back." He put his fat, stubby index finger in my face. "If you're running a scam on us, I'll come back here and put *you* in a dumpster."

"Tell the Mediator that I'm so sorry about all this. I know he wanted to wrap up the business today."

"Whatever. You keep talking, but I'm not listening."

Two of the thugs quick-walked away to the left, and two others walked to the street in the opposite direction. The lead man walked in the bar as the remaining one kept his vise grip on my shoulder.

"What's your boss's name?" I asked.

"Why? Are you going to add him to your Christmas list?"

I blasted him in the chest with my omega-gun. It was to test my new heavy stun setting. He was instantly unconscious. However, he was far too heavy for me to gently lie him down on the ground, so I let him collapse. I stepped around the body and into the dark bar I went.

Red smoke. Blue smoke. Yellow smoke. This was a smoking bar, and everyone was doing it. I pulled a cloth from my jacket and covered my nose and mouth with my left hand before I gagged. The air was warm and had a toxic feel to it, as if I were in a drug den. It was crowded with men and women in cheap clothes, drinking, dancing where they stood to a holo-jukebox. So crowded that no one noticed my weapon in my right hand as I made my way to the back, following the lead bouncer.

Any building in Metropolis meant the distance between the front of a place and the back of it could feel like it were the length of a marathon. That was how I was feeling. I kept moving and moving through the endless crowd, the smoky air getting worse, the music louder, my eyes watery, and my mood worsening. My main problem was I didn't know what Fritz the Mediator looked like. I only knew he was in this bar, and the hovercar he drove, which was parked nearby.

The bouncer was leaned over talking to a guy at a booth with a dainty female on either side. There were tons of empty and half-filled glasses on the table in front of the women, and a mobile computer in front of him. The man had a crew-cut and wore purple neon shades, a fluffy shirt with a dark vest, and a ring in each earlobe.

A hand clutched my shoulder from behind. "I think we need to take you to that dumpster," the voice whispered in my ear.

I shot him without even turning around. Immediately, the place erupted in chaos, people running, diving over the counter. I had turned and taken a knee. The other three were running to me with guns drawn. I shot all of them. One managed a shot, but if the establishment bothered to have its lights on properly, he would've been able to see me instead of hitting an innocent patron. I swung back around and blasted the lead bouncer in the chest. His hand-cannon fell to the ground and he crashed face first to the floor.

The Mediator was on the run! I bolted after him.

People were screaming. When I reached the back door, Fritz ran out. I stopped. I turned left instead and saw what I was looking for—another exit. That was the door I kicked open and ran out into the heavy rain. *No! Storm of the Century, not yet!* I had been right. At that original back door were three guys waiting with guns and rifles aimed. I blasted them with my omega-gun from behind.

I didn't need to look for Fritz. I had prepared.

I made it back to the Pony and got out of Angel's Beach as quickly as I could. On my dashboard display, I followed the moving dot. The sky traffic was crazy but manageable, so I remained in the fast lane until I got to my destination: the outskirts of Silver City.

Silver City was the center of Metropolis's robot production. I'd been there in my Blade Gunner and NeuroDancer cases. It was through those cases that I had learned that Silver City did have a small residential area, besides the endless miles of commercial mega-towers. The tracker I planted on the Mediator's hovercar led me straight to his home. If he had found it before he flew away, I would have said he was a criminal of above-average intelligence. Since he didn't, he was just a doofus who pretended to be more than he was. My assessment was confirmed when I walked into the building, typed his name into the tenant directory on the concierge center, and *voila*—there was his listing, along with his floor and apartment number.

The Mediator had a street reputation as the go-to guy for the criminal class. He set up the meetings of warring gangs and criminal megacorps when both sides had grown weary enough of the fighting and killing to want a truce, temporary or permanent. He was the guy everyone went to because they didn't trust anyone else. He setup the meetings and picked the time and place. He was the only one who communicated between the parties—no one else.

The man I chased right to his front door was as unimpressive as they came. *This was the operator who set up parleys for all these years among the most violent and unstable individuals, gangs, and corporations without a blemish on his record?* Not a chance. This man was too incompetent for all that. If I was able to bluff my way into his place, plant a tracker on his personal hovercar—a vehicle which shouldn't have been left unguarded to begin with—and find his personal residence, others a lot more savvy than I would have done so and deposited his body in a dumpster.

I was convinced that this man was an impostor. But then, who was he?

Time wasn't going to stand still for us. It was essential that I wrap up this case before PJ had to email me more photos of crazy maniacs entering the Dead Pool. This was a case that only added more lingering questions to my list. I didn't like loose ends. In the world of the private street detective, loose ends could get you killed.

The elevator stopped on the seventy-sixth floor, and I strolled out with a long duffel bag in my left hand and my omega-gun in my right.

It wasn't lost on me that every door I passed in the giant hallway had a security camera. Some were static, but a few followed me as I walked along—I could only guess if it was motion-tracking or manual control. As I approached Fritz's apartment, I noticed its above-door camera was already pointed at me. I wasn't only good at shooting human targets from afar; I shot the camera to pieces with one shot. The wires fizzled and there were a couple of sparks.

I rang the doorbell. It was my habit to always stand to the side of a door when I rang a bell; it's what police, fire, and ambulance personnel do. The shotgun blast through the door left a hole large enough for a four-foot midget to jump through without having to duck. The door was splintered, and the wall across from the door had a gigantic black spot. There was smoke and I could hear a voice. I tossed my stun grenade in.

Boom!

It was the loud, photonic model that blinded and deafened you temporarily if you weren't close enough to be blasted flat on your back. I was in the residence and there was Fritz on the ground, half-unconscious with his shotgun on the ground beside him.

"Come on out here now!" I yelled.

From farther in the apartment, one person, then a second, peeked out from behind the wall.

"Is that how you answer the door? Blasting a hole through it?" I asked.

"Says the burglar who carries stun grenades in his pocket," the woman snapped at me.

Fritz was on the couch. His wife was on one side and his daughter on the other. I sat in a facing chair, gun in hand, watching. They said nothing but their dirty looks said enough.

"So you're the Mediator?" I said to Fritz. "Liar."

"Liar?"

"No one so stupid as you could be the Mediator."

"Stupid?"

"I'm sitting in your home, genius. I followed you here from the bar. I found your home because you're dumb enough to have your name in the lobby directory."

Both the wife and daughter quickly turned their heads to look at him.

"Where's the real Mediator?" I asked.

"I am the Mediator."

"No, you're not. How do I get to him? I need to set up a meet."

"With who?"

"I'll tell the Mediator, which isn't you. Does the real Mediator know you're passing yourself off as him?"

"Since you don't believe I'm him, you can leave."

I stood up from my chair. "I came here to do some honest, illegal business, and I have to waste my time with the likes of you. I'll leave then. Maybe Classic Cyborg was wrong about you. He has been out of the game for a long time. You're just a joke."

The vid-phone rang. Fritz didn't even ask me if he was allowed to move. He stood up and picked up the phone handset next to the couch. "Yes," he answered the phone on audio-only. He lowered it from his head and reached out to me with it. "For you."

I cautiously took the phone and put it to my ear.

"Mr. Cruz," the voice said.

"Are you the real Mediator? Because I can't be wasting my time."

"You have a secretary who screens your clients. I have him. Lots of people try to meet me, but most of them are not worth my time. What does Classic Cyborg want me to do?"

"Arrange a meeting."

"All three of them?"

"You already know the players?"

"It's my business to know these things, Mr. Cruz, or I wouldn't have the rep I have. Pink Machete, Harder Steel, Robo-Stein, Classic Cyborg?"

"Yes."

"Anyone else?"

"No."

"Will you be joining Classic Cyborg at the meet?"

"Yes."

"Is that wise?"

"Who do you have your money on in the Dead Pool?"

"You, of course."

"I can't say that I'll ever understand the criminal world."

"Since we're chattin,' there's a rumor going around that the Exterminators were...eliminated. Any truth to the rumor?"

"Those Up-Top cyborgs should have stayed Up-Top."

"You're not suggesting you killed them?"

"I'm not suggesting anything. That's what happened."

"Amazing. Okay, back to business. Where's my fee?"

"Come to my office. Classic already pulled it out of his bank."

"Then I'll call you later."

"Call me where?"

"I have your personal mobile, Mr. Cruz."

"Then we'll talk when we talk."

"Goodbye, Mr. Cruz."

He hung up. I handed the phone back to fake-Fritz.

"Now that was the real Mediator," I said. "What's his name?"

"Fritz."

"His name's Fritz too."

"His name was always Fritz. I changed my name to Fritz. Everyone who works for the Mediator is named Fritz."

"Is your name Fritz?" I asked the wife.

"No, you idiot," she grunted at me.

I looked back at Fritz. "I'll let you and the family deal with your home repair chores, then."

I heard his wife and daughter cursing me under their breath as I left.

The first thing I did when I got back to my vehicle was scan it for tracking devices. I found one. It wasn't there when I had parked to go into the fake Fritz's apartment tower. I got into the Pony with a smile. I didn't take offense to the act. It was probably the real Fritz making sure I wasn't a doofus. Since I was clearly being watched, I shot out of the parking spot. I'd use every possible trick to lose any possible tails.

I was glad to arrive back at the Concrete Mama. The plan was a nap before going back to the office. I had slept a scarce few hours in three days with this case. The Pony was secure in its spot, and rather than go straight to my place, I took the elevator straight down to the lobby to check in with the Boys.

When I stepped out one of the cyborg ex-police vets was standing right there.

"Mr. Cruz."

"Anything new and exciting?" I asked.

"Only two things." He smiled.

"Two things? What two things?"

"You'll have to go to your apartment to find out."

Now I was smiling. "Does one of those two things communicate with such words as 'ga-ga-go-go'?"

"Possibly."

Room number 9732 on the one hundred-fiftieth floor was where I lived. I walked through that door with a spring in my step. "Honey, I'm home!"

I heard the giggling.

"Cruz, you cheated. It was supposed to be a surprise."

My wife popped out from her hiding place in the kitchen with a giggling Cruz Jr. wrapped up in tan attire, his tiny black fedora, and bare feet.

Now, I didn't want to work. I was happy crawling on the carpeted floor playing "hovercar smash-up" with Cruz Jr. He had an endless supply of toy hovercars but didn't need them. Children could play for hours and hours with one of their little shoes and be happy as could be.

Dot looked amazing as always (yes, yes, I'm biased. I'm the husband.) wearing a high-end gold-colored top, ivory belt and pants, black heels, and a white neck scarf. She was making something in the kitchen that smelled good—guess she didn't like the food I had cooked last week and was still eating, but I didn't blame her. I'd even eat food cooked by the Hellspawn (my parents-in-law) over mine.

"I have a case that's sticking to me like a fungus," I said out loud to Dot.

"A fungus? That's never good. As long it's not a 'save the world case,' and I'm not seeing you have shootouts on the news or jumping out of Martian flying saucers."

"That was one time!"

"What? The flying saucer or the shootouts?"

"The flying saucer," I said.

"Twice."

"Once. The first time I wasn't jumping anywhere. I was abandoned in the spaceship and had to land it. I walked out." I tickled Cruz Jr. "Isn't that right, Cruzie? You saw your dad come out of that flying saucer. There was no jumping."

"Oh, Cruz Jr. might have gotten into your home office."

I sat up on the floor. "And?"

"And he might have pulled some of your pictures from your whiteboard, but I put them back. You have a case with Electric Lady?"

"You know her?"

"Everybody comes to Eye Candy."

My wife was so right. She worked at Eye Candy Image Salon, which was always packed with customers from the time it opened until its late night closing. Women came from every corner of Metropolis to be made to look like movie stars with its "fashion police" of makeup artists, hairdressers, manicurists, pedicurists, skincare techs, tattoo artists, wardrobe stylists, and even dressers to assemble their wardrobe, if needed. The establishment was owned by Prima Donna, the Matron Queen of Metropolis fashion, but my wife was her second-in-command—a Senior VP, I liked to say.

I got up to see the damage.

"Cruz, I told you I picked up after him."

When I entered the room, I did a quick inspection. Everything was as tidy as I left it. My whiteboard with the players in my Classic Cyborg case were still there. Cruz Jr.—who again was really a teleporting ninja—would have gotten on the chair and jumped on the desk to get at the whiteboard. He liked pictures, especially faces, so the board would have been irresistible.

I walked back out to the kitchen. Cruz Jr. hadn't even realized that I had left; he was too busy with his hovercar smash-up game.

"Who's this?" I asked her, showing her a picture from my whiteboard.

"Who's that?" she asked, looking at me confused. "That's Electric Lady."

I looked at the picture again—it was my picture of Dr. Silver-Rose.

I came in through the door of the office. "How long does it take for a Storm of the Century to actually start storming?" I asked.

PJ, sitting at her desk, pointed at me. "Don't say that. You'll jinx the city. Do you want to be washed away into the Great Oceans?"

"I want this Storm of the Century to go away."

"The only thing that needs to go away is this Classic Cyborg case. You have other clients that need work done."

"I'm trying." I shuffled past her desk to my private office. On my desk were stacks of messages. I really did need to wrap up the case, but I knew it would be soon—very soon. "PJ!"

She appeared at my open doorway. "I'm right here."

"I don't have time to do it, and with your bionic fingers, you can get through it faster than me. I want you to find every picture of Electric Lady and of Dr. Silver-Rose that you can find."

"What am I looking for?"

"Something that doesn't fit. It may be nothing, but we have to cover the bases."

"Easy. I'll get it done quick."

"Quick or slow, it needs to be done thoroughly."

"Thorough and quick." PJ was gone. Already I could hear her bionic fingers on the keyboard.

I'd asked my wife why she remembered Electric Lady, though I knew in the image salon business you had to remember *every* client that came in. However, my instincts said there was more, and I was right. Dot told me that Electric Lady seemed to go out of her way to be noticed by staff every time she came in. Later, police had stopped by to "casually" ask if she was a frequent client—and she was.

I had my own research to do. The stack of messages would have to wait until tomorrow. I sat down at my computer and logged in.

"Cruz!"

I jumped up from my desk and ran out of my private office to her desk. She was watching the security monitors. I had spoken to the real Fritz the Mediator, only yesterday and today, in front of us on the screen, a dark-hued man in a dark suit and oversized shades was coming up in the elevator.

"Why did you yell?"

She pointed, but I saw it as soon as I asked the question. In the parking bay was an army of men—thugs in flowing coats that often meant lots of guns underneath.

The office door slowly opened, and the man came in alone with a grin.

"Don't shoot," he said, mockingly. "Left my men with the limo."

"How can I help you, sir?" PJ asked in her professional voice. Underneath her desk, she had her shotgun in her hand.

"I'm here to see a Mr. Cruz, and there you are. Fritz the Mediator."

"Mr. Fritz," I replied.

The Mediator walked to me and shook my hand. "A pleasure, Mr. Cruz. My men tell me that you found the little toy we left on your vehicle."

"Yeah. The Pony doesn't like tracking devices."

"The biggest threat for me in this business has always been dealing with people with a bag of rocks for brains. Such people get people like me killed. I had to make sure you weren't one of those people. You hear so much about someone. You have to spend all your time sifting rumor from fact. You've passed all the hurdles so far. The only question is: can you keep it up?"

"Don't you worry about my boss," PJ said.

Fritz grinned. "I better be careful. I heard she's punched more than one sorry sack through a window or a wall." He returned his attention to me. "Mr. Cruz, I came to tell you that I've been in touch with the other parties."

"You've spoken to all three of them?"

"Yes."

"Pink Machete, Harder Steel, and Robo-Stein? All of them are in hiding."

"Are you surprised?"

"Everyone's looking for them."

"You mean you and the cops are. Mr. Cruz, you may be good in your world, but legit operators like you will always be at a distinct disadvantage in mine."

"I'm more than happy to stay on my side of the street, but those on the other side keeping messing with me and the Average Joe and Jane. How did you find them so fast?"

"I have trade secrets too, Mr. Cruz. I found them."

"An only-criminals-can-find-criminals kind of thing?"

"Something like that, but I'm not a criminal. I'm a legitimate businessman."

PJ and I burst out laughing. Fritz started laughing himself.

"I didn't know I was a comedian too," he said.

"That was funny," PJ said. "You are a comedian. I used to say I was a legitimate businesswoman all the time in Neo-Paris."

"Oh, France. Nice. What happened?"

"They laughed at me and put me in jail," she answered.

"Okay, you found them. Now what?" I asked.

"The meet happens tomorrow. Keep your mobile handy. Make sure to wear an extra raincoat."

"Raincoat?"

"The storm's supposed to start tomorrow." I rolled my eyes. Fritz saw my face. "Sorry that doesn't meet with your approval, but tomorrow's the day. In my experience, you do these things as soon as possible, before any of the parties have time to plan anything asinine."

"Maybe we'll get lucky and the rain will wash them away into the Great Oceans."

"I hear you and Classic Cyborg are the new dynamic duo. He gets washed away, so do you. Wear that extra raincoat, please. Goodbye, Mr. Cruz."

The Mediator strolled out of Liquid Cool.

I made the call from my office desk. Classic's face appeared on the vid-phone screen.

"Cruz," he greeted.

"Tomorrow is the big day."

"Yes, it is."

"I'm going home early to get some extra sleep."

"I'm already home, but I don't think I'll be doing much sleeping."

"I really hope this doesn't go sideways tomorrow."

"You still think that?"

"I don't know what to think. I'm telling you what I hope. And the fact that the Storm of the Century is supposed to break tomorrow like a bad omen is not at all sitting well with me."

"Cruz, I didn't know you were superstitious."

"I don't mind rain at all. However, I do mind tsunami-like rainfall at the same time that I'm meeting three crazy cyborg maniac killers."

"You don't have to worry. You did all the work the last two times while I sat back. This time, I'll handle any situations that need to be handled."

"Don't worry. I'll have my weapons with me."

"Cruz, weapons aren't allowed in parleys."

"What?"

"No weapons."

"No weapons? But those crazy maniacs—their bodies are weapons."

"That doesn't count."

"How can it not count? Franken-borg's arms were cannons that dissolved mega-towers."

"If he were alive, we wouldn't be having a parley. The rules are simple: the principle parties only, no men, and no weapons. Seriously, no weapons are allowed. Law enforcement may classify some cyborgs as weapons, but not the mean streets. The Mediator's people will check, and they'll take everything off of you that you shouldn't have—from all of us."

I sat there dumbfounded.

"Are you still joining us, Cruz?" Classic seemed to enjoy my internal panic.

"Classic, I've never hidden behind another person in a fight, but I swear if this goes sideways in any way, you're my human shield."

Classic laughed. "It's a deal."

LAST CYBORG STANDING

The real Fritz called three minutes past six in the morning. I was so anxious I hadn't gotten much sleep. For most of the night, there was an excess of thunder that neither Dot nor I had ever experienced before. It really did look like the water of the universe was pooling up behind an invisible barrier in the sky. When everyone talked about being washed away into the Great Oceans, we were being facetious. But it looked like the joking wasn't a joke after all; it really felt like that was exactly what would happen.

I didn't much believe anything weather-people said on the news. The only weather they could predict was the weather happening in real time. However, all of them were saying that this was the day. Dot said it. Even I felt today was the day. After all, I was a glass-is-half-empty guy when it came to life. In wrapping up the Classic Cyborg case, I asked: When would be the absolute worst time for the Storm of the Century to hit? Today, of course.

The vid-call came in, but it was audio-only. It was Fritz the Mediator, live. I recognized his raspy voice.

"It's an old warehouse. Used to be called The Retro-Fit. You have forty minutes to get there. If you're not there by 6:45 a.m., go back home," he said and hung up.

I got dressed quickly, without making any noise to wake up Dot or Cruz Jr.—especially Cruz Jr. I didn't want him waking up Dot with his crying. Then I was out the door.

As I sat in the Pony, I felt completely naked. No guns? Why the hell was I going to a meeting of crazy maniacs without any weaponry, especially when the crazy maniacs were killer cyborgs? If something happened, how was I going to defend myself? Use harsh language? I started up my vehicle and was on my way, but I was not going to be at ease until this day was over.

I flew out of the Concrete Mama parking garage and my mouth dropped. The sky looked like a giant black force hanging above the supercity. It was surreal. The constant rumbling of thunder. The random flashing of lighting. I knew everything there was to know about the performance of my hovercraft. However, I realized that I had no idea how well either a normal hovercar or my own high-performance hovervehicle would operate in a serious thunder and lightning storm. I'd never experienced one before. Could that much water pounding down on a hovercar do something to the hoverengine? Could the average hovercar become a flying lightning rod in such a storm? One of the basic rules of defensive driving was that if you had concerns about your vehicle, your physical or mental state, or the environment you were flying into, don't drive!

I wished it were that simple. I glanced at my dashboard clock. Only twenty minutes for me to get to the meeting. Thankfully, the rain hadn't started, but I was driving in the slow lane, the closest sky lane to the ground.

I'd arrived in a district very close to the Hinterlands, which, again, would be a place I wouldn't want to be at the time of a major storm. The very place reminded me of being washed away. Several men stood waiting, holding heavy umbrellas even though it wasn't raining yet. I saw Classic's hover-monster truck parked, and I set my Pony nearby. There were three other parked hovercars in different areas, which meant everyone was here.

There was no reason to wait. I stepped out of the Pony and walked to the men with the umbrellas. Immediately I noticed how big the men were and their glowing eyes behind their shades. More cyborgs?

"Hands up while we pat you down," one of the hulksters said to me. I would have called them thugs, but if they worked for the real Mediator, they were a higher class of criminal—professionals.

I lifted my arms as one of them handed his umbrella to another and thoroughly patted me down. His hands moved in such a way—fingers turning and twisting, palms independently pressing and lifting—that they were clearly bionic. Afterward, he scanned my body with a device.

"Am I the only one here who isn't a cyborg?" I asked.

"I'd bet on it," the man said.

I didn't like that he used the word "bet." This wasn't just a kidnapping case for us. This was the final chapter of this Dead

Pool, where even I was listed as one of the "gladiators" in their sick game.

The man cleared me, and I stood with them waiting. We watched the vehicles. I didn't like the waiting, and I didn't like the thunder above my head in the sky.

Classic came next. We heard the squeak of his driver's side door and out stepped the ex-gangster cyborg legend. I expected him to wear something more appropriate, but he was in an immaculate suit jacket over his bare cyborg chest, with matching pants and shoes with no socks. He was dressed for clubbing. He approached us, buttoning his jacket. The routine was the same for him: pat-down and scan.

"Cruz," he greeted.

I nodded. "Are we all going clubbing after the meeting?"

"It's an important meeting."

"I hope your clothes are stormproof. A lot of rain is supposed to be coming down, and you don't use umbrellas like me."

"A little bit of rain never killed anyone."

"You're right, but a lot more than a little bit of rain is coming. Remember, I'm not an invincible cyborg like you."

Classic smiled. He looked up to the sky. "The rain won't come until this is all over."

Somehow, I felt that Classic was right. My attention turned to the other three hovercars in the distance. "What's taking them so long?"

"No one wants to be first," Classic answered.

I turned to the Mediator's men. "Why don't you do something? Maybe call them from left to right, so they don't feel slighted. I'm sure you'd like this to be over too so you can put those commercial umbrellas back in the box dry and get a full refund."

The men looked at each other. One of them nodded. The man who did the pat-downs and scanning again handed his umbrella to another man. I heard doors opening and slamming in the distance. The figure approaching from the leftmost hovercar was Harder Steel. The man in the middle was definitely Pink Machete. The figure coming from the last hovercar was unusual. He looked like he had a goat's head.

Harder Steel strutted to us and stopped, smiling. "Classic Cyborg," he greeted.

Classic didn't respond. He only stared at him.

"Hands up for the pat-down and scan," the Mediator man said.

Harder Steel raised his long cyborg arms in the air. He was patted down and scanned when Pink Machete reached us.

"Mr. Classic Cyborg. Finally!" Pink Machete shouted. "Why didn't we do this sooner?"

Classic remained quiet.

Pink Machete's body was searched and scanned.

"Too bad we won't get to see your machete," I said.

Pink Machete smiled at me. "One day you will, Cruz."

"Strangely, I don't think so." I looked up at the sky. "Maybe the coming storm will wash you into some gutter somewhere, never to be seen again."

"Gentlemen, no threatening," another Mediator man said. "This is supposed to be a cordial meeting free of threats."

"Oh, it's nothing," Pink Machete said to the man. "Cruz and I are best friends. We talk like this all the time. We're always joking around."

"What do we have here?" I said.

We all watched Robo-Stein arrive. He had a silver goat head with horns that curved back and touched the top of his shoulders.

"Gentlemen," he said with a nod.

"Are you serious?" I asked. "Everyone is dressed nice, even Pink Machete, and you come here with a big goat-head."

"Robo, I got to agree with Cruz," Pink Machete added. "You look downright ridiculous. It isn't Halloween, dude."

"I wanted to wear a head that I hadn't used before," Robo-Stein said. "To mark the occasion of this meeting. Arms up?" he asked the Mediator men.

"Yes. Pat-down and scan."

The same man did so again.

"If you can hold onto this device for me," he said and handed him what looked like a small clicking device.

"What's that?" I asked.

"Nothing," Robo-Stein replied.

"Then why did you bring it?" I looked at the Mediator men. "Destroy that thing. He's up to something."

"Mr. Cruz, we don't need you to tell us how to do our jobs."

"Hold onto it for me," Robo-Stein repeated.

"You can have it when you come back out. Gentlemen, you can make your way into the warehouse for your meeting. You will walk in single file. Mr. Cruz, you go first, then Mr. Classic

Cyborg, Harder Steel next, Pink Machete, then Robo-Stein. Mr. Cruz, please start walking." The Mediator man extended his arm to the warehouse in the distance.

In the cybernetic industry, Japan remained number one on Earth. The US and China battled back and forth for the distinction of second place. Retro-Fit was some old cybernetic manufacturing megacorp that had been bought out ages ago by a Japanese firm in Silver City. What remained was the shell of a gigantic warehouse that must have been state-of-the-art back when it was in operation. I led the column into the building and was glad to see the roof was intact, though parts of the wall had fallen away with the passage of time.

It was all open space inside. There had clearly been upper levels in the past, but those floors had been removed. It looked like there had been offices along one side of the wall on the ground floor, but they too had been removed. Daylight—if that's what you could call it with this overcast sky—came in through the holes in the walls and the above skylight.

"This was the premiere bionic production megacorp in Metropolis in its day. Now look at it," Pink Machete said. "Old and wasting away. The old generation, replaced by a new, younger, better generation."

"Why are we meeting?" Harder Steel asked Classic.

"My daughter, Electric Lady, was kidnapped by one of you. This has all gone far enough. All I want is her freed, unharmed. That's all I care about. Release her, and I'll leave Metropolis forever and never come back."

"Forever is a long time," Harder Steel said. "What if it was me? What guarantee do I have that you'd walk away?"

"My word."

"Your word?"

"I have never broken my word in my life—as a gangster or in my new life."

"Forgive and forget?"

"Yes."

"There's a problem, Mr. Classic Cyborg," Harder said, stepping closer. "All my men are dead. Someone killed them and I still don't know who. Who killed them?"

"How would I know? Ask your friends here," Classic said.

"My men are all dead. Pink Machete's men are all dead. Franken-borg was supposedly killed by your sidekick here, and his gang is all dead too," Harder said. "Then, I come back out on the street and hear that Ferrous Metal was also killed with all his men. Even some up-and-coming cyborg gang leaders are permanently off the streets too. Then I hear that some mean cyborg killers called the Exterminators, who I'm not ashamed to admit I was afraid I'd have to tangle with in the near-future, were killed by, once again, *your* sidekick."

"This meeting isn't to talk about your problems," Classic snapped.

"You want to talk about your problems, but we can't talk about ours." Harder Steel was shifting his gaze from Classic to me and back again. "That's not how parleys work, Mr. Classic Cyborg. We talk about it all. Here's how things stand now. The major cyborg gangs in Metropolis don't exist anymore. The most powerful cyborg crime boss, Franken-borg, and top three Up-Top cyborg crime bosses who were moving to Earth were all killed by a skinny, punk private detective who was working for you at the time."

"What are you saying?" Classic asked. "That I hired him to do that? He's not that kind of detective and you know that."

"Mr. Harder Steel, it seems your cyborg systems are not working properly," I said. "With all that excrement building up, it's now reached your skull and your brain is swimming in it. It's called self-defense. Franken-borg tried to kill me. He's dead. The Exterminators tried to kill us. They're dead. No one has to hire me to defend myself anymore than someone has to pay you to defend yourself."

"You really killed Franken-borg?" Harder asked. "I still don't believe it."

"I don't care what you believe."

"Electric Lady told me she threw you through a door like a puppet, but then you do something that no one else could do—kill Franken-borg."

"When Electric Lady threw me, I wasn't wearing my special undies from the planet Krypton."

Classic held up his hand. "I'm happy to discuss this all as long as you want, but first I want Electric Lady released."

"I asked you what would happen if it turned out to be me, but I don't believe your answer," Harder Steel said, "any more than I believe your sidekick killed Franken-borg."

"Classic, he didn't kidnap her," I said. "He doesn't even know where she is."

"How do you know that?" Harder Steel asked.

"Because I already know which one of you kidnapped her," I replied. "I was there at the kidnapping. She told me she broke up with you. She said she wanted a real cyborg man, which wasn't you."

Harder Steel laughed. It was then that I saw them. Harder had upgraded his teeth. He now had razor sharp, shark-like teeth.

"Where's Electric Lady?" Classic was asking me now.

"Real man?" Harder Steel said to me. "What would you know about that? I was plenty of a real man for her." He looked at Classic, grinning. "I bet the real reason she ran off was to give birth to my child, or with my enhanced 'man-power,' multiple children at once."

"Your childish attempt to start something won't work," I said to him with contempt. "Classic, don't waste your time with him. Robo-Stein is the kidnapper. That's why he wanted that little clicker device. She's nearby. Let's leave these jokers here, get her, and maybe we can get home before the storm starts. If we're lucky, it'll wash them all away, and Mr. Not-So-Hard here can use his one-inch bionic member as a flotation device."

"You're not going anywhere, old man," Harder Steel snarled, "and neither is your sidekick. We know you killed our men to eliminate the competition. The only person walking out of this warehouse will be the King of all Cyborgs."

Classic dropped his jacket to the ground, and it seemed the man I had known was gone. Maybe that's all it took in the past, simply taking off his jacket. He moved too fast for my eye to perceive the motion, but Harder Steel caught his right hook in his own hands before it connected. I made sure to step back far enough so I wouldn't become collateral damage.

Harder's head lunged forward, and he tried to bite out Classic's neck with his steel shark-teeth, but Classic's neck was as bionic and impervious as the rest of Classic's body.

Harder Steel yelled out so loud we all jumped. Classic had crushed Harder's right fist as if it were paper, then ripped his entire arm out of its socket. Harder tried to counter-attack with his remaining arm, but, again, Classic moved faster than I could perceive. One second Harder was standing, the next he was buried in the concrete. It was like Harder exploded and pieces of him shot everywhere, even punching through the roof above us and different parts of the wall around us. I was lucky I wasn't hit by any shrapnel. In the center of the bloody mass in the concrete ground was the contorted face of the late Harder Steel, his eyeballs were hanging in their sockets, and his steel shark-teeth jaw had cracked off from the rest of his face. Harder Steel wasn't going to be King of the Cyborgs, ever.

I didn't even get a chance to breathe because I knew what was coming next. Pink Machete tried a sneak attack, attempting to hit Classic in the back. But the legend was expecting the move and hit Pink Machete with a backward kick without even looking. Pink was literally kicked through the wall about twenty feet away.

Something shot back in through another part of the wall. Pink Machete had jumped up and ran so fast that it was as if he had teleported to Classic. Pink Machete *did* have his machete. He extended his arms out in a T-formation with his body and out popped laser-edged machetes in each hand, but it wasn't over. Each of his arms then separated into three arms, each with their own laser-edged machetes. That was the gangster's secret. Everyone thought he had one big machete when in fact he had six of them.

Pink Machete attacked all at once in a move that was meant to literally cut Classic in half at the torso. It was a move that reminded me of the two unlucky parking lot security men Pink killed, probably before they even knew what was happening. However, this time the blades of all six machetes broke in half. I'd never seen that before—and obviously neither had Pink. I didn't even know that laser blades could break like that. Classic's cyborg skin was that powerful.

Classic flashed a devilish smile at Pink Machete, who stared back in shock. Classic's left hand swiped one way, and Pink Machete didn't have a throat anymore. Classic swiped with his right arm and Pink didn't have a neck anymore. Classic grabbed the body—what was left of it—smacked Pink's head away like a baseball and threw the body. It crashed through the back of the wall fifty feet away. Pink Machete wasn't going to be the King of the Cyborgs either.

This time I had made sure not to take my eyes off Robo-Stein with his staring goat head.

"This might be a good time for you to tell us where Electric Lady is," I said to him.

"That was always my plan," Robo-Stein said calmly.

The remaining cyborg gangster walked to the entrance and waved. He was signaling to the Mediator's men. Classic and I joined him. I noticed Classic's fingertips were full razor-sharp claws. Unfortunately, none of this violence was over.

One of the Mediator's men appeared.

"Can you activate the switch and allow Electric Lady to come in?" Robo-Stein said.

The man smiled. "Only three of you. Sure. Fritz said that we'd have another party." He walked away.

"She's not too far away," Robo-Stein said.

"Why did you kidnap my daughter?" Classic asked.

"I'll explain when she arrives."

We all looked up. It was raining.

Not now! I thought.

I saw the dust cloud first. My eye followed her until the Electric Lady stopped at the main entrance. She glared at Robo-Stein, but the look she gave Classic and me wasn't especially friendly either.

"Sorry about Harder Steel," Robo-Stein said.

"What?" she asked.

"He didn't make it. Neither did Pink Machete."

"I don't care about Pink Machete. What are you saying about HS?"

She brushed past us into the warehouse. We followed her. She ran to the bloody metal mess that had once been Harder Steel. Slowly, she knelt down.

"No!" she screamed.

When she jumped to her bionic feet, nodes all over her body began to flash blue. Her head turned and she marched to us.

"Who killed him?" she asked.

"Your father was entirely justified in his action," Rob-Stein defended. "Your boyfriend threw the first punch. Too bad he couldn't take a counter-punch." Robo-Stein was too composed for my liking. He was up to something—something bad.

"No happy reunion then?" Classic asked her.

"Is that what you were expecting?" she said with a level of hatred that I had rarely seen. "Well, I told him all your secrets! You're not as invincible as everyone thinks you are. I told him everything! Did you think you'd rescue me and we'd go off happily ever after into the sunset as father and daughter?"

"No."

"Then what?"

"Every man has to clean up their own messes. So does every parent."

Classic hit Electric Lady so hard and so fast that he literally punched her upper torso off. The body landed in the distance inside the building. She had died instantly.

Robo-Stein and I looked at each other. Neither one of us saw that coming.

"Thank you, Robo-Stein for returning my daughter." Classic said with a combination of relief and menace.

Robo-Stein had no idea what to say. I wouldn't have either. "I had planned to kill you and her, but you've seriously upset those plans." He looked at me and asked, "Did you know that was going to happen?"

"No."

He looked back at Classic. "Looks like you're as evil as you've always been."

"She said she told you my secrets."

"She did," Robo-Stein replied. "I think I understand the real reason for your fear of my brother. You were the older model, with side-effects. He was the newer model, with *no* ugly side-effects."

Classic nodded. "Yes."

"I have made some of my own modifications."

"I expected you would."

"It's as indestructible as you."

"What does your new bionic head really do?"

What I hated about these cyborgs was that they were moving too fast for me to see anything, and I was standing right there. I had only blinked once—normal eyes tend to do that—and Classic was gone. I heard a noise in the distance, and there was a new hole in the same part of the wall where the late Pink Machete had involuntarily exited the building.

"Did you just headbutt Classic out of the building with your goat head?" I asked Robo-Stein. "You're moving too fast. I missed it."

Robo-Stein laughed, then he stopped. "You killed my brother."

"Hey, that's not my fault. He was going to blast me with his building-killer arm weapons."

I ran. All I heard was Robo-Stein laughing. "Run, run, Mr. Cruz." I was almost out the door when I heard a loud thud.

When I turned, there was Classic Cyborg holding the collapsed body of Robo-Stein, who now had a new hole in the center of his chest. Blood sprayed out as Classic let go. Robo-Stein fell to his knees and then fell forward to the ground. There was a click and his goat head unattached and started rolling away. Classic crushed the head like an old tin can with his foot.

Classic Cyborg grabbed his jacket from the ground and put it back on. The King of the Cyborgs buttoned it. He had a self-satisfied smirk on his face. "We had a saying back in my days of ultraviolence: that was good TV," he said.

"I'll have to remember that one."

Since I hadn't seen the demise of Electric Lady coming from a mile away, I had to quickly re-evaluate my profile of Classic. His hands were back to normal—the clawed tips had retracted. The menace in his eyes was gone. I felt as I did before—that I had nothing to fear from Classic.

"Why did you kill your daughter?" I asked.

"My daughter was an official member of Harder Steel's gang. Do you know how one becomes an official member?"

"Kill an innocent person."

"The first one she killed was near where your wife works. Someone saw her and she was going to be arrested, but a decision was made, without my knowledge, to give her an alibi."

"Dr. Silver-Rose."

"Oh, you know already. Yes, she pretended to be her long enough—going everywhere and making a point to be noticed, leaving a nice, easy trail for police to follow to give her an alibi. An alibi she gladly used to beat the case. What did my daughter do then? She killed more people. Apparently, she enjoyed it. She wanted to be a real hardcore gang member. She never would have stopped, none of them would have. All of this, Cruz, was because of me. I was the catalyst for all this evil, so it was my burden to clean it all up."

"You killed all their gangs."

"Yes."

"I killed Franken-borg when no one thought such a thing was possible, and you took advantage of it."

"You helped me clean up the mess I created. All the cyborg gangs inspired by me gone—the next generation, the generation after them, even the gangs from Up-Top."

"You started the Dead Pool," I said.

"I did."

I shook my head. "You planned this from the beginning. What about Dr. Silver-Rose? What's her story? How does she fit into this?"

"She's my other daughter."

"That's it. You left the world of one daughter for the world of the other daughter. Your angel daughter and devil daughter. Your angel daughter kept you on the straight path. Where's her mother?"

"She died too, unexpectedly. You need a guide in life when you take a path that you're not familiar or comfortable with, even if you realize it's the right path."

"You sound like a mystic, which doesn't exactly match with what you've done in this warehouse today."

"Yes, it does. I'm cleaning up the mess that I alone created in this world. If I never was Classic Cyborg and did those things I did as a criminal, none of this would have happened. I would have had two angel daughters rather than one."

"What's the missing piece, Mr. Classic? You killed your wives, didn't you? Not on purpose, but you did. I found out that your good daughter became an expert oncologist too. PJ asked me why would someone do that when there's no more cancer in the world? But there is, isn't there?"

"I became the most powerful cyborg there ever was. No one knew how I did it. I became a legend because all the other cyborg gangsters had a vast array of attachments—axes, drills, giant clawed hands, and much more. I simply used my normal cyborg body to defeat them because I was stronger than any of them. But it came with a cost. The obscure scientist who I found, so many years ago, to make me into the Invincible Classic Cyborg did it by making me a mini-walking reactor. I'm powered not by advanced bionics, but, as some might say, the cosmic power of the atom. However, there is always a good and bad to such energy."

"You're Nuclear Man. Franken-borg was the Fission Man. I get it now. That's why the City really employed you. They needed you to stop the future generation of cyborg gangsters that Franken-borg represented."

"I left the gang world all those years ago and never thought about the ramifications. My secret scientist found someone else to be his creation. *I* was the prototype for Franken-borg. That psycho killed so many people."

"You didn't make him do it."

"I was responsible. Thankfully, Franken-borg was insane. He killed that scientist so there wouldn't be anyone else who could make an even better version. So the threat was contained. Unfortunately, Franken-borg did find out about me. I don't know how. Silver-Rose confirmed it by going undercover herself, as an illegal cyborg doctor. She pieced it all together on her own. Electric Lady found out somehow too. She and Franken-borg were conspiring against me. Franken-borg wanted to be unique, an only model. His goal was to kill me and become a legend. Then use his status to unify all the cyborg gangs under him. But Electric Lady—her plan was bolder. She wanted to create a legion of new criminal cyborgs. Harder Steel wasn't using her. She was using him."

"That's when you started the Dead Pool?"

"I started the Dead Pool because that's as long as I could hang on. I didn't know about the side-effects. Wide awake, everything is fine. But apparently, when I sleep my radioactivity is not completely contained. That radiation killed my first and then my second wife before I found out. And the radiation is killing me too. It always has been. No reaching the big 1-0-0 for me. I'm not dying, Cruz. I'm already dead."

"If I knew about your wives, I probably could have figured out all of this from the start. But then I couldn't do a thorough background check on you like most clients, with so much of it being classified."

"The perks of being an employee of the Gang Division and Intelligence."

"What about this crazy Dead Pool then? I'm not shooting you."

"You don't have to. All you have to do is say that you did. But you have to promise me one thing."

"What's that?"

"I want you to donate all the money to the Guardian Angels Initiative of the Metropolis Polish Catholic Church. They did such a good job with Silver-Rose. Maybe if they had more resources they could have saved Justyna too, and things could have been different. They'll have the resources now. You'll see to it."

"I will. Your plan did come together."

"I hired the right detective."

"How does this end then?"

"I'll go out there, take away the guns from one or two of Fritz's men, and let the others shoot me. You'll grab one of the guns from the ground and be the one who stops me with the final shot."

"How? Guns don't work on you."

"Your shot will. I'll simply unplug myself. All my final affairs are in order; my daughter of grace knows what to do. I had her go into hiding because I wanted to ensure none of them could get to her. One more thing. When I'm buried, I want to be in my best suit and my favorite red glasses. I have everything laid out on my bed. Silver-Rose and Trendy have access to my place, past all my security measures."

"It'll all be taken care of."

"Shall we go?"

"I've met many crazy maniacs, Classic Cyborg, but I suspect that you'll be one that I'll never forget."

"Cruz, it was nice knowing you too."

We shook hands and out into the beginning of the Storm of the Century we went. With the downpour, the men never saw Classic coming with those bionic legs of his.

Everything happened as he said. The Mediator's men got away, barely, slipping, falling, and stumbling in the torrential downpour. I shot Classic with one shot, but it was like shooting a tank with a spitball, though that wasn't how the streets were going to play it. I had put down Classic Cyborg. He remained there on one knee at the scene of the scuffle. One of his hands clawed into the ground, keeping his body from being washed away. Looking at him was eerie. His eyes were blank—he had turned himself "off" permanently. He was the last cyborg standing; I was the last man standing. The Dead Pool was over. There would be many others, but I would never know of them. As the real Fritz had told me: I lived on my side of the street; they lived on theirs.

The Guardian Angels Initiative got the biggest, single donation in their eight-hundred-year history. Lots of girls and boys would be helped and kept off those mean, neon streets courtesy of that good paying client and crazy maniac Classic Cyborg.

REVIEW REQUEST

Dear Reader,

I hope you enjoyed *Classic Cyborg*.

Can You Write Me a Review?

If you enjoyed *Classic Cyborg (Liquid Cool Series: From The Crazy Maniac Files)*, I'd greatly appreciate an honest review on one or more of the following sites:

Reviews are the best way for readers to discover good books. My writer's motto is simple: "Readers Rule!" Thanks so much.

Always writing,

Austin Dragon

CONTINUE THE ADVENTURE

Yes! Now that you've been introduced to the ***Liquid Cool: From Crazy Maniac Files*** mini-series with **CLASSIC CYBORG**, why not jump into the Main Series? The first two are FREE!

Your Next *Liquid Cool* Books!

- *These Mean Streets, Darkly* (Liquid Cool Prequel Short)
- *Liquid Cool* (Liquid Cool: The Cyberpunk Detective Series, Book 1)
- *Blade Gunner* (Liquid Cool, Book 2)
- *NeuroDancer* (Liquid Cool, Book 3)
- *The Electric Sheep Massacre* (Liquid Cool, Book 4)
- *I, Alien Hunter* (Liquid Cool, Book 5)
- *A.I. Confidential* (Liquid Cool, Book 6)

- *Liquid Cool Box Set* (Liquid Cool Prequel and Books 1-3)
- *Liquid Cool Box Set 2* (Liquid Cool: Books 4-6)

Also by Austin Dragon

See all my books in science fiction, horror, and fantasy at: http://www.austindragon.com/books

Want to know when the next Liquid Cool novels are coming out?

Join my VIP Readers' Club!
http://www.austindragon.com/be_a_vip

ABOUT THE AUTHOR

Austin Dragon is the author of the _After Eden Series_, including the _After Eden: Tek-Fall_ mini-series, the classic _Sleepy Hollow Horrors_, the new epic fantasy adventure _Fabled Quest Chronicles_, and cyberpunk detective series, _Liquid Cool_. He is a native New Yorker, but has called Los Angeles, California home for the last twenty years. Words to describe him, in no particular order: U.S. Army, English teacher, one-time resident of Paris, movie buff, Fortune 500 corporate recruiter, renaissance man, dreamer.

He is currently working on new books and series in science fiction, fantasy, and classic horror!

Connect with Austin on social media at:

Website and blog: http://www.austindragon.com

Twitter: https://twitter.com/Austin_Dragon

Pinterest: http://www.pinterest.com/austindragon

Goodreads: https://www.goodreads.com/ADragon

Other books by Austin Dragon

See all my books at: http://www.austindragon.com/books